Finding the Power Within

Seaside Wolf Pack Book 3

C.C. Masters

DEDICATION

Dedicated to everyone who has supported me along this journey!
Special thanks goes out to the Seaside Wolf Pack on Facebook for
always keeping me inspired and motivated.

Thank you to Ann Marie Ware, without you I would not be able to keep
writing.

Thank you to Sarah Reddish and Ellen Yates for all of your help getting
this book ready for public viewing!

Prologue

James

I sat across the table from the suspicious stranger in Austin's office. He had simply strolled into the house an hour before and asked if Austin was the pack master.

I immediately used the pack bond to find out which moron had let this guy into our home, but the wolves on guard duty swore they never saw anyone approach the house or the property. I'd be having harsh words with them later. He never should have been able to make it onto the heart of our territory, let alone into our home.

I watched this asshole silently. He had casually claimed to be Anna's father, but I immediately did *not* like him. He was relaxed and smiling, not at all concerned that he had just wandered into the home of a pack of wolves - uninvited.

He was tall and lean with hair so blond it was almost white. His eyes were a pale blue reminiscent of an icy glacier. He had a gracefulness that screamed warrior rather than dancer, and an aura of danger to match. He was dressed in a crisp white button-down shirt and grey slacks, looking more like he planned to spend the afternoon at a country club than infiltrate the home of a wolf pack.

He hadn't smelled human or wolf to me, but he gave off a sensation of *other*. When I extended my senses, I got a sensation of cold, rather than the warmth that my pack mates usually exuded.

Froston's explanation? He was *fae*. I had to hide my incredulous reaction to that declaration, but Austin hadn't expressed any doubt. Austin merely accepted the statement and asked him to have a seat. I hadn't been aware that the fae were anything more than stories told to entertain children but I trusted Austin's judgment.

"What makes you believe you're Anna's father?" Austin asked mildly.

Froston chuckled. "You doubt my word?"

"Anna was adopted as a baby by humans," Austin told him bluntly. "If you're her father then how did that happen?"

I watched Froston's reaction carefully, but he didn't flinch at the implied accusation of abandonment. "I've been watching her from afar, and I've decided that now is the time to bring her home."

That didn't answer anything. Where was he when she was born? Where was he when she had been adopted out to humans? When she had been struggling to figure out who she was the first time she shifted? The only excuse that would have been acceptable for his absence was death. That was clearly not the case here. What made him think that 'watching her from afar' was appropriate?

Austin had handled the situation with our unwanted guest diplomatically so far, but I was just waiting for a signal from him. This man's grin was infuriating and he couldn't give a straight answer to anything. The only thing he was clear on was that he was here for Anna.

Not going to happen.

Anna had never complained or spoken of her childhood directly, but I had the impression that it wasn't all butterflies and roses. Was this guy aware of what she had been through? Had he been 'watching from afar' as she suffered? I clenched my fists at the thought of any man standing by callously, watching Anna struggle.

"Thank you for watching over her for me, but I think it's time I brought her home," Froston told Austin with a smile.

A soft knock on the door drew our attention. *Fuck.* That was Anna.

Anna had been through a lot lately, and after the events of the cabin in the woods, I couldn't deny my feelings for her any longer. A small portion of my cold, dead heart had started to come back to life once she had stepped foot into Austin's office for the first time and glared at me with her chin tilted up in challenge. The night after being shot, lying on the ground with her soft body pressed against mine and my life bleeding into the dirt, I had realized that she had my heart completely. There was nothing that I wouldn't do for her.

I hurriedly stood and strode to the door, ignoring Austin's answer to the asshole. I only opened the door wide enough for me to exit and pushed Anna out of the doorway and further into the hall, shutting it behind me.

Anna looked up at me with suspicious green eyes. She must have just taken a shower because her scent was mixed with the fresh, fruity scent of her shampoo. Her pale blond hair was still damp and flowed down her back in gentle waves. She crossed her arms and widened her stance, making her challenge to me clear.

"Just cooperate," I ordered her, already knowing she was ready to test me.

"No," she answered simply, holding my gaze firmly. Defiance was clear in the tilt of her jaw and the flash in those gorgeous green eyes of hers.

I sighed. Under normal circumstances, I would find her boldness equally frustrating and hot. But today, I needed to get her out of here. I didn't want her anywhere near this outsider until we got some answers from him as to what he was really doing here.

I had just resigned myself to the idea that I was going to have to throw her over my shoulder to cart her away when the door opened behind me. I turned to face Froston coming out of the doorway with Austin close on his heels.

I cursed to myself and placed my body in front of Anna's to try and shield her from his advance.

"Anna!" The asshole boomed with a broad grin and open arms. "I knew I sensed you out here."

Anna peered around me to get a view of Froston. "Have we met?" She asked him cautiously.

"Not officially. I'm your father," he said warmly, dropping his arms but moving closer.

She looked at Austin for confirmation. "We haven't established that as a fact yet," he cautioned her with a frown.

Froston laughed. "Of course, she's my daughter, I can feel my magic coursing through her blood."

I saw Anna's face change as her curiosity piqued- sometimes that girl was more like a cat than a wolf. I held out an arm to keep her back at a safe distance.

Austin met my eyes with a nod and I sighed. We were both in agreement: neither Anna nor Froston were going to agree to walk away from this meeting, so the best we could do was stay by Anna's side to keep her safe.

I followed Austin back into the office to have a seat at the table, careful to keep my body between Froston and Anna. I already knew I wouldn't be able to keep Anna away from him, but I was determined to keep her from harm. He would have to get through me to get to her.

Now that they were close to each other, I could see a little resemblance between them. They were both blond, fair skinned, and tall. But Anna was almost a carbon copy of her mother, so a little bit of blond hair wasn't enough to convince me that she and Froston were kin. I couldn't see much resemblance between them beyond similar coloring.

I let Anna ask her questions, watching her reactions carefully. She seemed cautious, but hopeful. I hated the way that asshole tugged at her heartstrings by telling the story about her mother. I didn't believe a word of it; this fucker was trying to manipulate her.

"That was a nice story," I interjected. "But how do we know any of it is true?"

"Fae don't lie," Froston said simply. He held my gaze with his frosty blue eyes, unblinking.

I scowled and looked at Austin for confirmation. Austin communicated the truth of that statement via the pack bond. Even if fae were unable to lie, I doubted Froston was telling us the entire truth. Something about this guy just didn't feel right.

"We don't know much about fae," Austin said. "What you told us might be true, and I'm willing to give you the benefit of the doubt for now. But we'll be looking much further into this before Anna goes anywhere with you."

Froston sighed. "Well, that's going to be a problem." He stood up so Austin and I followed suit. Anna stayed seated and looked like she was going to be stubborn. Good. I was glad he hadn't gotten to her with his bullshit.

"I need my daughter now," Froston said with a smile. "Anna, dear, come here."

Anna stayed seated and just glared at him. I felt a little swell of pride at that. Wolves did not come when called like pets.

"I don't think so," Austin said firmly but politely. "Anna's going to stay here for now."

Anna nodded in agreement. "This is my pack, I'm not going anywhere."

I tensed. Froston had been polite up until now. But now that he knew he wouldn't get what he wanted with his partial truths and half promises? I mentally prepared myself for battle.

The smile never faded from Froston's face, he simply shrugged. "Have it your way."

He waved a hand and an invisible force knocked me back. I got to my feet in shock. What was that? I shook off my disorientation and circled for a better angle to attack. He had grabbed ahold of Anna's arm and was dragging her across the room.

"You're not getting her out of here," I warned him. Where did he think he was going to go? There was only one door to the office, and I felt Austin call for our pack-mates. In only a few minutes the room would be packed with our wolves.

Froston laughed in response and swirled a hand around. Magic was so thick in the air I could feel my skin buzzing from the charge. A portal straight out of a fucking sci-fi movie started to open in front of us.

Anna struggled to fight him off, and she got a couple of good hits in, but they lacked the necessary force to harm him. I growled in frustration at the invisible force holding me in place. I struggled even more desperately to break free as Froston carried Anna to the portal.

Anna shifted into her wolf as Froston flung her through the opening. She landed on all four paws and whirled around to face us. I could see nothing but snow to give me a hint as to where she was, and cold air was radiating out through the portal. She crouched, ready to leap back through to us. I silently cheered her on as I struggled to break free of the hold on me.

Hope soared in my chest as she leapt and flew through the air. She was going to make it. Right before she would have landed safely on our side, Froston stepped through, knocking her back as the portal closed behind him. Immediately as it shut, I was released from the hold. I gave a wordless howl of anger, rage, and frustration.

Our pack mates rushed in from where they had been trapped behind the door to the office, but I ignored them. I shoved the table, but it unsatisfactorily skidded only a foot or so. I picked up a chair and smashed it into the table, but the sound of splintering wood did nothing to calm my rage. I reached for a second chair and smashed it repeatedly into the ground, imagining that I was instead smashing it into Froston's smug face.

I felt a wave of Austin's energy reach for me, but I was in no mood to be soothed or calmed. I wanted to destroy everything in sight. I wanted to destroy Froston. I spin to face Austin. "We need to get her back!" I shouted.

I could see my own anger and frustration mirrored in Austin's eyes. "You're wasting time," he told me coldly. "You can destroy my office, or you can gather the pack and make a plan to get her back."

Chapter 1

Anna

I woke up disoriented and alone in the darkness. There was nothing but stillness around me - no scents, no sounds- it was almost as if I were in a vacuum. I started to panic when I couldn't see anything around me in the darkness, but then the familiar sight of my room in Austin's house slowly faded into view. The room itself was still mostly empty – I only had a bed and a nightstand. But just the familiar sight of the plain walls was comforting.

I shook my head in confusion, trying to clear out whatever cobwebs must have been cloaking all of my senses. I could see all the familiar items in my room now, and I felt silly for worrying. I was lying on top of my blankets instead of under them, which seemed odd. I ran my hands over the familiar bedding to comfort myself.

I turned my head slowly, examining my room with scrutiny. Everything seemed like it was in its place, but I felt a sense of wrongness. Something wasn't right here.

I rolled off the bed and stood cautiously, extending all of my senses. At first, I couldn't pick up any scents. But the moment I thought about what my room *should* smell like, I could suddenly pick up on the subtle scents that made this my home. That was strange. Had I hit my head? Why were all of my senses delayed?

There was still nothing but silence in my room. I couldn't remember what sounds were usually in the house, but there was always something. The silence felt like a heavy weight, pressing down on me. I took a deep breath and started to head for the door. I'm sure Austin would have answers for this.

I hesitated with my hand on the door handle and looked back towards my windows. The windows reflected only my own image back to me, and I couldn't see out. Have they always been like that? What time of the night was it?

The questions faded from my mind, and I couldn't remember why I had hesitated at the door at all. I wanted to go find Austin.

I turned the handle and stepped out into the hall. The hallway stretched out in both directions as far as I could see. Doors lined the hallway far into the distance and I felt the sense of wrongness tugging at me again.

I turned to the right and walked down the hall, almost as if another power was pulling me in that direction. With each step I took I felt more confident that I was going the right way. Why had I ever doubted myself?

I stopped in front of a heavy oak door with a metal door handle in the shape of a snarling wolf. I just knew Austin was on the other side of this door, waiting for me. I struggled to push the heavy door open, but it felt like the door was fighting me as if it were consciously trying to keep me out. The harder I pushed, the more determined I was to get in there. I needed to see Austin.

I stopped to take a breath, and the door quietly opened in front of me. Austin was watching me from behind his desk with cold eyes. I studied him carefully as I entered the room, trying to get a feel for what was going on.

His muscular form was impeccably dressed, as always, in a dark suit and red tie. His dark blond hair was styled as if he had just stepped off a photoshoot for GQ. But he watched me approach without a word of welcome, his face stony and his blue eyes icy.

I swallowed nervously. Had I done something to make him upset with me? I thought back to what happened earlier today, but my mind was blank. I didn't even remember going to bed.

I frowned, but the question fled my mind as Austin stood and walked towards me. I reflexively stepped back as Austin stalked me, menace rolling off him in waves.

"I told you I never wanted to see your face again," he growled hostilely.

I gasped in surprise and looked up at him with wide eyes as he came closer. Austin had never treated me this way before. Even when he was angry, I'd never felt truly threatened.

"Why aren't you gone?" he demanded as he stalked me.

I had taken more steps back without realizing it, and my back was now pressed against the door. He slammed his hands on either side of my head, caging me in between his arms as he stared into my eyes.

There was no warmth, no kindness to be found there. In his eyes I only saw hatred.

"I...I..." I stammered, utterly at a loss. My heart was pounding and I felt a bead of cold sweat drip down my back. This wasn't the Austin that I knew and loved. This was someone else, a monster.

He grabbed me by the arm and shoved me out into the hall. I tripped over my own feet as I tried to stumble away from him and fell to the floor.

"Get the fuck out of my house!" he roared before going back into his office and slamming the door behind him.

I tried to stand, but my body was shaking too badly. I stayed on my hands and knees on the floor as I tried to gather myself. I closed my eyes and took a deep breath.

I tried to tell myself that Austin's hatred and anger towards me didn't matter. That I was going to be fine. I had been on my own all these years, I could be on my own again.

My heart didn't believe the lies my head was trying to tell it. I was devastated and confused. What had I done to deserve this?

I slowly raised my head and used the wall to help me stand. As soon as I let go of the wall to take a step forward, the twins were in front of me. I blinked. I hadn't even heard them coming down the hall towards me.

They were both dressed in jeans and hoodies as if they had stopped here on their way to class, backpacks slung over their broad shoulders. They pulled off the hot college student look better than any guy I'd ever seen with their messy brown hair and muscular forms. If I had passed by them in my college student days, I would have been too shy to even make eye contact.

I looked at Mason and then Jason, hoping they would have an explanation for this. Or better yet, tell me this was a horrible joke gone wrong.

I didn't get any reassurance or comfort from either of them. Jason just smirked at me, and Mason had a dark look in his hazel eyes that made me nervous.

"We thought you would've gotten the message by now," Mason said coldly.

Jason laughed, but the sound sent chills down my spine. They both circled around where I stood in the hallway like wolves circling injured prey.

"Yeah, *Banana*," Jason said mockingly. "We thought you would've run out the door with your tail between your legs."

"Did you not understand when we told you we were done playing with you?" Mason asked with a smirk.

"We got what we wanted," Jason laughed. "Not that it was worth all the effort we put into it."

All the blood drained from my face. They weren't joking.

Mason sighed. "You were just a waste of time, but here you are, taking up even more of our time."

"But-"

"You better run, little wolf." Jason laughed.

Mason smirked at me. "I hope you're still here when Austin gives us the word to rip out your throat."

"I hope she gives us a good chase," Jason said as he circled around me.

"Are you kidding me?" Cody's voice interrupted them.

I turned to face him with relief. Cody was here, he would make things right. But when I met his Caribbean blue eyes, I saw only disgust. Cody was physically the most intimidating of the pack. At six and a half feet tall and 230 pounds, he was a wall of muscle. I had never had a reason to fear Cody before, he had always been warm and a little flirty with me. But now he was anything but flirty.

"I think we should just toss you into the ocean and let you drown - that way we won't get any of that disgusting half-breed blood on us." Cody stopped several feet away from me and crossed his arms, watching me with loathing in his eyes.

Tears came to my eyes. So it wasn't anything I had done? They had found out what I really was. There was nothing I could do about that, I couldn't change what was in my blood. Despair filled me, and I walked further down the hall, away from Cody, away from the twins.

I saw James watching me in the distance. A part of me wanted to rush towards him, begging him to make this right. But another part of me knew that he would never accept me now. I was tainted. Nothing but a disgusting creature.

I stopped in front of James. Where Cody may have been the biggest of the pack, James was the most terrifying. He was more lean than bulky, more sleek assassin than hulking guard. His dark hair and dark eyes made him seem at home in the shadows.

James watched me with cold, emotionless eyes, but didn't say a word. He merely pointed further down the hall. I trudged forward, feeling hopeless.

Caleb stepped out of a door in front of me. I wasn't even hopeful when I looked up to meet his eyes, I already knew what I would find. Disgust and hate. His usually warm brown eyes were cold and calculating, his brown hair mussed as if he had been running his hands through it.

He reached back into the room. "There's something I want you to take with you." He handed me something wrapped in a blanket.

I could feel the stickiness on the bottom of the blanket, but I set it down to unwrap it. I slowly folded back the corner of the blanket to see the gold and white coat of Tigger. Why would he wrap my pups in there like that? Were they sleeping?

Dread was in the pit of my stomach - I knew my pups would never lie still like this. Horror and despair hit as the two bodies of my beloved puppies were revealed. I stroked my hand down Eeyore's silky black coat and my hand came away with sticky red blood. I let out a howl of anguish.

My shoulders shook with the force of my sobs. They would have happily run to Caleb, expecting treats and snuggles. They never would have thought Caleb would hurt them. I can't even imagine the horror and betrayal they must have felt in their last moments...

I looked up at Caleb, unable to speak through my sobs.

He just looked at me callously. "You're next. That's what we do to mutts who try and weasel their way into our world. You don't belong here anymore than they did."

"Anna!" an unfamiliar voice called to me from a distance.

I frowned, taking a deep breath and trying to place the voice. There was something I should know...

I glanced back down to see the blanket with my pups gone. I looked up and down the hall, all the guys were gone as well. There was just the empty corridor stretching out as far as I could see.

I didn't want to get up off the floor from where I knelt, but something was urging me forward. I felt compelled to stand and walk further down the hallway. I stopped in front of a black door, carved with roses. I ran my hands over the sculpted roses, dread filling my heart. My fate was waiting for me on the other side of this door.

I wrapped my hand around the metal of the handle and thorns dug into my skin, drawing blood. I didn't flinch or draw away, this is what I deserved. Pain and agony is what a repulsive creature like me should get.

The door swung open and I stepped into the darkness, despondent and alone. The shadows parted and revealed my uncle's kitchen from when I was a child. I flinched at the shout I heard from the living room and scurried to the stove. I reached out with a small hand and stood on my tiptoes to reach the pot on the back burner.

I lifted the lid and peeked inside to see what I was making. I had been boiling pasta, but I must have been away too long. The water had all boiled away and left the pasta burnt and glued to the bottom of the pan.

Terror grabbed my heart and squeezed. I panted in fear as I tried to think of a way to fix this. They were waiting for me to bring them dinner right now. There was no time to make anything else and if anyone saw the wasted food I would be punished severely. Anxiety flooded through me and I trembled in trepidation.

A fist knotted in my hair and pulled me back from the stove. I tried not to trip as I was dragged back by my hair, that would only make things worse.

"What the fuck is your problem, you worthless little piece of shit?" my uncle raged at me as he threw me to the ground.

I curled up in a ball to try and protect myself, tucking my hands in so my fingers wouldn't get broken if he stomped on me.

"You're useless, even as a slave," he thundered as he aimed a kick to my back. I was forced to uncurl as he grabbed my arm and pulled me up, dragging me back to the stove.

He shoved my face into the pot, steam from the hot pasta burning my face. "What the fuck is this? You can't even boil pasta?"

"Not the face, please," a deep voice mocked from behind us.

My uncle let out a breath filled with frustration. "You can deal with this right now, I'll take her back when you're done."

He shoved me back towards the newcomer and I looked up to see Danny, the first man who had ever touched me. Danny smiled at me, but he had a sinister glint in his eyes that frightened me. We were suddenly back in his frat house, where I had learned that violence wasn't the only way a man could hurt me.

"You and me are going to have some fun," he purred, gripping my arm painfully. I made my body go limp. I had already learned the first time that it hurt less if I didn't struggle.

"Morpheus, that is enough!" I heard the stranger shout.

Danny faded away, leaving me alone again. There was an amused chuckle that echoed all around me. I stood and whirled, looking for the source, but there was no one in sight.

The room slowly started to fade back into the shadows. All around me, the darkness that I had woken up to was slowly consuming the world and coming for me. I desperately looked for a way out, but I was completely surrounded. It sucked me in and I was gone.

Chapter 2

Anna

I slowly opened my eyes to darkness. Panic set in and I trembled, afraid to move. Horror and terror overwhelmed me as I laid here alone. A small part of my brain realized that I had just awoken from a nightmare, but I struggled to break free of the emotions that held me captive.

How many nights had I spent like this? Terrified that the slightest movement would draw attention to me and cause the torment to start all over again. Slowly I broke free from the nightmare and slid back into reality.

I took a deep breath and closed my eyes again. The darkness was here all the same whether I had my eyes open or not. I went through some of my mindfulness exercises, trying to push the panic and the fear away. It had been years since I had felt this so strongly.

I chanted my mantra to myself: *I am strong, I am not afraid, I will survive, I will be better.* Slowly, I got control over my breathing and heart rate. The panic faded into the background and I was able to think more clearly.

What had caused me to slide so far back into old habits? I had come so far over the years, I hadn't experienced one of these night terror episodes in so long I had forgotten how real they seemed.

I tried to pull myself back into my current reality and away from the past. What was the last thing I remembered? I shot up from the bed when the memory of Froston coming to the house and taking me through the portal surfaced. He had shoved me back through the portal while I was still in my wolf form. Who changed me back into my human form?

Light came into the darkness at my movement and I looked around in confusion. I was in a bedroom, not my own. The light was emanating from the walls in a soft glow, revealing the stone walls and old fashioned furniture. Had my movement triggered the actual walls to start glowing?

I stood up from the bed and listened carefully before stretching my sore muscles. I didn't hear any sounds, no one was near. I felt too vulnerable, standing here naked, just waiting for someone to come into the room, so I shifted back into my wolf form. I shook out my coat and stretched my back. My entire body was sore. How long had I been laying in that bed?

I trotted over to the door but was stopped before I could get close to it. There was an invisible barrier that blocked me from the doorway. I paced in frustration, testing the boundaries of the invisible cage I had been placed into. I investigated every inch of my prison, taking in all of the scents and looking for any way out.

There were no windows in the room, but there was an archway that led into a bathroom. The walls were all made of stone, and it was clear that the door I couldn't reach was the only way out of here. I pushed away my feelings of panic and helplessness and tried to convince myself it would be okay. I wasn't a frightened child locked in a room. I was a wolf.

If Froston or anyone else thought that they could push me around because they thought that I was just a sweet, helpless female then they were going to be in for a big surprise. I wasn't the timid Anna anymore, I wasn't going to hide from confrontation or quiver in fear. My time with my pack had taught me to stand tall with my head held high. I am a wolf in the Seaside Wolf Pack and I am a fighter.

I tried to hold back my urge to shred something with my claws in frustration. Froston, I refused to call him my father, had most likely placed me in here for a reason. He obviously wanted me to think that this was something other than a forceful kidnapping. I was going to have to be smart to get out of here.

I was going to have to play Froston's game in order to get an opportunity to escape. He seemed to like playing the role of a caring father, but it was going to grate on my nerves to indulge him after everything he had done. I huffed in frustration but debated on what to do next.

The room itself was pretty, as far as prisons went. The giant four poster bed I had awakened in was decorated in dainty blue lace and there was an impressive looking wardrobe next to a feminine vanity. The room was clearly meant for a female. The other side of the room held a couch and a small table and chairs. It reminded me of a large studio apartment.

I decided to make myself presentable in the hopes that I would be given the opportunity to talk my way out of here. I trotted over to the wardrobe and switched back to my human form. I disliked feeling exposed, so I looked for something I could cover myself with.

The wardrobe contained a large selection of dresses, but no pants. The dresses ranged from thin gossamer to stiff ball-gowns. I decided on a lightweight, lacy dress in white.

Hopefully, this would put Froston at ease and cause him to underestimate me, so I could make a plan of escape. There were no shoes in the wardrobe, only a selection of thin slippers to match each of the gowns. I sighed in disappointment. The stone floors were going to bruise my feet if I had to wear these all day long.

After I had dressed and used the bathroom, I stared at the door. Was anyone out there? I threw a pillow from the bed at the invisible barrier and saw it shimmer before the pillow bounced back towards me.

I narrowed my eyes. Froston had told me that I had broken the barrier that he had placed on my magic. Could I break this?

I stood in front of the barrier and placed my hands on it. With my eyes closed, I reached down inside of myself for my magic. I didn't have to struggle as much this time. I reached past the magic that allowed me to shift, and delved into the deeper well that I must have inherited as part fae. I ignored all the emotions that came with that realization and focused on the task at hand.

I wasn't sure what to do once I felt my magic, so I decided to experiment. I tried imagining myself grabbing handfuls of it and flinging it at the barrier.

Nothing.

This time I tried to envision a wall of my magic burning a hole through the barrier. The only thing I accomplished was giving myself a headache. I let out a frustrated sigh, I don't think I was doing this right.

I backed off and paced in front of the barrier. I was desperate to get out of here, but a part of me was also afraid to fully embrace my magic after what happened last time. I could still see the vision of Ben's charred remains in my mind.

I was gathering my courage to try again when the door started to open. It was strange, because I couldn't hear the sound of the door opening, or the footsteps of Froston entering the room. He paused in front of the barrier and placed his hands on it, his eyes focused in concentration.

I narrowed my eyes in suspicion. It looked like the barrier that was the bane of my existence did more than just keep me here, it also kept me from hearing what was going on outside my prison. What was he trying to hide from me?

I watched the barrier shimmer as Froston removed his hands and then easily strode through it without hesitation. I briefly wondered what would happen if I shoved him back through while holding on to him. Would the barrier allow me to cross if we were touching?

Froston was through the barrier before I had to opportunity to attempt it, but that didn't mean I couldn't try when he was on his way out.

"Glad to see you're awake. I had a feeling you would wake up ready to fight." He chuckled, but his amusement never reached his sad eyes.

I crossed my arms and glared. "Are you ready to take me home?"

He completely ignored my question. "You look so much like your mother," he murmured quietly, drifting closer to me.

I glared at him, barely holding in my anger and frustration. "Don't pretend to care."

James had gotten a photo of my mother while he was with the Canadian pack, so I couldn't deny that we really did look similar. But Froston should have been the one sharing pictures of my mother with me. I shouldn't have had to wait for James to go on some kind of covert mission to get one.

He sighed with resignation and took a seat in the chair before gesturing for me to join him. "We're alone now; no one can hear our conversation."

I watched him cautiously and tried to push aside my anger. I didn't trust him, but I needed him to trust me if I was going to be able to get out of here. I took a seat and tried to compose myself. Yelling at him wasn't going to get the information that I needed or get me back to my pack. Not trusting myself to speak, I simply raised an eyebrow at him.

I was waiting to hear what possible explanation he could give for this. Why would he throw me through some kind of magical portal and lock me in this stone room? That wasn't how you should treat your long-lost daughter. Even worse than that, he'd harmed two of the men who had taken me in and given me their protection.

Froston rubbed his hand over his face in a human-like gesture. I tried to remind myself that he wasn't human, and that I shouldn't be thinking of him as if he were the caring father I always wanted.

"Anna... there are some things I want to explain to you." Froston searched my eyes carefully.

I didn't say anything, I just waited. He was right, he did have a lot to explain.

My dear father must not have seen what he hoped for, because he sat back with a sigh. "I was sent to the human world to fetch you."

I held back the angry growl that wanted to rise inside of me. After all this time, he didn't come back for me because he had located his lost daughter? He came back because he was *sent*?

"I had someone watching over you," he told me defensively, probably sensing my flare of anger. "I was concerned when Evelyn died, but I saw that you were being taken care of by a pack."

I felt a flash of betrayal. Evelyn was hired by my father? I thought that she had watched over me out of the goodness of her heart.

Realization struck. Austin had asked me where Evelyn had gotten all of her money. I guess now I knew the answer.

I tried to push away the bitterness that was rising within me. I had been tormented as a child, with Evelyn as the only person who cared for me. But she had never stepped in to protect me or tried take me away from my abusive uncle. She let me go back home to him every night, knowing what awaited me.

If she was a paid caretaker, why couldn't she just adopt me? Was her story about being hunted by a pack even true? I swallowed the lump forming in my throat and took a deep breath. Evelyn was not here for me to ask, but my father was.

"Why-" My voice broke and I cleared my throat.

"I didn't dare to get too close to you. I couldn't risk anyone finding you or realizing our connection," Froston told me forlornly.

I crossed my arms over my chest, trying to keep my heart from thawing. "Why not?"

He looked off into the distance as if searching for answers. "It's complicated."

I felt my heart hardening. "So, uncomplicate it."

"Anna, don't trust anyone. It's not safe for you here."

"Not even you?" I shot back.

Froston smiled at me sadly. "Only if we're alone. I have a part to play when being watched. Things would only be worse for you if they realized how much I care for you."

I huffed in irritation. "Actions speak louder than words, and you haven't shown that you care for me at all."

Froston reached out for me, but I kept my arms crossed over my chest.

He looked disappointed but dropped his hands into his lap. "I do care for you, Anna. If I didn't I would not have been able to stay away from you all these years."

I scowled. Did he think I was stupid?

"So what stopped you?" I asked him, not even trying to hide the accusing tone in my voice.

"There are things you don't know-"

"So tell me," I interrupted sharply. "Don't keep dragging this out."

He nodded as if I had just confirmed something for him. "I'm deeply indebted to the king. Our house is a noble house, but we continue to exist dependent on the king's will."

Froston looked at me to see if I was following so I gave him a nod. "Magic runs deep in our blood. Legend has it that the gods formed our ancestors out of pure elements. That's why we have such a strong connection to the elemental magic around us."

I frowned, thinking about the fire that had come bursting out of me. Using magic still seemed like a foreign concept to me; my brain struggled to put magic in terms of the science that I was familiar with. Gods forming people out of elements didn't fit with the scientific explanations for the world.

"So we are magical and indebted to the king. Why am I here?" I asked bluntly.

He chuckled. "You're here because King Illian wants something from you. I wasn't the only one who felt the flare of magic that identified your position. One of the princes was in the human world and felt it as well. I did all I could to make sure that I was the one to bring you here, but we were closely watched. If I'd given even a hint that I wasn't wholeheartedly doing the king's bidding, someone else would have been sent for you."

Froston leaned forward to signify the importance of his next statement. "You do not want to be in the care of anyone but me."

"So… you kidnapped me to keep me safe?" I asked doubtfully.

He sat back in his chair. "If I hadn't, someone else would have."

I watched him carefully. I didn't sense that he was lying but he clearly was not telling me everything.

"What does the king want from me?" I asked warily.

Froston sighed. "He needs a weapon."

My eyebrows rose in alarm.

"You wouldn't have to harm anyone," Froston assured me hurriedly. "Just demonstrate your power, so that King Illian can tell the Summer Court that we have an entire army…like you."

"I'm not going to hurt anyone," I told him firmly.

Froston smiled at me affectionately. "That's why we need to teach you how to use your magic now that you've broken my barrier. I'm sure you don't want to accidentally harm anyone in your pack?"

I shook my head, my stomach clenched in anxiety. I had gotten lucky that my fire had only harmed my attackers. What if I had burned James while I was clinging to him? Or what if Austin and Cody had been standing too close? Tears came to my eyes at the thought. I had absolutely no control over what happened that night, and I'd never forgive myself if I harmed anyone that I loved. I barely forgave myself for harming my enemies - the image of Ben, burned and broken, trying to crawl away from me was forever burned into my memory.

I swallowed nervously. Maybe being here could be an advantage in the long run, but I needed to know more about what I was getting into. I knew nothing about the fae, I hadn't even known they existed. When the barrier broke around my magic, I had never expected to be told that I was part fae. Sam had told me that panthers down in South America had shamans who could use magic, so I had just assumed that I was an unusual wolf.

Froston was here now and he owed me an explanation. "I don't know anything about the fae," I told him hesitantly. "Can you give me a crash course?"

Froston laughed. "Human mythology usually splits the courts into Light and Dark, Seelie and Unseelie, but the closest English words for them would be Winter and Summer. Both are separated from your world by a veil that we need to use a portal to cross. Both courts can cross into the human world, but there is no direct link between Winter and Summer."

My heart dropped when I realized that I wasn't even in the same world as my pack any longer. How was I going to get back to them?

I tried to focus on what Froston was telling me and not let despair overwhelm me. He was explaining how most of the fae in the Winter Court had powers related to winter, death, and destruction.

"I would think that makes Winter more powerful." I interrupted.

Froston smiled with amusement. "Life can be just as powerful as death."

I shrugged unhappily. "What if I can't 'demonstrate my power'? I've failed at just about everything I've tried to do with it."

Froston gave me a softer smile. "You're still just a child. It takes time."

I made a face. "I've been on my own for years," I told him defensively. "I've built a successful life for myself; I think that makes me anything but a child."

He smiled at me affectionately, but didn't argue.

I took a deep breath. "So after I prove myself to the king, I can go home?"

He avoided eye contact so I pressed further. "How do I even get home? Where are we? Why did you take me to the Arctic? Who were those other men? Why didn't they freeze to death instantly in the subzero temperature? Why didn't I?"

Froston looked surprised at my barrage of questions so I paused for a moment to give him time to start answering me. I was most concerned with any information he would give me on how to get out of here and back home.

Movement caught my eye and I turned to see the door opening once again. This time a tall, dark-haired man stood at the door, staring at me from the other side of the barrier with a smirk on his face. I sat up a little taller and looked at Froston. He had a slight frown that he quickly hid before turning his back to the door.

Froston turned to me so that his face was not visible to the man at the door. "I need you to play along for now," he said urgently. "This man is dangerous to both of us."

I sighed but gave a quick nod. I didn't know what was going on here, but I was hoping it wouldn't hurt me to follow Froston's lead for now. I was going to trust that whatever he was doing here was meant to help me and not harm me.

Froston turned back to the door with a grin on his face. His attitude and mannerisms had changed back to the jovial character when I first met him. He let the stranger in the door, and there was no sign of the caring father that he had been playing only a moment ago.

Which was the real Froston, and which was an act?

My gaze went to the stranger as he crossed the barrier and moved into the room. He had wavy dark hair that fell almost to his shoulders, and green eyes that were even brighter than mine. The stranger was wearing all black, but the cut of his clothes was more old fashioned than Froston's business-like slacks and button down. His dark shirt had an open neck and snug breeches tucked into knee-high boots. He was tall and lean, and had an almost ethereal beauty, unlike the rugged good looks of my wolves. But where my wolves radiated warmth, and Froston radiated the fresh coldness of a winter day, the stranger had a darkness about him.

I extended my senses further to get more of an awareness of him. The darkness that exuded from him wasn't frightening at first. It was almost seductive in the way that it drew me in, so I hurriedly backed off and tried to shut off those senses.

Froston gestured for me to stand. "Anna, I would like to introduce you to our Prince Mandrake."

I stood and smoothed down my dress, unsure of how to greet a prince. "Um, nice to meet you," I murmured.

The prince looked amused by my obvious discomfort, but didn't say anything. He gracefully took a seat in the chair that Froston had vacated, while Froston stood behind his chair. After he was settled he waved a hand for me to sit across from him.

I tried to hide how nervous I was as I sat and pasted a smile on my face. Hopefully, it didn't look as fake as it felt.

"Anna," He said my name slowly as if savoring it. "I'm glad your father finally brought you here."

My eyes flicked to Froston and he gave me what I thought was supposed to be an encouraging look. Luckily, the prince wasn't waiting for a response from me.

"We'll be starting our lessons tomorrow. I've made time for you in the afternoons."

I looked at him curiously. "What lessons?"

Froston cleared his throat, but the prince leaned forward to speak in a playful manner. "Now, Anna. I don't expect you to observe pointless courtesies when we are alone. But if we were in public, I would have to punish you for your disrespect."

I just looked at him blankly before shifting my gaze to Froston. What was he expecting from me?

"They don't have royalty where Anna lives in the human world, my prince." Froston told him cautiously. "Anna, you should address the prince as 'Your Highness' when speaking to him."

I turned bright red but mumbled an apology with 'Your Highness' tacked on the end. I looked up through my lashes to see the prince with a grin on his face. I wasn't sure if he was amused by how uneducated I was, or by how embarrassed I was. But either way, I didn't like the way his eyes quietly mocked me. But Froston had cautioned me that this man was dangerous, so I held my tongue.

"My unique talents are best suited to teach you what I need you to do for me" the dark prince declared with a smirk.

I hadn't missed the double entendre, but I wasn't sure how to respond. Froston didn't miss a beat. "We are both grateful to you for your help, Your Highness."

"I'm looking forward to it," the prince murmured as he ran his eyes slowly over my body as if he were thinking about devouring me. A shiver ran down my spine as tendrils of his magic reached for me. My body might be responding to whatever magic he was trying to use on me, but my heart was already full. I had absolutely no desire to get involved with this man, I wanted to go home to my wolves.

"How long do you think it will be before I can go home?" I blurted out. "Your Highness." I added as an afterthought. I was not looking forward to spending time with this guy, especially not alone. I didn't like the way that he made me feel, and I missed my pack.

The prince laughed but Froston looked nervous.

"I take it you haven't told her our plans?" The prince asked, not taking his eyes off me. "No matter, we'll have plenty of time to discuss it." He stood and Froston motioned for me to stand as well.

I thought about being defiant for a split second but stood as Froston directed. I forced myself to smile at the prince as he held out his hand for mine. I gave him my hand cautiously, but he merely held it for a moment.

"It was a pleasure to meet you, Anna. I look forward to our time together." The prince held my gaze as he slowly raised my hand to his mouth and gave it a gentle kiss. I tried to ignore the heat that flooded through my body, but I couldn't hide the flush that rose to my cheeks. What was going on with me? I felt like my body was betraying my heart, was this some kind of fae magic? It was way too soon for my hormones to be affecting me this strongly, I wouldn't be going into heat again until late December.

The prince gave me one last smirk before turning to the door. "Froston, I require your assistance."

"Of course, Your Highness." Froston murmured in response.

I opened my mouth to object. There was no way they were going to give me little bits of info that just caused me to have more questions, then walk away without giving me answers.

Froston shot me a look behind the prince's back and waited until the prince had crossed the barrier with a shimmer. Interesting. Did the barrier only work on me?

"I'll explain everything," Froston assured me. "Just give me some time."

I ground my teeth in frustration but gave him a nod. He breathed a sigh of relief then followed the prince through the barrier, leaving me alone in my prison.

Chapter 3

Austin

I straightened my shirtsleeves and took a deep breath. Cody had gathered the majority of the pack here today for a meeting. All our team leaders were here, but we had left a skeleton crew to guard our boundaries.

My pack was organized into teams of six wolves, the members of each team were expected to remain in close contact with each other at all times. Each team had a strong team leader and five other wolves whose skills complimented each other. This organization helped to keep my pack of over fifty wolves close and easily mobilized in case of emergencies.

News of Anna's disappearance had spread through the pack quickly and tempers were high. My pack might be civilized and well disciplined, but we were still wolves. Having a stranger come into our territory and take our most precious female was going to rile even my most dependable wolves.

The loss of Anna had struck painfully deep in my heart. She hadn't been gone that long, but I already felt the emptiness that echoed in the house without her warmth and her scent. The thought of her bright smile had gotten me through quite a few stressful days. Having Anna here had given me a renewed sense of purpose. She inspired me to work harder to make a better life for my pack. The thought of coming home every day to a house without her left me feeling empty inside.

I strode down the hall to where my pack was gathered and tried to tuck my feelings away. My pack was waiting for my orders and needed me to be strong and confident. Cody and Trevor were attempting to keep order, but my pack needed direction and an outlet for their frustrations. As pack master, I could feel anger radiating throughout my pack. I needed to give these guys something to do before that anger boiled over into senseless violence.

I stepped into the room and Cody's eyes flicked towards me with relief. I knew things were bad if Cody was at the end of his rope. Cody and Trevor were the two largest wolves in the pack, so normally they wouldn't be having a problem keeping control over the rest of the guys. Even when we were in our human forms, we were still influenced by the instincts we had inherited as wolves. Our shape didn't change that.

"Enough!" I shouted, putting the full weight of a pack master's authority into the command.

Heads immediately snapped towards me, and there was silence in the room. I didn't like using my abilities as pack master to control my wolves, but in this instance it was necessary. I relaxed my hold on them once I had everyone's attention.

"Everyone have a seat," I told them briskly. There weren't enough chairs or couches in our kitchen/dining/living room area for everyone, so some of the lower ranking wolves sat on the floor.

"I know there have been rumors going around." I met the eyes of each one of my team leaders, gauging their reactions. Most gave me nods before lowering their eyes. One of them, Blendel, looked at me defiantly before lowering his eyes - he was going to need some special attention.

"Anna has been taken by the enemy," I announced bluntly.

Angry grumbles and discontented murmurs drifted from pockets in the room. I made note of which teams that came from. I had debated on just how much I should tell my wolves. Would announcing that Anna was part fae put her in even more danger? Was it fair to my pack to withhold that information if we were going to be going up against the fae?

"Just who is our enemy?" Blendel challenged. "There's talk of fucking faeries and shit."

I met his gaze head on and let him feel the weight of my stare, putting my full power behind it. He quickly dropped his eyes, backing down from his challenge.

"While most of us have been under the impression that the fae were nothing more than myths and exaggerated fairy tales, myself and other pack mates have stood in their presence and can assure you that they are real." I looked around the room as I spoke and was met with incredulous and disbelieving looks.

James picked that moment to walk into the room and stand behind my right shoulder. Some of my more cantankerous wolves quieted with his threatening presence. While I tried to be an approachable leader with an open-door policy, James made most of my wolves nervous with his mere presence.

James narrowed his gaze on Blendel after scanning the room. "You afraid of fucking faeries and shit, Blendel?"

Blendel scoffed but stayed silent, submissive for now.

I cleared my throat. "This meeting was called before the events that occurred earlier this morning. I originally planned to deliver some news that will be a pleasant surprise for most of you."

I paused, giving the pack a moment to take in my words and shift gears. The fear and uncertainty in the room decreased somewhat now that their curiosity was piqued. Good. That was the goal. "I've decided to recall our teams from overseas. We have withdrawn our bids for the next round of government contracts and will be regrouping here in Seaside."

There were quite a few murmurs of surprise from all around the room. The government contracts had been a major source of income for the pack for years now. But we had come to the point where our businesses and jobs here in the states could support us for now. I was relieved to be bringing my entire pack home.

I thought I'd be bringing them home to safety from the chaotic Middle East, but with the events of this morning I wasn't sure it was going to be any safer here for them. I wasn't willing to let Froston keep Anna from us. He had acted like a caring father while he was here, but why did he really take her against her will? There was more to this than we knew. Whatever the reason, I wasn't sure we would be able to get her back without a fight.

I waited until the pack had settled once again. "Our brothers will be home within the month and will need us to help them reacclimate to being here in the U.S.." I saw quite a few knowledgeable nods around the room. It wasn't easy for everyone to come home, there was an adjustment period that could be more difficult for some.

Rich raised a hand cautiously and I nodded at him to give him permission to speak. "Do we need to prepare accommodations for them?"

I frowned. My original plan had been to ask Anna if she would be willing to open up her former home and Evelyn's house to two of the teams coming back. Evelyn's home wasn't far from here, but Anna had lived forty five minutes away in Port Idris. Port Idris was through the tunnel and to the west, closer to the center of our territory and only an hour from Emporia. That would give that team the ability to cover the western portion of our territory. The third team would be able to stay here with us in the mansion. But now that Anna was gone... we had bigger problems to worry about.

"Details will follow on that, Rich," I assured him confidently. "I'll be assigning work details to prepare a place for them in the near future."

Rich nodded, reassured by my words. He had probably been concerned that I was considering splitting up the overseas teams and placing them among the existing teams. That would be far from ideal, as each unit was close and it was difficult to integrate new team members into a tight knit group.

I looked around the room to see that most of the pack was settling down with the news of reinforcements coming. Tony caught my eye and asked for permission to speak. I gave it to him with a nod.

"But we're going to get Anna back?" he asked hesitantly.

"Of course, we're getting her back," Trevor grumbled. "We don't leave our pack members with the enemy."

"Is it a rescue mission or a war?" Henderson asked cautiously.

Tension rose again in the room at the mention of war. A war between supernatural races could be disastrous and everyone knew it.

I raised my hand for silence. "Right now, it's just a rescue mission," I assured them. "A rogue fae has taken one of our females and we're going to get her back." I honestly hoped that was the case.

"If we don't get her back, we're never going to get another female to join the pack," Henderson said forlornly. "If we can't keep our females safe..."

There was silence in the room. I was a little surprised to hear that members of my pack craved more females after our previous failure, but I could understand the desire to have more females like Anna. However, there was only one Anna and we needed her back.

"While we are working to put together a rescue team, I need everyone on alert." I told them firmly. "Anna's smart, and she'll find a way to contact us if she can. Stay aware of anything out of the ordinary, or anything that could be a signal or a message."

James stepped forward. "Trevor and I'll be meeting with each of your teams to give you specific assignments and work details to prepare."

I gave him a nod. "The meeting is adjourned for now. I need you to stay on the premises until your team meetings are complete."

I turned on my heel and walked out, the room exploding into conversation after I left. I was leaving them in the capable hands of Cody and James for now – I had called a meeting with the council. I deflated a little as soon as I was out of sight. It wasn't easy to project an aura of confidence when fear for Anna's safety had taken root within my core. I was worried about her and I was worried *for* her.

There were many reasons why Froston might want to take Anna. I was hoping that the affection he had displayed for her in our meeting was genuine, but he had been difficult to read. There was a pit in my stomach that churned with worry. I hated to even consider it, but usually when a rival pack would take a female it was for breeding purposes.

Anna was a young wolf in her prime and many would want to possess her as a status symbol because of her beauty and her pure white coat. Anna was so much more than that to me, I could care less what color her coat was. What made Anna so beautiful was the pure soul that shined from within her.

I also worried because it was well-known that females went into heat twice a year. Most females experienced their fertile weeks in June and December and December was approaching quickly. I felt sick at the thought of anyone using Anna like that. I hadn't confessed any of these concerns to my pack-mates and I doubted that these thoughts had occurred to everyone.

The twins fell into step behind me, I decided to bring them with me to the council meeting as my security. Their emotions were running high, and I didn't want that energy feeding into the already frenzied energy swirling around the pack right now. They were another reason why I needed to appear absolutely confident that we could get Anna back. I needed the twins to believe in me and follow my lead.

Mason and Jason were on edge and they needed a time-out from the pack. They needed to feel like they were doing something to help Anna. Otherwise, their restlessness would result in them acting out. The last thing I needed was the two of them abandoning the pack and embarking on a rash and unplanned rescue mission. If we wanted Anna back, we were going to have to work together.

We climbed into Cody's SUV with Mason driving and Jason in the back. I waited a moment, knowing that an inquisition was coming. Their hearts were in the right place, and I would be lying if I said that I didn't feel the same combination of loss and frustration as they did. They just needed a little guidance on how to manage those emotions.

The twins flicked glances at each other, obviously conversing silently with their bond. I sat back and waited for them to finish, I was guessing that Mason was going to be their spokesperson.

"So, boss," Mason started cautiously. "What's the plan?"

"The plan is to consolidate our allies against our enemy," I told him calmly.

"So we just leave her there? How can we just abandon Anna? We need to get her back now!" Jason shouted from the backseat.

I met his eyes through the rearview mirror. "We don't know where Anna is. Just where are you going to get her back *from*? We can mount a half-assed rescue attempt that 's going to fail and leave us in a worse place than we are in now. Or, we can gather intelligence, get our allies on our side, and get our girl back."

Jason settled back in his chair with a sigh of frustration and rubbed his face with his hands. "We need her back." I could see the desperation and the helplessness in his eyes, so I didn't hold his outburst against him. Deep down, I felt exactly the same.

"We are going to get her back." I told him softly. "Anna is tough and she's smart. We know that she has not just survived a lot, she also managed to beat all the odds against her."

Jason gave a nod, but his teeth were gritted in frustration. "I just need to do something now, I can't just sit here and pretend that everything is fine."

"We are doing something." I told him firmly. I already had Trevor's team prepping for a mission up north. I had a feeling that Anna's story had begun in the Arctic wolves' territory when she was born, and that's where she was now. Telling the twins that they had to remain in Seaside while I sent another team up north for Anna was going to be a fight for another day.

The twins were a valuable asset to the pack, but they were still young and could be emotionally volatile and impulsive at times. We needed cool heads and rational thinking to get us through this. In most circumstances, I could trust James to be the voice of caution and reason, but time would tell if he could maintain a level head when

Anna was in danger. I'd never seen James let a female into his heart before and I was worried about what Anna's loss would do to him. He was usually tightly controlled, but dangerous. Would losing Anna make him lose control? Could I stop James if he lost all sense of caution and went on attack?

Jason sat back in his seat and crossed his arms with a scowl. Mason watched his brother with a frown. He was drawing back into himself, no doubt he was thinking the situation through.

Crisis averted for now, I settled back in my own seat and pulled out my phone. I could only handle one problem at a time. Right now, I needed to make a plan for how I was going to get the council on my side and willing to take on the most powerful creatures I had ever encountered. The fae might seem invincible, but everyone had a weakness. I just needed to find it.

Chapter 4

Anna

I paced anxiously, waiting for Froston to return and give me the answers that he'd promised. When the door opened, it wasn't Froston that stepped over the threshold, it was a teenage girl with bright red curly hair and blue eyes. She was barely over five feet tall and had a dainty bone structure that made her light on her feet. She was wearing an old fashioned blue dress, something I would have expected a woman to wear in the medieval ages, not now.

I watched her cross the barrier easily as if it weren't there at all and I huffed in frustration. I really was the only person that couldn't cross the stupid thing. The girl entered cautiously and gave me a shy smile before she curtsied. Once again, I was at a loss as to how to respond appropriately so I gave her a smile.

"Good evening, my lady. I was sent to dress you for dinner?" She kept her eyes down as she spoke but peeked through her lashes at the end to gauge my reaction.

I perked up. Was I going to get out of this room? "Thank you, but you can call me Anna," I said politely.

She brightened up at my answer and gave me a huge smile.

"What's your name?" I asked curiously.

She giggled. "My name is Caylee. I was hoping you would be nice." Her curiosity seemed to overwhelm her shyness. "You just came from the human world, didn't you?" she asked eagerly.

I nodded, looking a little closer at her. Caylee looked and felt completely human, and I didn't sense anything to tell me that she was a supernatural.

"Is that where you're from?" I asked gently.

She flounced towards me, her shyness completely forgotten. "Yes! I was brought here for good luck, you know, on account of my red hair."

I blinked in surprise. "Do you like it here?" I asked cautiously.

"Oh, yes," she told me enthusiastically. "I've been here since I was just a child, but I never want to leave." She shuddered in horror. "I can't imagine going back there."

My jaw dropped in surprise and she smiled at my reaction. "It's going to be even better for you, because you aren't a human at all so you don't have to be a servant." She leaned in to whisper conspiratorially, "And I heard that Prince Mandrake has his eye on you."

I inhaled a sharp breath. "Could you tell me more about him and the rest of this world? This is my first time here."

Caylee giggled again but happily started to chatter away as she went over to the wardrobe to look through the dresses there.

She told me that Prince Mandrake was the youngest son of the king, and all about how handsome he was, and how every female in the kingdom wanted his attention now that the other two princes were wed.

I cleared my throat to interrupt. "So, we're in the king's castle?"

Caylee laughed. "No, silly. This is your father's castle. Prince Mandrake is visiting. It's a great honor to your father to have him request to meet you."

"So, if my father has his own castle, then he must be important?" I asked hesitantly.

Caylee giggled. "Your father is one of the nine lords that answer directly to the king. They have castles that circle around the edges of the king's territory and protect our lands."

"Protect us from what?" I asked curiously.

Caylee shrugged. "Whatever's outside?"

I frowned at her, that wasn't much of an explanation. "So, there's a king, three princes, and nine lords. What about everyone else?"

"Well, there's a bunch of minor lords who answer to the lords like your father. But there are also 'lesser fae'. They don't have all the magic like the lords do, but they can do little tricks like shapeshifting." Caylee shuddered. "Usually you can tell the difference because the lesser fae aren't as beautiful, and some of them are considered to be deformed."

I frowned at Caylee, but she hurriedly reassured me. "I'm sure that a lady like yourself won't have any dealings with them."

This was incredibly uncomfortable, I felt like I had stepped out of reality and into a bad movie. I didn't belong in a castle, or with a prince. I belonged at home with my pack.

A sharp pang of longing shot through me as I wondered what my pack was doing now. Were they in a panic after I disappeared? Were they worried?

"You look sad," Caylee said softly. "Do you already have a love?"

I nodded. "I do."

"Is he… a human?" she asked with wide eyes.

I couldn't help but smile. "No." What would she think if I told her I had more than just one love interest? I decided not to say anything more on the subject. I'd never met her before, and I didn't know if I could trust her. Plus, this time alone with her was valuable. I needed to gather as much information as possible.

"What dress do you think I should wear?" I asked thoughtfully, gazing over her shoulder into the wardrobe and trying to draw her attention away from my love life.

That did the trick, because Caylee went right back to chattering away with her bubbly enthusiasm about what dresses would most please the prince. I fought the urge to roll my eyes, I'd prefer to wear a dress that would repulse the prince, not attract him.

"Who else is going to be at the dinner?" I asked Caylee once she had paused to take a breath.

"Just you, the prince, and your father," she said breathlessly. "This is your chance to entice him while you don't have any competition."

I sighed. *Great.*

"Tell me more about the fae. How big is this kingdom? How often do people travel to the human world? How many humans are here?"

Caylee paused and gave me a strange look.

"I don't want to look uneducated in front of Prince Mandrake," I told her, trying to look self-conscious about my ignorance.

41

She nodded wisely. "Yes, you want to make sure that you don't give him the impression that you're stupid. I heard that he prizes wit among his lovers."

It took everything I had not to roll my eyes at that, and I tried to look interested.

"There are quite a few of us humans here," Caylee said thoughtfully. "Most of us were taken as children and work as servants. Some of the lucky ones are taken as lovers once they are old enough." Caylee leaned towards me. "Usually if you have a child for one of them you're taken care of for life, you get the choicest positions here."

"What about the children?" I asked curiously. "What happens to them?"

Caylee sighed. "Some of them have magic and get to be guards or special assistants to the fae. Those without magic are just the same as us regular humans."

"How often do people visit the human world?" I asked curiously.

Caylee giggled. "Only the princes and those who have the king's permission can go." She tugged on the strings to lace up the corset on the dress and I grunted as it cut into my ribs. I was definitely not a fan of fae fashion.

Caylee motioned to the vanity. "Sit, so I can do your hair."

I gently lowered myself to the stool and struggled to breathe as the corset pressed on my lungs. "Any chance we can loosen this?" I gasped out.

Caylee eyed me critically. "You're already more... curvy than most of the fae females. I don't want the prince to think you have a thick waist."

I raised my eyebrows and struggled to get the words out. "He's already seen me without a corset, so it's too late for that."

She took in a sharp breath and looked dismayed. I stood up so that I could talk and tried to reassure her. "And I'm fine with the prince thinking I'm thick."

Caylee looked so scandalized that I couldn't help but chuckle. "Honestly, Caylee, thank you for trying to make me look attractive, but I would rather be able to breathe." I turned around to give her access to the laces in the back.

She pinched her lips together but started to loosen the corset. I sucked in a breath of air in relief once I felt the corset give enough for my lungs to expand completely. Caylee didn't seem too upset, because she went right back to chattering away at me as she brushed out my hair.

I didn't get any useful information on how I could get out of here, but I tried not to worry. Caylee tried to be as helpful as she could, but court gossip wasn't what I was looking for. I didn't care which males were the most handsome, or who was looking for a new lover, or who was sleeping with who.

"So, the fae don't marry?" I asked Caylee curiously.

She shrugged. "Not really. They don't really form emotional attachments like we do, they are constantly switching alliances and taking new lovers." Caylee paused. "I guess the exception are the princes and the nine lords. They're expected to marry and have powerful babies to serve the kingdom."

I raised my eyebrows. "But do the humans in this world marry?"

Caylee looked at me in surprise. "Some do when they give up hope of getting a fae lover. There's no point in having human babies, they'll just grow up to be servants."

"And you're okay with that?" I asked her. "You wouldn't want your child to be a servant, but it's acceptable for you?"

Caylee cocked her head to stare at me. "No one's ever asked me what I wanted to be before. I think I should be able to attract one of the fae if I'm careful."

I looked at her in disbelief. "But why do you want to stay in this world?" I asked softly. "Why not go back to the human world and go to college? You could be anything you want. You don't have to be a servant or have a baby for someone who doesn't love you."

Caylee laughed. "The human world is inferior to this one. Only an idiot would want to go back."

Caylee seemed so sure of what she was saying, but I had a feeling that the fae were brainwashing human children from a young age to stay here to take advantage of them. They were convincing kids like Caylee that her best option was to be a servant to them to keep them in line. That hardly seemed fair.

Caylee didn't seem like she was willing to change a lifetime of preconceived notions right now, but maybe I could show her she had more options over time. I sighed. I don't know why I was thinking of ways to get Caylee home to the human world when I wasn't even sure I would be able to get back myself.

Eventually Caylee stepped back to view the final product and sighed. "I think this is the best I can do."

I couldn't help but laugh a little at her dismay at not being able to make me into someone the prince would find attractive. Hopefully, he would realize that I didn't belong here with the fae and would send me right back to my pack. If only I could be that lucky.

I stood up to look in the mirror. Caylee had dressed me in an old-fashioned ball gown with a full skirt and corset. It was an icy blue color that reminded me of Cinderella's dress when she went to the ball to meet the prince of her dreams. I felt the urge to laugh hysterically at the ridiculousness of my own situation – dressing to meet a prince was the opposite of a dream come true for me. I wanted no part of this type of life.

I leaned toward Caylee and took ahold of one of her hands. Froston had already warned me that the prince was dangerous. I was trying to put on a brave face and not let my inner fears get to me, but deep down I still felt small threads of panic and anxiety trying to get out.

"Should I be afraid?" I asked Caylee quietly.

She avoided my eyes and licked her lips nervously. "He's not as…temperamental as his brothers," she told me in a whisper. "But those that displease him tend to quietly disappear."

Caylee looked around the room anxiously. "He'll keep a smile on his face and look amused by those that oppose him, but…"

I let out a breath, I definitely needed to be cautious here. This wasn't a game.

I released Caylee's hand and gave her a warm smile. "What do you like to do for fun around here?"

She looked relieved at the change of conversation and started chatting about the various festivals that took place in the castle. I nodded along to what she was saying but tried to think about what my strategy for tonight should be.

I needed to be strong enough that I wouldn't be taken advantage of, but polite enough that I wouldn't be challenging the dangerous prince. With a sigh, I realized that the best strategy for tonight would probably be to speak as little as possible. I was way over my head here.

All too soon, Froston was at the door and ready to bring me to dinner with the prince. My stomach was a pit of dread.

He had changed into clothing that resembled Prince Mandrake's from earlier today, but instead of black, he was dressed in white and silver. Going by the clothing choices, it seemed like the fae were trapped in the past. They also didn't seem very fond of technology, and instead relied on magic. Caylee had showed me how to control the lighting in my room, which had to involve magic because the walls themselves glowed with light. When I asked Caylee how it worked, she had just tilted her head in confusion.

Froston dismissed Caylee and held out an arm for me to take. I hesitated. "Do we have to do this?" I pleaded with him. "If the prince is so dangerous, shouldn't I stay far away from him?"

Froston sighed. "Unfortunately, he's taken an interest in you. It might have been a flash of your power that caught his attention, but he seems to be fascinated by how...different you are."

I frowned. It seemed like I didn't fit in anywhere. I wasn't human enough to fit in as a human, I wasn't wolf enough to blend in with the wolves, and now I wasn't fae enough either? Where did I fit into the world?

"I'll do everything I can to keep you safe," Froston promised.

I nodded in resignation, but it didn't escape my notice that Froston had not promised to keep me safe, he just said he would try.

I couldn't help but look around with wide eyes as Froston lead me out of my prison and through the castle. He smiled at me affectionately and gave me a guided tour as we walked. His castle reminded me of something from King Arthur's times. The stone walls of the hall were broken only by narrow windows that looked like they could be used by archers firing at invaders down below. There were woven tapestries hung on the walls depicting fae hunting, doing battle, or in nature.

I've always been fascinated by history, and in any other circumstances I would have been delighted to walk through a castle that was steeped in thousands of years of history. But being a prisoner in a crazy, unknown world kind of put a damper on that. The tour did ease my apprehension a little; I felt less like a prisoner being walked to her sentencing.

The grouping of guards around a giant doorway gave me the hint that we had reached our destination. Apparently, Prince Mandrake normally traveled with an entourage of men dressed in black. I could pick up on the faint auras of magic that surrounded each of them, but their power was miniscule compared to what I had felt with Froston and the prince.

I took a deep breath before stepping through the doorway into what Froston called his 'hall'. It was pretty much what I would have expected a king to have in his castle if we were in the *Lord of the Rings* movies. I had to give my head a little shake to remind myself that this was reality, it seemed so strange.

The prince stood as we entered and ran his eyes over me. "Anna," he purred. "You look absolutely ravishing."

I blushed and murmured something that ended in 'Your Highness' but allowed him to pull a chair out for me to sit.

He licked his lips when his eyes caught on my cleavage and I squirmed uncomfortably. This was super awkward, especially since my father was sitting right next to me.

"May I begin the meal, my prince?" my father asked smoothly. "My servants have prepared a spread that should please you."

The prince flicked his eyes over to my father and gave him a nod, seeming amused at Froston's attempt to draw his attention away from me. I was more than grateful for the interruption and kept my eyes down as the two of them chatted about mutual acquaintances.

I kept my ears perked for anything that could be useful for my situation, but could barely hide a yawn when most of it seemed like pointless gossip. Most of it was about other fae trying to get into favor with the prince and my father.

"Are we boring you, Anna?" Prince Mandrake asked with a smirk before taking a sip of his wine.

"Of course not, Your Highness." I said with a blush.

He set down his glass of wine. "I think it's time we talked about something that will probably be of interest to you – your future here."

I swallowed nervously, and my eyes flicked over to Froston. I hated that my initial instinct was to look to him for reassurance, so I straightened up in my chair and met the prince's eyes. "That would be something of interest to me." I was proud of myself for keeping any hints of sarcasm or worry out of my voice.

The prince looked entertained by my reaction, so I doubt that I fooled him.

"You will be spending your afternoons with me for the foreseeable future," he told me with a smirk. "I have all kinds of things that I want to teach you."

"About magic?" I asked curiously.

He raised an eyebrow.

"Your Highness." I added.

"The prince has the unique ability to absorb magic into himself." Froston informed me. "Any errant magic that you might release will be easily taken care of and you don't have to worry about harming anyone accidentally."

I detected a hint of warning in Froston's voice. He was probably telling me not to attack the prince, even if he managed to provoke me.

I was already wary of the prince. If Caylee's and Froston's warnings hadn't already been enough to worry me, then the dark swirl of energy around the prince would have done the job. Now that I was sitting close to him, I could feel the pull of his dark magic even more than I had before. I tried my best to not get distracted by it.

"What kind of magic will I be learning, Your Highness?" I asked cautiously. I was more than a little worried about what the fae might require me to do on their behalf. But I was also curious. Would working with the fae give me some control over the magic that had burst out of me and burnt my attackers to a crisp? The fae might intend to try and use me as a weapon, but I wanted to make sure that I would never unintentionally harm someone.

"The first thing you need to know about magic is that everyone has their own special blend," the prince told me, swirling his wine glass in his hand. "Your father is an elemental with an affinity for cold and ice, but your mother was a wolf with a special connection to the earth. I'm interested to see what powers you might develop."

Froston nodded in confirmation before turning to the prince. "Anna works as a healer among the humans," Froston told him. "Humans don't use magic to heal, but I think she might find her affinity there."

The prince scoffed. "I have a feeling it's going to be more than just healing." He leaned in towards me, his darkness reaching out to me.

I swallowed nervously. The prince's eyes were focused on my own and I could feel his power drawing me in closer to him. His power was seductive, but also terrifying at the same time. The darkness called for me to relax and give in to it, but it had a sense of finality. I think if I had closed my eyes and let it envelop me, I would have been taken by death.

There had been times in my life where I would have found comfort in the sweet release he was tempting me with. But right now, I had too much to live for. I struggled against the pull with everything that I had inside me. I felt like I was stuck inside of a riptide, swimming with every last bit of energy inside of me.

The prince laughed when I managed to break his hold on me with pure willpower. Sweat dripped down my back and my hands shook with the effort. Froston smiled at me proudly. Were they both completely insane?

"My father is what the humans might call an incubus," the prince told me with a smirk. "His powers lie in beauty and seduction. But my mother was the Morrigan."

I inhaled a sharp breath. I knew enough about mythology to recognize the name. The Morrigan was considered to be a goddess of death. But how much of mythology was fact, and how much of it was fantasy? I'm sure that I would be finding out as I spent more time with the prince. Before, I had been wary of him. Now I was terrified. Was that why he had done it?

I hoped the prince was finished with his games after that display. I felt like I had just run several miles at a full sprint, and I wasn't sure I would be able to fight off another one of those attacks.

Froston and the prince switched to another language to talk between themselves, leaving me to either wonder what they were talking about or get lost in my own thoughts. I was grateful that they were ignoring me and tried to use the time to pull myself together.

Dinner went by in agonizing slowness and servants brought in round after round of more food. I sampled each dish that was brought in, but I was too nervous to really enjoy any of it. Exhaustion had hit me so hard that just lifting my fork to my mouth wasn't worth the energy expenditure.

The language they were speaking was beautiful and almost musical. I guess I should have wondered earlier why a group of people in another world spoke English. But it was obvious now that they had only been doing so for my benefit, I was going to ask Caylee about that the next time I saw her. Towards the end of the meal, I wondered why they had even required me to be here. Was it just so that the prince could frighten me? What would have happened if I hadn't broken free of the prince's compulsion?

Finally, dinner was finished. The prince dismissed both Froston and myself, giving me a wink. I fought hard to suppress my shiver, I did *not* want any more of the prince's attention.

Froston escorted me back to my room in silence, and this time I was too tired to do more than just place one foot in front of the other. Once we had passed through the barrier that Froston had placed on my room, he spoke.

"I hope you realize now that I've been telling you the truth. It's dangerous for you in this world."

I nodded in agreement. "I wish I had never been brought here."

Froston flinched as if he were hurt, but what did he expect? He had dragged me here, away from my pack, and let the prince attack me.

"Get your rest tonight, Anna," Froston told me softly. "I'll do my best to keep the prince occupied and distracted, but you're still going to have to go to the lessons with him."

I sighed and looked up at him in resignation. "I just want to go home."

"I know." Froston told me gently. "I'll do my best to get you back to your pack, but I can't make you any promises, and it's not going to happen anytime soon."

I turned away from him to hide the tears in my eyes. He sighed but walked to the doorway.

"I'm changing the barrier. You'll be able to come and go as you please, but only myself and a few others will have permission to enter. The sound barrier will remain, so you will have some privacy."

"Thank you," I murmured.

Froston turned back to me after he finished. "I hope you understand that things won't go well for you if you try to escape. If the prince takes you into his custody…"

I paled. I definitely did not want that to happen.

Froston and I said goodnight, and then I was alone. I struggled with the dress for a few minutes, but quickly gave up. There was no way I could get this corset untied by myself, I needed Caylee to undo it for me.

Exhausted, I walked to the bed and threw myself on it. Despite how uncomfortable I was lying there in the dress, I was asleep in moments.

My night was anything but restful. I tossed and turned, only to be plagued by nightmares when I finally managed to drift off to sleep. It had been a long time since I've had nightmares this bad, they seemed so real. I finally woke towards the end of the night and just laid in my bed, staring at the ceiling. Sleeping felt like it was draining the energy out of me, not replacing it. If I was back home, I would have put on a movie to distract myself. But the fae's strange mix of magic and technology didn't include movies.

Instead, I thought about my pack back home. I tried to picture what they would all be doing right now. Were they worried? Did the twins feel abandoned? Did James have control over his temper? Was Austin making plans to get me back? Was Caleb taking care of the pups? Was Cody keeping everyone together?

Chapter 5

Anna

When Caylee brought breakfast late in the morning, I was still lying there, just staring at the ceiling. She did her best to try and cheer me up, but honestly it was a lost cause. I was physically and emotionally drained, it was all I could do to get dressed for my first lesson with the prince. Because I had gotten such a late start on the day, it was already afternoon by the time I had eaten breakfast and Caylee had dressed me to her satisfaction.

Caylee led me through the castle, and with each of my tired steps my apprehension grew deeper. I wasn't sure what to expect from my daily lessons with the prince, but after dinner last night I knew it wasn't going to be pleasant.

We stopped in front of a set of doors that had a group of guards in the front, indicating that the prince was inside. Caylee's constant stream of chatter had included some information about the prince and his guards. He had a large contingent of guards that traveled with him wherever he stayed. They were made up of mostly men with mixed blood: human and fae, but also included some of the lower ranking fae. You could always tell where the prince was in the castle, because there would be a group of at least five men dressed in all black outside of the room.

Caylee had laughed when I asked her why Prince Mandrake wouldn't want more powerful fae as his guards. Surely the prince would want the best? "Why would a powerful fae agree to be a servant when they should be a lord?" Caylee had laughed. It looked like the social structure of the fae was based on power as well as pedigree.

"Just you, my lady," one of the guards told me gruffly as we approached the door. "Your maid will have to wait outside."

I sighed but thanked Caylee for bringing me here. She gave me a small smile as I took a deep breath and braced myself for an afternoon with the prince. I tried to focus on the importance of learning how to use my magic. I needed to learn how to control it, but also pick up on anything that would help me fight for my pack if the need arose.

One of the guards opened the door for me, and I was surprised to step into a room that didn't look like it belonged in a castle at all. I walked into a large gym that could have been in any fitness center back home. There were mats on the floor for stretching or fighting, weight benches, and a plethora of free weights. Any equipment that would have required electricity to work was missing, though. Apparently the fae had not invented exercise equipment that could run on magic.

"You look surprised."

I jumped when the prince's voice came suddenly from behind me.

"I wasn't expecting anything so modern, Your Highness," I replied as I turned to face him. Today he had his shoulder length dark hair pulled back, making his sculpted cheekbones even more prominent. He was dressed all in black again, making him look sleek and stylish.

He chuckled. "Froston is quite fond of the human world and enjoys many of the comforts they've developed over the years."

I looked around, trying to imagine Froston carrying all this stuff through a portal into the Arctic the way that I had arrived here. It didn't seem practical or possible, but it did make me chuckle at the mental image of Froston carrying a weight machine on his back.

"You wear your thoughts all over your face," the prince told me quietly. "You won't last long in our world if you don't learn to control that."

I gave a frustrated huff. "I'm not well-suited for this world in a lot of ways - so it might be best for you to just send me home."

The prince laughed out loud as he circled around me, moving more gracefully than I could ever hope to be. "If your father wasn't one of my most important allies, I'd be tempted to keep you for myself."

Another piece of the puzzle fell into place for me. I'd been wondering why the prince had been willing to let Froston handle my kidnapping and confinement. I guess I was incredibly lucky that he considered my father a powerful ally.

"The two of you have been friends a long time?" I asked the prince, more to make conversation than out of any real curiosity.

The prince laughed again. "Friends?" He shook his head in amusement and motioned for me to join him over on the mats. I was guessing that was a 'no' to being friends then.

"You and I have a lot of work to do today. I want you to meet the king soon, and I want to show him what you can offer us." He stepped closer to me and I reflexively took a step back before I even realized what I was doing. That seductive darkness still radiated off him, and I would prefer to be as far away from that as possible in my current mind's state.

The prince cocked his head at me with laughter in his green eyes that were eerily similar to mine. "I'm not going to harm you, my sweet Anna."

I blushed but held my ground as he came closer and reached for my hands. His hands were calloused as he gently took ahold of mine. That surprised me, I would think that a prince wouldn't have many duties that required manual labor.

"Now that we're alone, you can call me Drake," the prince offered as if he was being generous.

My heart fluttered nervously as we stood close to each other and I felt his magic reaching for me again. Dark tendrils wafted off of him and floated towards me, I instinctively recoiled but there was nowhere for me to go.

"Normally, fledgling fae are taught from birth how to manage their magic. But you have some unique circumstances," he explained quietly.

I nodded. Unique was one way of putting it.

He gave me an amused smirk. "Because you're utterly clueless, I'm going to take a short-cut to show you how this works."

I blushed but tensed up when I felt his magic surrounding me and pressing in on all sides.

"We're going to connect and I'm going to channel magic through you. I'll have control over the magic itself, but you'll feel exactly what I'm doing and be able to replicate the process on your own later."

I stared into Drake's eyes and it was like the world dropped away, leaving only the two of us. My anxiety intensified, just what was this magic lesson going to entail?

"Just relax," I heard him murmur as his magic reached inside of me. I panicked and tried to fight him off, but his magic slid inside of me easily. I knew the moment that we made the connection because it was like our minds melded together.

I could feel him in every thought and crevice in my mind. He combed through all my thoughts and emotions as easily as I would shuffle a deck of cards. The invasion was violating and the ease at which he did it was disconcerting. How could I protect myself from someone like him? How could I ever hope to protect my pack from the fae?

Pay attention. I felt rather than heard his words as he delved into my well of magic. As much as this invasive process horrified me, I did see how it was useful as I felt him handle my magic.

I could feel the control he had over the flow of magic and his intent as he wove it around me. He had my complete attention as he pulled my own magic from me and used it to blow a gentle breeze through my hair.

I couldn't help but smile when he created a cloud of fireflies that surrounded us before flying up to the ceiling and dissipating in a shower of sparks.

I felt him release his hold on my magic and urge me to try to do the same. I fumbled to direct the flow of magic the way that he had, but I was able to access it much easier than I ever had before. Now that he had shown me what I should be doing, I was able to clumsily mimic the motions that he had gone through. He had to keep giving me little nudges when I floundered, but I was able to follow his directions.

We worked together for hours. Sweat beaded on my face and dripped down my back as I struggled to follow the prince's directions. We worked on using what the prince called elemental magic by making breezes that fluttered through our hair. I was completely hopeless at the illusion magic that he had used to create the fireflies, so he eventually abandoned his attempts to teach me that.

"Let's try fire," Drake announced. "You seemed to have some affinity for that before."

I swallowed nervously. Letting loose an out of control blaze of fire was not something I was willing to risk.

Through our connection, the prince picked up on my thoughts. "I told you before, I can absorb any errant magic that you let out. That's one advantage to inheriting part of my father's magic."

I observed him thoughtfully. Drake told me before that his father was like an incubus to the humans, and now he had told me that he could absorb magic. Was the out of character attraction that I sometimes felt for him due to him trying to use some type of incubus magic on me? I had thought that an incubus was a type of demon who used humans and fed off their sexual energy. Were demons real? Or had humans named different fae as demons?

Drake probably heard those thoughts, but he didn't react to them. "I know you can use fire," he said impatiently. "Close your eyes and focus." The prince delved back into my magic to demonstrate. He created a small fire above our heads that quickly burned out. I tried to do the same, but my fear kept getting in the way. I was afraid to let the fire out, just seeing Ben's charred remains in my mind.

The prince released my hands with a disgusted snort. "Your father has allowed you to stay with the humans for far too long. You've become soft and helpless, a frightened rabbit right before the hounds are released for the hunt."

I glared at him, but he was partly right. I was soft. I cared about the people around me and I loved my pack. But he was wrong about me being helpless – I'd do anything to keep them safe. I let my anger simmer inside of me and used that to fuel the magic to create a small flame.

Drake watched me with narrowed eyes. "Interesting that you link your emotions to your magic, I haven't seen that before."

I shrugged. "That's what works for me."

"Let's see what you can do when you get truly angry, then," the prince murmured.

He combed through my mind, bringing forward a memory of Kelsey when she had deliberately tormented and embarrassed me in front of a guy that I thought was cute my freshman year of college. At the time, I had been in tears and confused about why she would do something like that. We were friends, weren't we?

"Get tough!" Drake shouted in my mind. *"Have some self-respect! You just let her push you around like that? How could you expect anyone to respect you or see you as an equal?"*

Looking back on it now, I was embarrassed at the way I let Kelsey treat me. I was angry at her for the emotional roller coaster she had kept me on over the years, but I was angrier at myself for letting her do it. I shouldn't have let her manipulate me, I should have seen through her 'best friend' act. I never should have let her keep drawing me in every time I thought I had enough and was ready to walk away.

But she always had a reason and an apology waiting for me once she had pushed me too hard. And I had never had a true friend before to compare our relationship to. I hadn't even realized how fucked up it was – I was just grateful for the good moments that we had together.

All of that was over. I had my pack and my guys now. I knew what true friendship and family meant now. I knew what it was like to be accepted for who I was.

"Hold on to that determination," Drake told me. *"You need to believe in yourself and hold your head high. Use your emotion, but don't get lost in it."*

I focused on the anger that he had drawn out of me and used it to form a ball of fire bigger than a basketball. Heat came off it and warmed my hands but I let it dissipate with a thought.

"That was good, but you can do better."

We kept working with the prince trying to goad me into emotional reactions. But by the end of our session, I was able to independently use my magic to do a few simple tasks.

I couldn't fight the huge grin that stretched over my face as the prince withdrew from me and I was left alone in my own head. This experience had been anything but pleasant, but I was learning how to use magic!

Drake shared in my grin for a moment, before he remembered that he was an arrogant ass and put his trademark smirk back on his face. "That will be enough for today."

I only nodded. I had accomplished a lot, but it had also taken a lot out of me. For the second day in a row I felt like I had run a marathon.

The prince started towards the door, but turned back to me. "Oh, and Anna?"

"Yes, Your Highness?" I mumbled quietly.

"Let's keep our unorthodox training methods to ourselves. If anyone asks, you flung fireballs at me as I absorbed them."

I nodded in confusion, but the prince was out the door before I could ask any questions. Now alone in the room, I plopped down on the floor and laid on one of the mats. I'd just rest for a minute before making the hike back through the castle to my room.

"My lady?" I heard Caylee's voice call out to me.

I reluctantly sat up and Caylee giggled when she saw me on the floor. "The prince asked me to bring you back to your room before fetching you something to eat," Caylee told me with a sly grin. "He said you worked up an appetite?"

I blushed. "Not the way you're thinking."

Caylee pouted in disappointment but reached for my hands, so she could pull me to my feet. She chattered enough to make up for my silence as we made our way back through the castle. I was so tired that I had to keep my eyes on the ground to keep from tripping. That was the reason why I didn't notice when I almost walked into a female fae.

She was just as tall as I was, but waif-thin where I was curvy. Her blond hair was a few shades darker than mine and braided into an elaborate up-do that must have taken hours to perfect. She was wearing an elaborate gown with a corset that made her waist look tiny. If this was what a female fae was supposed to look like, then I understood Caylee's dismay at not being able to make me fit in their mold. The female fae narrowed her eyes at me and circled like a lion would circle around injured prey. "I don't see what's so special about you," she practically spat at me.

I stood up tall and straightened my shoulders. I was so not in the mood for this right now. I already had my fill of the Kelseys of the human world, I had no desire to meet the fae version. I simply ignored her and continued walking. Caylee's jaw dropped but she ran after me once she realized I wasn't going to stop.

The female gave a very unladylike snort of disapproval as I walked away from her, but she didn't pursue me.

Once we had turned a corner and were out of site of the stranger, Caylee whispered to me in a panic. "Don't you know who that was?"

"No, Caylee. I don't know who that was, because I haven't met anyone other than my father and the prince since I've been here," I said sarcastically. "And I don't care who she is because I don't like bullies." There was no way I was going to let a mean fae female make me feel like less than her. I was a badass fire-throwing Arctic wolf now.

I immediately felt bad for my sharp tone when I saw Caylee wilt. I'd let my stress and exhaustion get the better of me, and I'd taken it out on the one person who had shown me kindness here.

"I'm sorry, Caylee," I said gently. "It's been a really rough day. Maybe we could talk about her once we get back to the room?"

"Of course, my lady," Caylee answered quietly. "I'll run you a hot bath as soon as we get back so you can relax."

I was too tired to argue with her or let her know that I was perfectly capable of running my own bath, so I just nodded in agreement. I never thought I would be so happy to see the door to my prison here in the fae world, but I eagerly went into my room and sat on the couch. I slumped down and closed my eyes, hoping for a few moments of peaceful rest.

True to her word, Caylee headed right into my bathroom to turn on the water. There was a moment where I wondered how the fae had hot running water without electricity, but I decided to just let that one go for now.

Chapter 6

Anna

The next couple days were more of the same. The prince would show me different ways to use my magic, and I would clumsily fumble my way through it until I could manage the task on my own. I practiced my magic on my own tirelessly, because my pack was going to be depending on me to protect them, and I wasn't going to let anything stop me from succeeding.

I slept for most of the time that I wasn't in the lessons or practicing, but my sleep was fitful at best. I wasn't sure if it was magic use that kept me feeling drained and exhausted, but no amount of sleep seemed to help.

During the night when I tried to sleep I was plagued by nightmares, and my only real reprieve was in the early mornings. I tried my best to get through the days, but with every day that passed I missed my pack more. I had a constant physical ache that reminded me of their absence, like a part of me was missing.

The prince had started out teaching me how to manage basic elements like wind and fire, but eventually I graduated to more complex magic. I discovered that it was easier to focus on my intent behind using magic and let it flow through me, as opposed to trying to force it to do what I wanted.

During our lessons, the prince was gradually becoming less of an asshole to me. He didn't even care when I lost my temper and yelled back at him when he was pushing my buttons. Sometimes I even thought that he enjoyed it.

Today, Drake was waiting for me in our practice area with two other people. One was a young girl, who looked like she was about ten years old and had her hair in pigtails. The other was an older man in his seventies or eighties.

Drake hopped to his feet when he saw me in the doorway and sauntered over with his trademark grin looking even more wicked than usual. "Anna, you're in for a treat today."

I looked at the two humans nervously. "What am I learning today?"

"Today, we are going to be focusing on one of my specialties – compulsion."

My jaw dropped. "Compulsion? You can manipulate people?"

He gave me a feral grin. "I can. Today you're going to learn how to project an emotion onto another person. Once you get better at that, you'll be able to subtly influence another's thoughts."

I crossed my arms over my chest. "Why would I want to do that?"

He laughed. "Why wouldn't you? Anything you want can be yours."

"Have you done that to me?" I asked softly. "Manipulated me?"

He smirked. "I've tried, but you're surprisingly resistant. That makes me think that you might have an affinity for it."

I frowned. "Can we learn something else today? Maybe like making portals back to my world?"

The prince laughed heartily but reached for my hands. "My sweet little buttercup. I should be hurt that you're trying to run away from me."

I rolled my eyes but held my tongue. I would like nothing more than to run far away from here and never come back.

"As much as I would like to indulge your every request..." the prince said mockingly. "Your father is one of the few fae in the realm who have that ability."

I tilted my head to regard him. That was why my father was such an important ally to the king. It also explained why the prince was being gentler with me than he would probably like to be.

"Why do you really want me here, anyway?" I blurted out. I was more than tired of the subterfuge and games that were part of our daily routine.

The mocking smirk faded from his face and he looked at me honestly. "I need you. The kingdom needs you." He sighed and dismissed the two humans. They looked relieved and didn't waste any time getting out of the room and away from the prince.

Drake took my hand and led me over to one of the benches. "I'll be honest with you, Anna," he told me seriously. "There's a lot of tension between us and the Summer Court right now. My father can be… antagonistic at times."

I swallowed nervously. I was supposed to be meeting this king soon so that he could evaluate my progress and see whether or not I would be of use to the kingdom. A part of me hoped that he would decide that I was completely useless. But I had a feeling that the prince wouldn't agree to simply send me home to live my life if I was deemed a failure. From what Caylee had told me, he definitely seemed like the vindictive sort.

"You don't know a lot about our world, but let me tell you the basics," the prince stated. "The Summer Court is made of the most perfect, beautiful, and powerful of our kind. The Winter Court is made up of everyone who doesn't meet their standards or who has been rejected and turned away," he explained. "There are a lot more of us than there are of them, but there are quite a few of the fae here that would do anything to get back into their good graces."

"And you don't?" I asked curiously.

Drake smiled. "I was born into the Winter Court, and I would never be accepted in Summer. My mother, the Morrigan, was one of the most powerful fae alive at the time, most would consider her to be a goddess. But her powers of death and destruction would have never been welcomed at the shining Summer Court. She carved out a powerful kingdom here and made a haven for everyone who had nowhere else to go."

"And your father?"

He chuckled. "What's the phrase the humans use? It's better to 'reign in hell than serve in heaven.' He might be king here, but would merely be a noble there."

I was surprised that the prince was opening up to me. He had just been mocking towards me so far.

"What happened to your mother?" I asked softly.

Drake shrugged with surprising vulnerability on his face. "She was just gone one day. I used to think she would be back at any moment, but now? I don't think she's coming back."

I gave his hand a squeeze and he looked at me in surprise. "I'm sorry, it sounds like you must have had a difficult time growing up."

He gave me a half-smile with his full lips. "You have no idea."

Drake stood back up with poise. "Let's get back to work, Anna. I need you to strike fear in the hearts of the Summer Court fae."

I couldn't help but laugh. I doubted that the sight of me would ever strike fear into the hearts of anyone, let alone some of the most powerful creatures in existence.

The prince shared a smile with me. "One of you might not be so frightening, but an entire army? That would give them pause."

"How could you fake an army?" I asked incredulously. "They're going to notice that I'm just one person."

Drake laughed. "We aren't so obvious as to present them with an army. We just need them to think that we have been breeding with the wolves regularly. Once they get a sense of the raw power that you possess, they'll back off."

I just looked at him dubiously. I was like a clumsy child just learning how to write with a crayon whereas the prince was a master artist using magic. I doubted that anyone would be impressed with me.

The prince just seemed entertained by my doubts. "Magic is like a muscle, my darling. The more you use it, the stronger you'll get. And I intend to be giving you some very good workouts," he purred.

I rolled my eyes at him, but he gave me a wink before striding back to the door to ask the guards to send us new 'victims' to practice on. It looked like I was not going to be able to get out of this lesson so easily.

The prince saw the stubborn look on my face when he turned back to me. "Anna, Anna, Anna," he murmured as he strolled in my direction. "As a wolf, you should know that you're either the predator or the prey. And believe me, *no one* will ever mistake me for prey."

I lifted my chin defiantly. "Haven't you ever heard the saying: 'If they stand behind you, protect them. If they stand beside you, respect them. If they stand against you, defeat them?' Just because someone is weaker than you, it doesn't give you the right to take advantage of them. It gives you the responsibility to stand up for them."

The prince scoffed. "There's no room for weakness in our world."

My eyes flicked to the doorway when I saw one of the guards shove a human girl inside and then pull the door shut behind him. She backed up, looking terrified. I can't imagine what the guards must have told her before pushing her inside.

I walked towards her slowly with a smile. "Hello, there. I'm Anna. What's your name?"

The girl gave me a shaky curtsy. "My lady, my prince. My name is Gloyers."

The prince pushed passed me and gave her an evil grin. "Excellent." He grabbed a hold of her arm and pulled her to the center of the room, motioning me to follow. I reluctantly trailed after him. How was I going to get out of this? The thought of letting the prince harm this poor girl made me sick to my stomach.

"Take her hands," the prince directed me. "When you're first starting, physical touch can make it easier."

I reluctantly took her hands and the prince positioned himself behind me, placing his hands on my hips. "I'm going to connect with you, and then guide you through what we need to do to the human."

"Gloyers," I corrected him.

He gave a snort, but otherwise ignored me. I felt the familiar sensation of the prince's magic invading my mind. I didn't try to hide my discontent with today's lesson plan, but it didn't seem to bother him at all.

What should we make her do? I felt the prince debating in my mind. Usually, he kept his thoughts blocked off from me, but today I could feel his thoughts flicking through my mind, faster than flashes of light. I struggled to process them into something I could understand or put into words. I did understand that his usual compulsions had to do with inspiring lust in others, but he wasn't interested in doing that with a human child. I was grateful for that.

He came to a decision and I felt wicked glee emanating from him. *"Watch and learn."*

Whatever he was about to do, I knew it wasn't anything that I wanted to be a part of. He delved into my magic to use it for his purpose. But where usually I was content to let him guide my magic, today I struggled against him. I felt his ire and we grappled for control. I was surprised that I was able to hold my own with him for so long.

"Fine." I heard him in my mind. *"We'll do something else today."*

This time when he delved into my magic, I felt him pull it into himself instead of using it for a purpose. I fought against his draw, but he was too strong. I felt my magic gradually draining away from me and my body growing weak. I desperately fought against him with everything I had, but my struggles were completely useless. I hadn't felt so helpless since I was a small child. I felt like a butterfly being crushed in the hand of a giant.

It seemed like an eternity had passed before he finally released me, and I tried to stumble away. I would have fallen if he hadn't taken me back in his arms.

"You can go," he told Gloyers. She ran out of the room and the prince and I were left alone.

I tried to push him away, but he held on tighter. His darkness pulsed against me, feeling stronger than ever. With his body pressed against mine, I was surrounded by his scent and it reminded me of a dark night in the forest.

"This is a lesson I need you to learn," he murmured into my ear in a low voice. "We can feed on humans and weaker fae to make ourselves stronger. You can call this a payment for the lessons I've given you, since you clearly have no intention of coming to my bed."

Dread flooded through me. Had he tried to manipulate me into sleeping with him? There had been a few moments where I felt a flash of uncharacteristic attraction for him. I had wondered why. Because although the prince might be physically handsome, he was nothing like the men I loved back home.

"There's a part of me that wants to take you for myself," the prince murmured as he rubbed his face in my hair. "I want to conquer you and make you mine."

Fear flowed through me, sharp and cold. "Is that what you want?" I asked him. "Would that make you happy? Having a puppet? Wouldn't you prefer for someone to choose to be with you?"

Drake was silent for a moment and I held my breath. I realized that I was in a lot of danger here. I was as weak as a newborn kitten right now, and if he attacked again I wouldn't be able to defend myself. If he tried to use compulsion on me, would I even be able to stop him?

"They do choose me. They choose me for my wealth and power," the prince said bitterly. "But that's not something you want, is it?"

I was shaking as I chose my next words carefully. "Maybe you need to be the first to love? Open your heart to someone?"

The prince snorted. "There's no such thing as love for princes." He tightened his grip on me. "Others won't be as kind or gentle with you as I am. I heard you've already had several visits from Morpheus. You need to decide who you want as an ally and who you want as an enemy." He released me with a rough shove and I fell to the floor.

"We're done for today," he announced before striding out of the room without a backwards glance.

I stayed kneeling on the floor and closed my eyes. Helpless tears dripped down my face and splattered on the floor in between my hands. I had let my guard down with the prince and forgotten just how dangerous he was. I thought that he had been opening up to me, but had he just been manipulating me? Was he even capable of kindness and empathy?

I wanted to believe that some of the good inside of him had been peeking out earlier, and that he had just reverted to his old ways when I challenged him. But after today, it was clear that I could never trust him or let him in again.

I heard Caylee's soft footsteps as she approached. "My lady?"

The exhaustion had set so deeply into my bones that I could barely raise my head to speak with her. My hands braced on the floor in front of me were the only thing keeping me in an upright position.

She gasped as she took in my condition and tried to help me up, but she was just too small and slender to be able to bear my weight for the length of time it would take us to get back to my room.

Caylee wrought her hands nervously. "I don't want to leave you here alone like this, my lady. If any of the other fae come in here..."

"It's alright, Caylee," I mumbled. Her intentions were sweet, but if any of the other fae attacked me like the prince had, she wouldn't be able to prevent it.

"Should I get your father?" she asked nervously.

I gave her a nod and she darted off.

I fought to keep my tears inside. I didn't want to become like the prince – cold and manipulative. I didn't want to learn compulsion. I had been afraid of what the fae would do to me, but now I was also afraid of what they might make me become.

It wasn't long before Caylee and Froston came through one of his portals into the gym. Froston helped me up but once he realized he would have to support almost all of my weight to walk, he decided to just pick me up and create a portal back to my room.

He laid me on my bed gently and sent Caylee for some tea.

"What happened, Anna?" he asked softly.

"The prince." I couldn't keep the bitterness out of my voice.

He sighed. "The prince drained you?"

"Yes." Tears came to my eyes again and I hated myself for it. "I was helpless, I couldn't stop him."

Froston frowned. "I doubt he truly wanted to hurt you, it was more likely that he wanted to teach you a lesson in power."

"Well, he accomplished both," I said resentfully.

Froston sat down on the edge of my bed and smoothed my hair back. "I should've known that my previous warnings wouldn't have been enough." He sighed. "I forget how different things are in the human world. If you show weakness here, another fae will take advantage of that. You're lucky that the prince didn't really want to hurt you. Our enemies won't show the same restraint. You need to be prepared for what's to come."

I just gave him a dirty look and closed my eyes. As much as I hated to admit it, he was right. I needed to stop whining about how the prince hurt me and pull myself together. I needed to become stronger so that he wouldn't be able to do that again.

Froston leaned down and laid a kiss on my forehead. "Get some rest, you'll feel better soon."

Chapter 7

Anna

I gazed up at Austin as we walked down the moonlit beach. The sand was cool under my bare feet, but Austin's hand was warm in mine. The stars twinkled up above us and the moon glimmered over the gentle waves of the sea. He smiled down at me and gave my hand a gentle squeeze.

Austin was dressed more casually than usual in khakis and a short sleeve button down shirt that revealed his tats. His dark blond hair was looser than his usual style and his blue eyes were bright with excitement.

The last time that we had planned a date, the night had ended in disaster. We had tracked our enemies down, but in the process James had been shot and I had discovered my fae side. I was glad that we had another chance now.

"The surprise is just up ahead," Austin promised with a warm smile. "I've been looking forward to this night for so long."

"Me, too," I told him honestly. "I feel like we needed some time alone together."

He sighed. "I know what you mean. I love my pack, but sometimes I just need to step back and be just a man or just be a wolf."

I squeezed his hand. "I get it. You feel like you can't be yourself sometimes - that you need to be what everyone else expects you to be."

Austin looked at me in surprise. "Exactly."

I laughed. "I'm not just a pretty face."

"I never thought you were," he murmured. We stopped walking and he pulled me up against him. Gently brushing a stray lock of hair out of my face, he leaned in closer. "The moment I met you, I knew that you were something more. Something that I had been looking for my entire life."

My heart pounded as I looked into his eyes, but I knew he was right. There was something between us that I couldn't deny. I wound my hand around the back of his neck as our lips met.

The kiss started as just a gentle brush of lips but deepened into something more tender and sweet. I sighed as he pulled away, but he grinned at me. "The night is just getting started."

He led me over to a blanket where a bottle of wine and two glasses were waiting for us. I sat carefully and arranged my dress, so my legs wouldn't get tangled in the gauzy fabric. I frowned when the dress flickered from blue to pink and then back to blue again.

"I picked out something sweet for you." Austin drew my attention and the strange dress was quickly forgotten. He held out a glass for me to take. "Would you like the honor of making the toast?"

I paused to think, but then I smiled and held up my glass. "To many more nights like this."

He grinned. "I can promise you that we will have *plenty* more nights like this." We clinked our glasses together and I took a sip. True to his word, Austin had picked out something sweet for me. It made me smile because I know he would have preferred something dry.

"What are you thinking about?" he asked softly.

I leaned forward to give him a peck on the lips. "I was just thinking how you're just as sweet as this wine."

Austin laughed and put an arm around me. "I'm glad I chose well, then."

I leaned into him and enjoyed the warmth that his body gave off as the cool sea breeze swirled around us.

"Tell me one of your secrets," Austin murmured into my ear. His low voice sent shivers down my spine and made forming any thoughts difficult.

"A secret?" I pondered for a moment then smiled. "I hid a secret stash of chocolate somewhere in the house."

Austin laughed. "That's not the type of secret I was looking for."

I shrugged. "I don't really have deep, dark secrets."

"That's not really true, now is it?" Austin flashed an evil grin before his face smoothed back into a warm smile.

I blinked in surprise but shook my head to clear the image. I must have imagined that.

"What if I tell you one of my secrets instead?" Austin paused and then gave me a gentle kiss. "You're so sweet and delicious... I could just eat you up."

I giggled but kissed him back. Our kisses deepened and he pulled me onto his lap. I pressed my body up against his and groaned when he cupped my bottom to pull me close.

I moved to straddle him and threaded my hands through his silky hair. He moaned as I rubbed up against him and ran his hands over my body. I lost myself in the sensation of his mouth on mine and his hard body against me. I slid my hands under his shirt to feel the chiseled planes of his abs.

Austin pulled away from me to lift his shirt over his head but I started to feel a pull on my magic, similar to what the prince had done. It was more faint and subtle, but still there. I pushed Austin back from me with an accusation on my lips. He laughed, and before I had a chance to get the words out his face morphed into that of a stranger's. I screamed and tried to pull away, but the stranger held me tight to his body with a malicious grin.

"We're just getting started, my dear. I intend to enjoy every moment of this." His laughter echoed all around me with a sense of familiarity. I felt like I should have recognized it, but the memory floated just beyond my grasp.

This time when I tried to pull away, I used more than just my body. I pulled my entire sense of self away from him. He looked at me in surprise as the scene around us slowly dissolved.

"This isn't over," he snarled.

I pulled back again and felt something snap. A moment later I sat up in my bed with my heart pounding and a thin sheet of sweat covering my body. The soft glow of light started to emanate from the walls from my motion and I sat on the edge of my bed to think. Even though I must have been sleeping for hours, I felt more exhausted than when I had first gone to bed. I tried to hold on to the last vestiges of the dream that were slowly fading away from me.

I'd been having strange dreams lately, but this one was suspicious. During the dream, I had felt a drain on my magic – similar to what the prince had done to me. I narrowed my eyes. I think I needed to learn more about how to protect myself. And I was going to have a lot of questions for my father the next time I saw him.

I was a little angry at him for how casually he had acted when I told him about what the prince had done to me. But I was even angrier with myself. I had been thinking of Froston as if he were the caring, loving father that I had always wanted in my fantasies. But this was reality. I had been letting myself be weak, thinking that he would take care of me. I was on my own, just like I had been my entire life.

I'd survived a lot and I would survive this. Even better than survive – I would come out stronger. I would get my rest tonight. But tomorrow? I was going to be ready to fight. I was done passively waiting for the little scraps of information that Froston and the prince were willing to dole out to me. It was time for me to take control of this situation.

I laid back down to go to sleep. I needed my rest if I was going to be able to take on the prince again, but how could I protect myself while I was sleeping? That thought wasn't enough to keep me from drifting back to sleep.

Chapter 8

Austin

I strode down the hall in council headquarters with the twins following behind me. Mason had settled down and was more contemplative than angry. But Jason was still glowering as he trailed behind us.

I hesitated at the door to my father's office with my hand on the door handle. My father had been such a constant and overbearing presence in my life for so long that his absence left me unsure of how to feel. The sting of his betrayal still smarted, but deep down I hoped it wasn't true.

A part of me hoped that he would have an explanation for all of this once he was found. The night that Cody, Anna and I had been taken captive after James was shot was still fresh in my mind. I found it difficult to believe that my father was behind that.

Why would he be behind the failed attempts to kidnap Anna when he had easy access to her as part of the council? Why would he order James killed while he was on the way to the house in the woods to confront us? As much as James and his cousin disliked each other, they were still bound by blood. Reed was a member of the council and would have been honor-bound to take revenge for his cousin's death. Or had my father thought he could escape detection all together? Never be caught?

Whomever 'the boss' was had never arrived that night. After going through the house, Caleb was convinced that it was my father behind it all. Not too long ago, my father had confessed to setting Caleb up to take the fall for some spyware he had installed on the other council member's computers. So, it was possible that he was behind the attacks on us, but the unexpected appearance of the fae had put doubts in my mind. It just didn't feel right.

My ears perked at the sound of someone in the office and I turned the handle apprehensively. The door swung open to reveal my brother, along with his new fiancé, Jessica.

Justin sneered at me from behind my father's desk, but Jessica just frowned at me from where she sat in his lap. Jessica and I had a difficult history – she had joined my pack temporarily in the hopes of becoming my mate. However, she had not been a good fit for me or my pack.

"Ready to relinquish your temporary council member status?" Justin asked as he twirled a strand of Jessica's hair around his finger.

I rolled my eyes. "You sound confident. Just because you took over my father's pack doesn't mean you'll automatically be named to the council. I heard that you're having a difficult time maintaining the pack. Rumor has it that more than a few of your pack mates want out."

Justin scowled and pushed Jessica away before standing. "We'll see about that."

I merely shrugged. "You're welcome to use the office for now, I have a council meeting to get to anyway."

Justin took a step towards me. "You think you've won?"

"Won what?" I asked in exasperation. "There has never been a competition between us. You were born first. You get the pack. That's always been a given and I've never challenged that."

Justin narrowed his eyes. "You never accepted my authority; you left the pack and started one of your own," he snarled. "You've always done everything you could to prove that you're better than me to our father."

"I left the pack because you made my life a living hell," I growled. "I was being a good brother by stepping aside and letting you have your place, despite you doing everything to instigate me into a fight."

"Father said he regretted that I was born first," Justin spat out. "I needed to prove to him that I was better than you." I felt Justin calling power to himself from his pack and braced myself. He was gearing up for a fight.

"Father is gone," I told him quietly. "You have your pack, and I have mine. Let it go."

Justin slammed his hands down on the desk. "I'm going to destroy you and take everything you value for myself," he snarled. Jessica backed away from him slowly and tucked herself into the corner of the room.

I felt the twins vibrating with anger behind me, but they knew better than to try and usurp my authority by challenging Justin themselves. I sent some soothing waves of energy in their direction, they were already on the edge and I didn't want Justin to tip them over. I hadn't expected the disappearance of my father to push Justin over the edge.

I held Justin's eyes. "I have no reason to fight you, but if you even think about harming one of my pack members – I'll completely crush you." I reached for my power and brought it forward, making sure that he could feel the full weight of it bearing down on him. I rarely needed to make a display like this, but I needed him to understand that if he tried to take me on, he would lose. Badly.

Justin held my eyes for a solid minute and I was steeling myself for an attack when he looked to the floor. I held in my surprise, but Justin wasn't cowed. If anything, the anger that I sensed from him was even greater than before. I wanted nothing more than to walk out the door, but my eyes flicked over to Jessica.

She was still cowering in the corner, her hand covering her mouth. My eyes narrowed when I saw the shadow of old bruises on her wrists. Her eyes widened when she realized what I had seen, and she hurriedly pulled her blouse to cover the exposed flesh.

Jessica avoided my eyes and Justin laughed. "Having regrets, brother?"

I took a step closer to him, still holding my power so that he could *feel* the threat I was about to deliver to him. "Dominance fights are one thing, but harming a female?" I loomed over him. "I'm content to let you have the pack for now, but if I hear you're abusing them – I will put a stop to it."

Justin just smirked at me. "Calm down, they're just love bruises. Your female doesn't like to play rough sometimes?"

My eyes flicked back to Jessica and she gave me a shaky smile and a nod. As much trouble as she caused in my pack before, I had no desire to see her harmed. And I certainly wouldn't stand by if my brother was harming her or taking advantage of the lower ranking wolves in his pack.

My stare-down with Justin was interrupted by a knock on the door. I stepped away from Justin but didn't turn my back on him. I wanted to have at least one eye on him until we had more of a resolution.

Mr. Phillips stepped in the door when Mason opened it after a nod from me. "If you boys want to fight for the council seat, it's going to have to wait. We have business to discuss with Austin."

Justin glowered at Mr. Philips, probably not pleased at being called a 'boy'. Neither was I, but that was an argument for another day. Mr. Phillips was right to interrupt a petty fight in between the two of us on council property. This was a neutral zone and we should both know better. We were both pack-masters and needed to be setting a good example for our packs, not indulging in petty squabbles.

"We'll finish this discussion later, brother," I told Justin. I glanced at Jessica before following Mr. Phillips through the door. She squared her shoulders back and gave me a glare, but it was lacking any real heat.

I sighed to myself. I was going to have no choice but to try and contact my mother again to find out what was really going on in that pack. She had refused to speak to me since the news of my father's betrayal surfaced, and she probably blamed me for everything that had happened.

I pushed all thoughts of my father's pack away as we walked down the hall and to the room where the other council members waited. Anna was my priority right now. I needed help to be able to take on the fae and get her back.

The twins trailed behind me as we made our way to the council meeting room, but stopped in the hall outside of the council chambers. I gave them some last minute orders via the pack bond to make sure that they behaved while I was out of sight.

Mason hesitated but communicated back to me that they weren't pups that needed to be watched. He wanted to prove they were just as reliable and valuable as Cody. Jason just looked sullen.

I hid my surprise from them. The twins had come as a packaged deal with Cody, and I was in the habit of treating them like errant little brothers. Maybe it was time for me to take a step back and let them have a little more responsibility.

I sent them a couple images of what Cody would usually be doing in this situation – talking up any of the council members pack members he could find. Cody excelled at being the affable, fun guy that the wolves from other packs wouldn't mind hanging out with and letting little tidbits of info drop. Mason and Jason both straightened up and gave me determined nods.

Mr. Reed watched our interaction from inside the council chamber with amusement and gave me a smirk when I entered. "Where's the giant wolf you usually bring with you?"

I raised an eyebrow. "I'll let Cody know you asked about him."

I took my seat at the table and folded my hands in front of me. Mr. Morgan and Mr. Reed had been struggling with each other to be the one to fill the hole that my father had left and were now glaring at each other to determine who would be the one to lead the meeting.

Mr. Phillips rolled his eyes. "Austin, why did you request this meeting?"

I put a neutral expression on my face, but my blood pressure spiked. I desperately needed to make sure that the council was willing to back my fight to get Anna back. Every word that I was about to say had to be perfect.

I cleared my throat to give me a moment to clear my mind and allow the dueling council members to take their seats. "I wish to discuss an unexpected interaction with the fae."

There was complete silence in the room and I evaluated each council member carefully. If there were any wolves that knew about the fae, it would be the men in this room. They exchanged glances around me, as if debating what to say.

"You were approached by one of them?" Mr. Reed said cautiously.

"I was."

"You're not the only one," Mr. Morgan informed me quietly. "We've received several other reports from around the country. They seem to be approaching more isolated packs, though. I'm surprised that they contacted you. They asked to purchase females?"

My eyebrows rose. "No. They took my female." They were asking to purchase females from other packs? My heart sunk. What were they planning to do with Anna?

"Anna?" Mr. Morgan said in surprise.

"Does he have another female?" Mr. Reed asked caustically.

"Technically, she's not his female to begin with," Mr. Morgan spat.

Mr. Phillips sighed. "Let's be realistic. Things have changed since our meeting with Anna. Austin, how is your relationship with the lamia?"

"Better than ever," I stated pointedly. "Caleb is using his contacts among them to gather more information on the fae."

Mr. Morgan's face turned red and he focused on the wall above my head, unwilling to meet my eyes. "How much do you know?"

I shrugged. "I'll be getting his report when I return to the pack later today."

Mr. Phillips tapped his fingers on the table. "The fae are one of the things that we usually only discuss with new council members." He shrugged. "The fae have been gone from this world for so long, that no one had any concerns about them until now."

"But the pack in Canada is aware of them," I stated bluntly.

"They have to be," Mr. Reed informed me. "They guard the gateway into the realm of the fae."

I sat back in my chair as all of the little pieces of information fell into place.

"This is an informal discussion, of course," Mr. Morgan stated as he watched me carefully. "But I believe that you'll best your brother to become the next permanent council member."

I hid my surprise. Justin wasn't the only one who assumed he would take our father's place on the council. It wasn't long ago that these same council members were giving me a difficult time about Anna and the way I was running my pack.

"I hope you'll be able to best your brother," Mr. Reed muttered. "The last thing we need is that asshole here all the damn time."

I hid my smile. Apparently, I wasn't the only one irritated by my brother's presence. Mr. Morgan continued as if he hadn't heard Mr. Reed. "We've always know about the fae, of course. This stays in these walls…"

He gave me a hard look to make his point and waited for me to acknowledge him before continuing. "The wolves are distant cousins to the fae. We're descendants of lesser fae who stayed behind when the veil was closed."

I sat back in my chair and kept my expression neutral. "And that's not made common knowledge because?"

Mr. Reed shrugged. "The lamia originally negotiated for all fae to leave this world. Our presence here was a secret at first. But my guess is that as we evolved into what we are now, the council decided that the fewer who knew the truth, the better."

"I think we can all agree that we have become something other than fae," Mr. Morgan added. "We are an independent race, and announcing to the world that we are merely a version of lesser fae would destroy that independence."

Mr. Phillips cut in. "Because of that, I think we can all agree that it's best if the fae stay out of this world."

"I think that's best for a lot of reasons," I murmured. "But do I have your support to get Anna back?"

The council members exchanged looks. "How do you plan to do that?" Mr. Reed asked snarkily. "Only they can cross through the veil."

I frowned. "Let me worry about that. My question is – do I have your support if it comes to a battle?"

Mr. Phillips snorted. "I think you lack an understanding of what the fae are. One of them could destroy all of us. Facing down an army of them? That's hopeless."

I leaned forward. "And yet, it was done before. I doubt that the fae left this world to us by choice."

Mr. Morgan tapped his fingers on the table in front of him. "Yes, but that was a feat accomplished by the lamia and the witches. Not us."

I shrugged. "And I'm in negotiation with the lamia. We all know the witches will follow their direction."

Mr. Reed watched me carefully. "Come to us again when you have the support of the lamia and the witches and we will discuss this again. Until then? You should hope the fae are generous and decide to return your female to you."

I gave a sharp nod, but internally I was fuming. "And when I get her back, do I have your assurances that she is mine to keep? No more discussion of sending her off to other packs?"

Mr. Phillips laughed. "Son, if you can get her back, you earned her. You won't get any opposition from me."

The other council members nodded in agreement. At least I'd won one battle. Now that the topic of the fae was closed, the council started to discuss petty matters and I tuned out. My next project was going to have to be getting the lamia ready to take on the fae.

Chapter 9

Anna

I woke this morning with a purpose. I felt more refreshed than I ever had since coming here. Caylee was surprised to find me already up and dressed by the time she came to my room with breakfast. Normally, I would be too tired to do much and would just let her primp me before the lessons with the prince.

Today, Caylee watched as I gobbled up my breakfast within minutes and popped back up to my feet. "Um, my lady? Are you alright?"

"I feel better than ever!" I told her with a grin. "We're going to pay my father a visit this morning."

Caylee paled. "My lady, your father asked that you stay in your room unless you're with him or the prince."

"That's fine, we're going to find him," I told her confidently as I strode to the door.

Caylee followed after me hesitantly. "Perhaps I could find him? And let him know that you need to request a meeting?"

"Don't worry, Caylee. I'll make sure you don't get in trouble."

Caylee sighed but led the way. "He's usually in his office at this time of the morning, my lady."

Froston was in his office with two other men. I hesitated at the door and frowned. They both looked familiar, but it took me a moment to place them. I narrowed my eyes when it came to me - these were the two men who had helped Froston kidnap me.

"Anna." Froston stood in surprise and walked over to me. "I wasn't expecting to see you this morning."

He looked like he wanted to push me right back out the door, so I widened my stance and crossed my arms. "There are some things that I would like to discuss with you."

One of the men behind him chuckled and my hackles rose. I knew that laugh, and I never wanted to hear it again. I pushed past Froston to confront my nightly tormentor.

He met me with a grin. "So, you finally figured it out?"

"Morpheus…" Froston warned.

Morpheus just laughed, not breaking eye contact with me. His eyes were all black, no white, no color. Just an endless dark that felt like it could suck you in.

I narrowed my eyes at him. "What is *wrong* with you?"

Morpheus smirked and started to walk towards me. I was proud of the way I held my ground, but I couldn't help but let out a low growl when he reached forward as if he was going to try to touch me. He must have thought better of it, because he dropped his hands.

"Morpheus, Talen, will you excuse us so that I can have a word with my daughter?" Froston asked smoothly.

Talen shrugged one elegant shoulder and walked to the door, but Morpheus winked at me with one of his unusual eyes. "I'll be seeing you."

"Don't count on it," I said darkly but he merely waved a hand at me as he shut the door behind him.

The moment they were gone I turned my attention back to Froston. "Did you know what he was doing to me?" I hissed at him.

Froston was taken aback. "Doing to you?"

"At night. In my dreams." Hearing Morpheus's laugh in the flesh had brought back flashes of the nightmares that had plagued me since I got here. I had to push away the emotions that they brought up and focus on the here and now.

Froston's face darkened. "I did not. But he and I will be having words." He sighed. "Anna, the fae aren't like humans. Fae like Morpheus will play games with humans and weaker fae just because they can. That's just his nature."

I crossed my arms. "What other dangers did you forget to warn me about? How can I protect myself from things like that?" I was furious. Froston had to have known that other fae might attempt to attack me. At the very least, he should have helped to prepare me to fend off their assaults.

Froston sighed and motioned for me to sit. "Anna, I'm doing everything I can-"

"It's not enough," I interrupted. "You have elemental powers, just like me. Why aren't you teaching me how to use them? Why would you just hand me off to the prince, when he has dark powers?" Hurt bled into my voice. He was supposed to be my father. Fathers were supposed to treasure their daughters, protect them, keep them safe. Froston had already abandoned me once, but now he was intentionally leaving me helpless and alone with predators.

"Anna, you don't understand what's at play here." Froston shook his head.

"I don't care. At least teach me how to protect myself, I can take it from there." I stared defiantly at Froston, waiting for his argument.

Froston sat back in his chair and stared at me. "You're right."

I sat up a little straighter. "You agree?"

He nodded slowly. "I do. I think you and I need to spend some time together."

I gave him a bright smile. "When can we start?"

He stood. "Now." A portal opened in front of us that led back out into the Arctic and snow swirled inside the office.

I stood. "I'm not dressed for that, I'll freeze to death."

Froston smiled at me indulgently. "I know you were distracted your first time through, but you should have noticed that none of us were touched by the cold."

He was right, I did think that was odd.

"The first lesson I'll teach you is how to control your environment. You want to create a small bubble around you and fill it with warm air, creating a barrier between yourself and the outside," he explained. I squinted as I watched magic surround him.

I reached for some of my own magic and tried to mimic what he had done. Warm air surrounded me, but dissipated just as quickly as I created it. I shivered as the cold air flowed through the portal, chilling me to the bone. Froston chuckled. "You need to create your barrier first."

I watched carefully, but I couldn't see how he was making a barrier. "Can you connect with me and use my magic to do it?"

Froston looked startled. "That's not a safe way to learn how to use your magic, Anna. I know it might seem like an easy shortcut, but it's dangerous."

I frowned. The prince had mentioned that he didn't want me telling anyone how he was teaching me magic, but I had just assumed that he didn't want anyone to know that he was being kind, and damage his reputation as an asshole. He hadn't mentioned that it was dangerous.

"Why is it dangerous?" I asked cautiously.

"You're forming a connection with another person. The more often you do it, the easier it is for the connection to become permanent." Froston frowned at me. "It's similar to the way that wolves bond when they decide to pick a mate."

I just stared at him blankly. I didn't know anything about the way that wolves picked a mate. I had just assumed it was done the same way that humans did it. You fell in love and then pledged to spend the rest of your lives together. I was surprised to hear that a magical bond was involved.

Froston shook his head. "I'll do it for you this time, but I expect you to pick up on how to do it for the way back."

I gave him a nod, eager to see where he was taking me. It was probably too much to hope that he would bring me back to my pack.

The chill in the air disappeared and warmth surrounded me. The cold wind was still blowing through the portal, but it didn't touch my skin. I smiled, this is something that could be useful.

Froston took my hand and we stepped into the Arctic. Another portal formed in front of us as soon as the first one had closed. This time it led out into a beach and I eagerly stepped through.

"Now break the barrier around you so that you can feel the warmth and the sand under your feet," Froston instructed.

I failed utterly the first few times I tried, but Froston was patient and kept explaining what I needed to do. Eventually, I got it and I slipped off my shoes to wiggle my toes in the warm sand.

I glanced at Froston, who seemed amused by how delighted I was. "I'm going in the water!" I called to him as I ran forward. I splashed into the water and giggled as a small wave broke. The ocean spray showered me so that my dress was soaked up to my thighs. The water was warm, and I tilted my head up to feel the rays of the bright sun on my face.

I had been trapped in Froston's castle for days. Until I was here, I hadn't realized how depressed I had been. I really did *not* want to go back.

Froston was waiting patiently by the edge of the water for me to return, so I reluctantly made my way back to him. "This was one of your mother's favorite places to visit," he told me softly. "She would run right to the water, just like you did."

I looked up at him in surprise, he hadn't spoken much to me about my mother. Was he starting to open up?

"Did you come here often?" I asked curiously.

"As often as we could." Froston had a faraway look in his eyes, as if he were reliving the memories now. "I purchased this island for the two of us. Your mother hated living in the cold north."

My jaw dropped. I don't know how much money an island cost, but I was pretty sure that it was more than I would ever see in my lifetime. I briefly wondered where Froston got the money from, but that was not the most important question right now.

Froston shook his head. "We can talk about the past later. Now that we're here, let's do what we came here to do."

I nodded regretfully, but stepped closer to him, ready to learn.

"Elemental magic is all around us. There's magic in the earth, in the sea, in the wind, and in the people around you. I have a feeling that you're going to have the easiest time with magic from the earth and sea, just like your mother."

He raised his arms and pulled a breeze around us. I smiled, this was something I could do. I mimicked him, twirling a breeze around him and ruffling his hair.

"Good," he told me with a smile. "But this time I want you to try and use the magic around you, not inside you."

I struggled for a while as he tried to coax me through it, but my frustration grew the more I failed. "My mother could do this?" I asked him with a frown. "I thought she was a wolf."

Froston smiled. "She was, but she had more fae blood than you would think. She struggled even more than you are right now."

I plopped down on the sand and wiggled my butt to get comfortable. "How long did it take her to learn?"

To my surprise, Froston sat next to me and gazed out to the ocean. "Years."

I huffed in frustration. "I can't stay with you for years. I need to get back to my pack."

"The prince isn't willing to wait years either." Froston said darkly. "He's been working with you every day and is going to want to see results soon."

"What if I can't do this?" I asked worriedly. "What if I'm a magical dud?"

"You're not," Froston assured me. "You've just spent most of your life being told that magic doesn't exist. You were conditioned to ignore that part of yourself, and now you need to reconnect."

"Aren't you the one that blocked my magic?" I asked pointedly.

He gave me a wry grin. "Enough talk. Let's get back to it."

Froston switched gears and focused on teaching me about barriers. You could make them out of air, out of water, out of earth, or even out of pure magic. He walked me through it again and again until I could make them on my own. They were nowhere near as strong and sturdy as his were, but I was getting the concept.

The skies had been darkening over us as we worked, and I felt a small drop of rain hit my nose. "Make a barrier over our heads." Froston ordered.

I did as he asked and had it in place just as the skies opened above us and let out a torrential downpour. I gazed up, fascinated by the way the water hit the invisible barrier and ran down the sides of the cube I had constructed around us.

A flash of lightning was followed by the faint roll of thunder, far away. I glanced at Froston. "Ocean storms can usually travel pretty quickly."

He grinned at me. "I'm counting on it. I think what you need is to absorb some lightning."

"Are you insane?" I objected in an embarrassingly high voice. "I'm not willing to risk getting struck by lightning. I'll die."

"You won't die." Froston soothed me as he looked out to the sea.

Panic hit when I realized he had no intention of getting us off this island before the storm made its way here. I looked around in horror. There was nowhere to take shelter or to hide. The island was circular and almost all beach. If lightning struck, we would be the most attractive targets.

Lightning struck out in the ocean again and this time the rumble of thunder was much closer.

"Froston." I tried to use my most reasonable voice. "I'm not ready for this. How do you even know I have enough fae-ness in me? I might be almost pure wolf."

He laughed out loud and sat in the dry sand underneath my barrier. "Anna, you need something to jolt you out of your human mentality. You look at magic as if it's something foreign and you doubt everything I try to tell you it can do. You fight your magic instead of letting it be a part of you."

"This isn't the way to do it!" I shouted over the sound of the wind and rain, completely losing any semblance of calm. "This is ridiculous!"

"This is an excellent way to get a jolt of pure energy," Froston told me as if I were the unreasonable one. "You need to replace whatever Morpheus and the prince managed to take from you, and you need to find your connection with the elements. This will open your eyes and let you connect with your magic on a deeper level."

I paced back and forth as the next strike of lightning was less than a mile away from us. This time the thunder that accompanied it was a sharp crack instead of a distant rumble. The storm had gotten stronger and wind whipped around us. The sight of Froston just sitting there nonchalantly infuriated me.

I ripped away the barrier I had created to protect us from the wind and the rain, but Froston just stood and laughed as he was bombarded. "Come, Anna."

He took my hand and pulled me to the water, starting to wade into the shallow part of the water. This was it. I was going to die. I was going to be struck by lightning, electrocuted by the sea, and no one would ever find my body. Tears prickled my eyes when I thought about the guys. Would they keep looking for me? How long would it take for them to give up?

I let Froston pull me into the shallows and tilted my head back, letting the rain run down my face and hiding any tears that might have escaped my eyes.

"This is it, Anna!" Froston said excitedly. "Open up your senses and feel the energy building."

I closed my eyes and tried to do what he said. I opened up all of my senses and tried to tell myself this would be okay. Every bit of common sense I had told me this was insanely dangerous. Mixing water and electricity was crazy. But maybe Froston was right. Maybe I did need to let go of all my human beliefs if I wanted to survive this.

I felt Froston's magic extending outward and I let mine do the same. My awareness expanded, and I felt what he had been talking about. The air was buzzing with a charge that was building. The energy levels got higher and higher, making it difficult to breathe.

"Pull it inside of you!" Froston shouted to me.

I started pulling in the energy, much like the prince had pulled it from me. Suddenly, the world exploded all around us and it was like we were floating in a pool of pure energy. I absorbed as much as I could inside me and I felt Froston doing the same. The energy around us faded and the world slowly came back into view.

My whole body was shaking, and I fell to my knees in the water. Froston held his arms out to the sky and laughed. "That was amazing!"

I shot him a dirty look, but it didn't put a damper on his giddiness. He pulled me to my feet then swung me around back to land. I stumbled when he put me back down, but didn't fall. My entire body was buzzing with energy, it was worse than the time I had eaten an entire bag of chocolate covered expresso beans, not realizing how much caffeine was in them.

Froston finally realized that I was not nearly as gleeful as he was. He placed his hands on my face and looked into my eyes. "You took too much," he said with a smile. "I can feel the energy ready to burst out of you. You're going to have to let some out before we go back."

I closed my eyes. He was right, I felt like my entire body was stuffed with energy. There was no doubt in my mind now that I wasn't a regular wolf. I definitely wasn't anything close to human. I really was fae.

With the magic buzzing inside me, I let my instincts guide me. The rain was tapering off now to just a slight drizzle but my clothes were clinging to me uncomfortably. Froston had told me that I could do anything that I put my mind to, so I tried to dry myself off. With a thought, I dissipated the water that had collected on my skin, clothing, and hair. It worked, but my skin crackled with electrical charge and my hair poofed out like I had stuck my hand in an electrical socket.

Froston couldn't hold in his laughter when he saw me. "A little more gently next time, Anna."

I glared at him and tried to pull my hair back. I wound it into a tight bun, but little hairs still stuck up all over my head. Froston kept laughing as if he were drunk. Maybe he was. Maybe this was how the fae got their kicks.

I scowled. He pointed a finger at me and zapped some kind of electricity towards me. Faster than I could think I instinctively formed a shield, blocking it from me.

"Excellent work, Anna," Froston told me proudly. "Do that before you go to bed and no one will be able to invade your dreams while you sleep."

I looked at the shield a little closer, making sure I would be able to replicate it later. If Froston had told me I could make a shield like this and tried to describe how I would do it, I don't think I would have been able to. But somehow I had used my instinct to create this? Once I was sure I had it figured out for next time, I narrowed my eyes at Froston. If he was going to fling electricity at me, I could retaliate. I focused on making a fireball in my hand as Froston watched.

He formed his own shield right before I flung it at him. "Good form, Anna," he called to me. "Use the ocean to attack me this time, though."

It was official. All the fae were completely insane.

Froston and I battled it out for a while on the beach. I let out all my anger and frustrations along with the extra magic I had humming inside of me. It felt good to let loose, but it was also satisfying to see just how far I had come. I was anything but helpless now.

I stood much more confidently now. I was certain that I could protect myself against humans and wolves. Next, I needed to hone my skills so that I wasn't helpless in the hands of a more experienced fae like the prince.

Froston flung an arm around my shoulders with a grin. "I haven't had that much fun in decades, we'll have to do this again soon."

I just gave him a dirty look before a thought struck me.

"I know what would be even more fun," I said slyly. "Visiting my pack in Seaside."

He gave me a squeeze. "It's not safe for you there."

"Why not?" I asked. "At least just let me tell them that I'm okay," I begged. "They're probably so worried!"

Froston gave me a kiss on the forehead. "I'll get them a message, but you have to keep your distance for now."

I sighed in disappointment. At least a message was better than nothing.

Chapter 10

Anna

The prince had sent word to my father that he was taking a break from our lessons today but was sending a healer in his place. That was fine with me. I still wasn't ready to face the prince after our last lesson. I was angry at the way he had treated me, but I was also angry that I had let him get away with it. I hated feeling helpless.

Froston had introduced me to Airmed, a healer for the king. She was tall, with white hair down to her hips, and an ageless wisdom in her eyes. She had the same delicate bone structure that I had seen in the other female fae that I had met. She also didn't seem very enthusiastic about being stuck with me.

Airmed had me watch her as she healed several people, but then simply turned to me and demanded that I do the same. I had no idea where to start. I dropped my hands from the guard's arm in frustration. "I can't do this."

The prince had brought an entire contingent of guards with him to my father's castle; apparently, he never went anywhere unless well protected. The guards trained rough, which meant there were plenty of injuries for me to practice healing. Most of the guards were gruff and wary but reminded me of the marines back home.

I felt a pang of longing in my heart when I thought about my marines and the rest of my pack in Seaside. I tried to set aside my emotions and focus on what I was trying to do. One of the guards was sitting in front of me, cradling his broken arm and waiting for me to heal him. I had tried everything I could think of but was failing miserably at the task.

Airmed huffed in frustration. "I don't want to have to report to the prince that you failed, yet again."

"Well, I don't want to report to the prince that you failed to teach me, *yet again*. But here we are." We both glared at each other. I met her eyes steadily, and maybe it was my wolf side, but I wanted her to be the first to look away.

Airmed lowered her eyes first and I felt a surge of triumph. Maybe it was because I was a lone wolf amongst the fae, but I felt more in tune with my wolfish instincts than ever. Or maybe it was because I was accepting magic as a part of who I was. When I had first met the twins, I had struggled with accepting the part of me that was a wolf. I had blocked all my instincts and thoughts that were wolfish and only let them out when I shifted.

The twins had shown me that I might have two different shapes; human and wolf, but I wasn't two different entities. For most of my life I had considered 'my wolf' to be something that took over when I shifted. But in reality, I had been suppressing half of who I was while in my human shape, and only being free when I shifted into a wolf. The truth was that I was just Anna, all the time, and it was okay to embrace my wolf half even when in my human shape. I was just starting to accept the part of myself that was fae, and I needed to learn to trust my instincts to do magic.

"Just watch," Airmed told me with exasperation.

I struggled to see what she was doing with her magic, I was getting better at sensing the flow but was still clueless about how to replicate the intricacies of what she was doing. I really did want to learn to be a healer, but the techniques I needed to learn were eluding me.

If I was really honest with myself, though, a part of me was holding back because I was afraid of harming someone. What if I poured my magic into one of these people and set them on fire? Or made them explode?

Airmed closed her eyes and I felt the flow of magic come from within her to stream into the guard.

I had observed this many times before, but I couldn't seem to get a handle on what she was doing, other than simply sending her magic into her patient. The guard grimaced as the magic wrapped around his injured arm and then sunk in. I leaned forward to see what the magic was doing but all I felt was a coolness emanating from the injury.

Airmed opened her eyes to examine the now-healed bone and the guard flexed his fingers with a grin. Yet another patient, easily healed by Airmed after I failed to do anything.

Airmed and I both sat back and eyed each other after the guard left. "Maybe talk me through what it is that you're doing again?"

She sighed but started again. "Reach inside yourself, connect with your magic, and then use it to fix what's wrong." She had been telling me the same thing over and over again but using slightly different words each time.

"But *how* do you use it to fix what's wrong?" I asked in frustration. I needed more than just a general statement.

She clenched her jaw. "You just... feel what's wrong and use your magic to force things back into place."

I exhaled. Maybe Airmed could heal instinctively because she had been doing this for so many centuries. "But what about when you were first learning? Did you struggle at all?"

She gave a snort. "I've always been able to do this, there was no 'learning' for me." She paused thoughtfully. "But using magic is like fighting a battle, you have to master it and force it to do what you want."

Once again, we were at a stalemate. Using my magic didn't feel like fighting a battle. The few times when I was successful at doing anything with my magic it had felt more like a release than a battle. When I had successfully used my magic, it was because I had let my instincts and emotions guide me.

Working with Airmed wasn't teaching me anything. "Do you have textbooks on healing?"

"Textbooks?" She stared at me blankly. "What would a book tell you about healing? You just need to do it."

I sighed and gave up. I guess it was too much to hope for that someone had written a book on the techniques used for healing. I could really use a book called something like *'Theory of Magical Healing'* or even better *'Magical Healing for Dummies'*. But I guess that wasn't really necessary for the fae since they lived for centuries and didn't need to teach or pass down information like humans did.

I stood up since that was our last patient of the day. "Thank you for your help, Airmed," I told her politely. "I appreciate you taking time to teach me."

She gave me a look. "You're welcome."

I smoothed my dress down before exiting the room to collect Caylee. Froston had told me that the prince was off doing princely things. I had my freedom for the rest of the day and I didn't intend to leave my room for any of it. I wanted to practice my magic so that I would be ready for the prince.

The next time we met, I wanted to be able to hold my own with him. He told me before that using magic was like a muscle, and I wanted to get my magical muscle bulked up like it was on steroids. I grimaced at the thought; that was bad, even for my terrible sense of humor. But I wasn't going to let Drake intimidate me or take advantage of me. I was going to stand tall and meet his challenge.

I lost myself in my magic once we got back to the room. Caylee was bored watching me sit on the floor with my eyes closed, so I told her to give me some time alone. She happily skipped off to go chat up one of the prince's guards; apparently she had been getting friendly with them during my lessons. I was a little worried that they might take advantage of her, but she laughed off my concerns.

Alone in my room, I worked on my magic for hours until I was able to access it with barely a thought. I practiced making barriers, breezes, and tiny fireballs until it was second nature. But creating a slight breeze or a shower of sparks wasn't going to help me impress the king or get out of here.

Being more confident in using my magic was going to help me stand toe to toe with the prince. And the more I practiced, the more natural using magic felt. I needed to get to the point where I trusted my instincts where magic was concerned. If I could instinctively form a complicated shield that blocked magic when Froston tried to zap me, maybe I could get to the point where I could heal just as well as Airmed using my instincts.

Chapter 11

Cody

I slid into the chair opposite Robbie with a bad feeling. He looked nervous and kept tapping on the table, making me even more apprehensive. His normally neatly combed hair was sticking up in all directions, as if he had been rubbing his hands through it. He had at least two days-worth of stubble, and his eyes were bloodshot and wild.

Robbie had called earlier this evening and had wanted to talk to me alone. His request wasn't that unusual under normal circumstances, a lot of the guys would call me when they needed me to be an intermediary between them and James or Austin. Robbie had been recruited as a much-needed psychologist for the pack. He would usually call me when he was worried about one of the guys, or if he was having a difficult time with one of them. Austin and I had put a lot of faith in him to take care of our guys.

But these were not normal circumstances and Robbie was already on the pack shit list. He and Quinn had both given us stories the night of the attack on our pack house that didn't match. Even worse than that, he'd let one of our enemies get past him and onto our territory to place a bomb. We didn't have any solid evidence to show that he was in league with the enemy, and I really hoped that he wasn't. I wanted it to be just a coincidence, but my gut was telling me otherwise.

Austin had given the order for us to quietly keep Robbie under surveillance. If he was working with the enemy, we wanted to control the flow of information that they received. Giving the enemy false information was sometimes more useful than nothing at all. Caleb was monitoring all of his electronic communications to trace them. We didn't have anything yet, but if we simply kicked Robbie out, our enemies would just plant another mole that we didn't know about. It was better to use the one that we thought we found.

Robbie had asked to meet in this hole in the wall bar in the middle of nowhere. We were the only patrons here, and the bartender looked like he would be pissed if we tried to order something from him. He was kicked back in his chair, playing on his phone, and completely ignoring us.

"Cody," Robbie started, tapping his fingers even faster on the table. He wouldn't meet my eyes, so this was not going to be a pleasant conversation.

"Um, you know I have-" his voice cracked, and he cleared his throat. Dude was about to kill me with the suspense.

I tried to keep my impatience to myself, intimidating him wasn't going to make him spit it out.

"I had a sister," he finally mumbled.

I frowned. I knew he had a sister that was mated into a pack somewhere in the Midwest, but her pack didn't want to take in Robbie along with her. Receiving a female into a pack was a huge bonus, but adding another male to compete was usually a no-go in most packs. Robbie, in particular, was a no-go because psychology wasn't considered to be an occupation worthy of a wolf.

"Did something happen?" I asked him quietly.

He finally stopped the incessant tapping and threw himself back into his chair with a sigh. As he let out his breath, all the tension flooded out of him and he finally met my eyes. What I saw there in his tired eyes was defeat. He had given up.

"I have something to tell you," Robbie stated dejectedly.

My stomach sank as Robbie told me his story. He had been approached by another wolf a week before we had even found Anna or knew she existed. Initially, he was just offered money to betray the Seaside Pack but turned it down. The same night that Evelyn had been killed, he was approached again.

This time, the wolf told him that his organization had his sister and would be mailing her to him in pieces if he didn't cooperate.

"Cody, you gotta believe me," Robbie said with a plea in his eyes. "I never meant to hurt any of you guys. At first, they just asked me to do stupid stuff. Asked me about which room Anna was staying in, or when we were having meetings…"

I couldn't help the low growl that came out. "Putting Anna and the rest of the pack at risk isn't 'stupid stuff'. You allowed the enemy onto our territory-"

"I didn't know what they were planning that night they attacked the house," he told me insistently. "He said they wanted to meet with me on the other side of the property, I didn't realize they were going to sneak onto our pack lands."

"And the bomb?" I asked angrily. "If Anna or anyone else had been standing close-"

"They weren't," he asserted. "I made sure no one was around."

"So you knew?" I asked in a dangerous voice. Robbie had better think really hard before he answered that question.

He paled and lowered his head in shame. "I knew."

I heard enough. Robbie was lucky that I had self-control. If James were here now…

I reached for my phone to call Aus, I was too far from anyone else in the pack to use the pack bond to get a hold of him.

Robbie reached for my phone to stop me and I looked at him incredulously, standing slowly. I leaned over where he was sitting and let him feel the full power of my anger and sense of betrayal. He shrunk down in his chair with a mumbled apology. Content that he was willing to submit, I looked back at my phone and cursed. No bars of service.

"This is what we are going to do," I growled at Robbie. "You're going to come back to the house with me quietly. You're going to fully cooperate, and you're going to tell us everything. If and I mean if we get Anna back and no one in the pack is harmed, we might let you live. But you're skating on thin ice right now."

Robbie gave a sharp nod. "They killed my sister," he whispered and raised his eyes to me. "I'm next."

I shook my head in disgust. The only reason he was confessing right now was to save his own skin? "You should have come to us." I told him angrily. "If you had told us that they had taken your sister, we would have done everything we could to get her back unharmed. We were your brothers in arms, and you betrayed us. For what? What did you gain?"

"Nothing," he whispered. "I lost everything that ever mattered to me."

I grabbed his arm and hauled him up out of the chair, pushing him ahead of me. He exited the bar first and I squinted when I walked out into the bright light. That's why I never saw them coming before it was too late.

Robbie's head snapped back, and I was hit with a spray of blood and other things I didn't want to think about. I immediately crouched to make myself a smaller target and hurled myself back into the bar, rolling behind the wall for cover. Robbie's body hit the ground with a thump in front of me.

"Shit." I looked around the bar desperately for anything I could use as a weapon. Nothing.

The bartender was gone, and no one else was in sight. I extended my senses and felt the presence of other wolves nearby who were not in my pack. I cursed again, glancing at my phone – still no service.

I felt the wolves outside, not making any effort to come in here after me. What were they waiting for? I tried to extend my senses further and felt something odd. Where the wolves felt like warm, glowing balls of energy, there were other spots that felt cold and dark.

For the second time today, my heart sunk. I knew what this was, that was how Aus and James had described the man that took Anna. But it wasn't just one this time, there were a bunch of them, and they were about to enter the bar, leaving the mysterious wolves outside.

I smashed one of the chairs and picked up the leg to use as a weapon. I wasn't going down without a fight.

Chapter 12

Anna

"Anna! I have a surprise for you!"

I tensed when I heard the prince call out in a singsong voice. A moment later he strode into my room followed by a group of his guards, dragging something between them. The prince had been absent for several days now, leaving me to work with Airmed and to practice on my own.

I was even more nervous when I realized that he had brought six of his guards along with his 'surprise'. What kind of a surprise needed that many guards? Probably not a good one.

I stood to peer in between the guards and try to see what it was amongst their circle without getting too close. I gasped when I picked up on his scent and saw a flash of Caribbean blue eyes.

"Cody!" I shoved my way through the guards without a second thought, elbowing one in the ribs when he didn't move quickly enough for me.

The guards released him, and Cody struggled to stay upright on his knees, swaying as he met my eyes.

I knelt to inspect his injuries. One of his eyes was almost swollen shut, he had cuts and abrasions all over his face and his clothes were torn and bloody.

I gently cupped his face in my hand and he gave a contented sigh. "Found you." He gave me a rueful grin and reached for me.

"What have you gotten yourself into?" I murmured to him as we embraced, and he breathed in my scent. I was thankful at how much stronger I had been getting, because Cody was leaning into me with all of his weight and I was able to support both of us.

I pulled back and steadied him when he swayed again. "I need to take a look at your injuries."

I shot a dirty look at the prince, who seemed to just be watching our reunion with amusement. What was wrong with that guy?

I brushed Cody's hair back gently and ran a hand down his jaw. Most of his facial injuries looked painful, but not serious. "I'm going to check your eye," I warned him before carefully pulling down his lower eyelid to get a look at the eye itself. His beautiful eye was bloodshot, but I didn't notice any obvious damage to the eye. "I need a flashlight," I grumbled to myself.

To my surprise, one of the guards reached into the pocket of his black uniform and pulled out a small keychain flashlight. He glanced at the prince before handing it over to me. I gave him a nod of thanks, but it was a little difficult to be truly thankful when I was guessing that he had a hand in this.

Cody's pupils both dilated appropriately so I felt a little bit better. I also couldn't see any obvious abrasions or tears in the eye.

The rest of my exam of Cody went a little quicker, but I got angrier and angrier at the more damage I saw. Cody must have been pretty out of it, because he didn't complain or ask any questions. He just grunted occasionally when I touched a sore spot.

The prince and his guards also didn't murmur a word, just watched.

"Can you stand?" I asked Cody.

He grunted but was able to get to his feet. I stumbled a little trying to hold up the weight of a 230-pound werewolf but managed to keep both of us on our feet until I could guide Cody over to the couch to rest.

I helped him lie down on the couch and he closed his eyes in relief. Once he was settled and I smoothed my hand over his brow, I jumped up in anger.

"What did you do to him?" I growled as I stalked closer to the prince.

A few of his guards moved to intercept me, but the prince waved them back. "That will be all, you're dismissed."

There was some hesitation, but all of them bowed and took their leave of the prince before heading out the door.

The prince and I circled each other. I was angry, and the amused smirk on his face was just infuriating me further.

"You don't like my gift?" he taunted me.

"What did you do to him?" I repeated, narrowing my eyes.

The prince laughed. "He didn't initially accept the gracious invitation that I extended to him. My guards had to convince him to come along."

"You did something else." Cody would never just lie on the couch peacefully while I spoke with the man responsible for taking me from the pack. He had to be drugged or magicked into compliance somehow.

The prince shrugged. "Consider it part of your lessons. I have a feeling that you will be much more motivated to heal one of your wolves than one of my guards." He flashed a grin at me. "I'm sure you can figure out how to unravel the magic on him…eventually. But you might need a few more lessons in compulsion first."

I seethed but the prince just gave me a haughty grin. "Are you ready to go back to learning?" He stopped circling me and stood still.

"Fine," I ground out. "But teach me compulsion first." I needed to fix whatever was wrong with Cody ASAP.

"And you'll work with my healer after?"

I gave a sharp nod of agreement. I hated that the prince had won this round, but I needed to fix Cody.

The prince grinned at me triumphantly and held out his arm. "I'll have my men settle Cody in somewhere while we go find some humans to practice on."

I held off on taking his arm until I could get some promises out of him. "He'll be safe from further harm? And Airmed will heal him?"

The prince shook his head. "He will be safe, as long as you cooperate. But healing? That's going to be up to you, my dear. I need to keep you motivated."

"I would like to keep him here, then," I told him firmly.

The prince raised an eyebrow. "I'm not sure your father would approve."

"I'm sure he wouldn't object if the request came from you," I told him sweetly. "I want to make sure he's close by, so I can spend all of my free time learning to heal him." I was slowly learning to play his game.

The corner of his mouth lifted a little. "Very well."

I sat down on the couch and smoothed Cody's hair back. "Hey, Cody?" He opened his eyes and a smile slowly slid over his face.

"Anna…" he murmured, still looking a little dazed.

"I have some errands to do, but I'll be back to take care of you soon." I told him softly. "My friend, Caylee, is going to be here with you."

He mumbled something and closed his eyes again.

I looked up to meet Caylee's worried eyes from across the room. "I'll take care of him, my lady," she said quietly.

"Thanks," I told her with a small smile.

I stood and reached for the arm the prince had offered me earlier, giving Cody one last look. I wanted to just curl up with him, but I couldn't leave him in the confused haze that the fae had put him in.

The prince led me out of my rooms and his guards settled in formation around us as we walked down the hall.

"You know, darling, if I didn't know you better, I would think that you and Cody were an item." The prince was obviously trying to pry some information out of me.

"If I didn't know you better, I'd think that you were jealous." I looked up at him as he laughed out loud.

"You little minx," the prince said with a grin. "I heard that you were the only female in your pack, but I didn't suspect that they were your own personal harem."

I rolled my eyes. "They're not."

"I have to admit that I find the idea of a harem to be quite tempting." The prince smirked at me. "Of course, I'd have to find a wife that wouldn't object."

"Why marry at all if that's the way you feel?" I asked curiously. Surely, a prince could do whatever he wanted.

He shrugged. "I'm expected to marry and conduct myself appropriately as prince of the realm."

We were both quiet for as long as it took us to get to our practice space. The distaste was clear on my face when he brought in a human man in chains for us to 'practice' on.

The prince rolled his eyes. "Due to your delicate sensibilities, I've had the guards bring us a prisoner. He was caught after raping several young girls."

I narrowed my eyes at the prisoner. He was filthy, with matted hair and torn clothes but his eyes were burning with rage.

"Would you like me to show you how we know he's guilty?" the prince asked slyly.

I tore my eyes away from the prisoner to focus on the prince. He was watching me with a mischievous sparkle in his green eyes that made me want to proceed cautiously.

"How do you plan to do that?"

The prince held out a hand for me. "Come, take my hand and I'll show you."

I let the prince pull me closer to the prisoner and closed my eyes as he directed. This time, he connected with the prisoner and brought me along for the ride. I saw flashes of memories and emotions that showed me what a sick man this prisoner was. Not only had he done the crimes, but he had enjoyed every moment of it.

I yanked my hand away from the prince, breaking the connection. I tried to hold down the vomit that was rising up and struggled to take deep breaths to clear my head.

"What do you think we should do with him, Anna?" the prince asked with a grin. "What punishment should we dole out?"

I shivered. "We should make sure he never hurts another girl ever again."

"My thoughts exactly." The prince smirked.

This time I walked willingly back to the prince and took his hand again. I remembered my father's warnings about how dangerous connecting like this could be, but I doubted that the prince would risk forming a permanent connection with me. He had to know what he was doing, plus I needed to free Cody from his compulsion. I needed to learn this as quickly as possible.

The prince guided my magic, twisting and weaving tiny strands of it, forcing his intent into his work. I watched carefully in dismay. I could feel everything he was doing, but there was no way I could replicate this. The magic I could do was clumsy and bulky, this was completely on another level.

When finished, the prince looked at me. I'm sure he saw the complete devastation on my face, because he laughed. "I'll let you try something easier," he told me. "Why don't you try to undo it?"

I took a deep breath and focused. I had watched him insert every tiny little weave of magic into this man and I could feel each strand emitting small amounts of magic from where they were now. I tugged on one of the small strands gently, trying to remove it without harming the prisoner. It came free and dissipated into the air when I released it.

One down, only a hundred left to go. I worked quietly with sweat beading on my face as I concentrated. It took me ten times as long to remove all the magic than it had taken the prince to put it there in the first place.

The prince stood back and admired my work. "Good job. I'm surprised you were able to do that without harming him. Maybe you do have some affinity for healing."

Before I could comprehend what was happening, the prince had pulled out a knife and slit the prisoner's throat. I stared in horror as blood sprayed out of the wound and the prisoner clutched his throat. I stepped forward to try to help, but the prince held me back.

"It's for the best, Anna," the prince murmured in my ear. "The magic would have lasted a short time, but he would have gone right back to his old ways once it faded completely."

The man slumped to the floor with a glazed and empty look in his eyes and blood pooled around his body. I pushed the prince away from me and he didn't object. "You just killed him!" I couldn't believe the prince had acted so callously.

The prince shrugged. "I didn't feel like re-doing it after you unraveled all of my work. The guards will have someone clean up the mess." He held out his arm for me to take but I pushed past him and headed for the door.

His laughter followed me. "We're done for today, but I'll see you tomorrow."

Caylee was surprised when I came back to the room after such a short time, our lessons usually lasted for hours. I knelt next to Cody and smoothed his hair back. It was time to apply what I had learned.

I turned to Caylee. "Would you mind finding something for him to eat? He's going to be hungry once he snaps out of this."

Caylee gave me a nod and scampered out of the room. I hoped Cody was going to be ready to eat when he woke up out of this haze. If he turned down food, I would know that something was seriously wrong with him.

I took a deep breath and started to work on him. I ignored everything around me and just focused on the small bits of magic glowing inside of him. I could do this.

It felt like hours later when I finally sat back down on my heels and Cody blinked in confusion. "Anna?"

"Yeah. Looks like you made a trip to hell to find me." I said with a tired smile.

"Totally worth it," he told me honestly, running his hand over the injuries on his face. His brow furrowed in concern. "Are you alright?"

I gave him a small smile. "Yeah, just tired. I'm more worried about you."

He sat up slowly and rubbed his head. "I don't remember coming here, I just remember having some weird dreams. Where are we?" He winced as he stretched out his body, obviously still in pain from all his injuries.

Caylee came back into the room, followed by a guard carrying a huge tray of food. I was relieved when I saw Cody perk up at the scent of food. "I'll explain while we eat."

Cody's jaw dropped multiple times as I told him about everything that had happened since I had been here. "You've been here for over a week?" Cody asked incredulously.

I nodded, and he frowned in confusion. "You went missing and I met with Robbie the next day. A bunch of guys jumped me. But a week?"

"Oh, no one told you?" Caylee piped up.

Our heads both turned to her in surprise. "Time moves a little differently here. A week here is like a day or two back home."

I think Cody and I were equally shocked. "That does make me feel a little better," I told them. "At least the pack hasn't been looking for me that long."

Cody reached for my hand. "Just a minute without you is too long."

I blushed and Caylee giggled. "This is your love?"

I turned even more red and Cody grinned at me. "Your love, huh?"

"Um, Caylee. Thanks for the food. Would you mind giving Cody and I some time to catch up?"

She winked at me. "Of course, my lady." She gave me a curtsy with a huge grin on her face and slipped out the door.

Cody picked up another turkey leg and looked at me thoughtfully. "All of this seems so…unreal. Fae? Another world? Magic?" He shook his head and took a bite.

"Yeah," I mumbled. "Almost as crazy as people who can turn into wolves."

He almost choked on his bite of turkey. "That's believable. But this?"

I couldn't help but chuckle before turning serious again. "I know this is the last place you want to be right now. But Cody? I'm glad to have someone with me." I had to swallow hard at the end.

Cody sat down his turkey leg and reached for my hand. "Anna, I'm glad I'm with you. I was going out of my mind thinking about all the horrible shit you might be going through."

I gave him a small smile. "I can't complain. They haven't locked me in a prison or anything. I feel terrible about making you guys worry about me, though."

He gave my hand a squeeze. "I'm just glad you're okay, *my lady*," he teased me.

Once I gave him a genuine smile he released my hand and then went back to eating. The man could really pack away some food.

"Froston promised to send word to the pack that I'm okay. I'll ask him to let them know about you too," I told him.

Cody swallowed his last bite and frowned. "The dude that kidnapped you? Is he really your father?"

I shrugged. "Maury hasn't announced the DNA test results yet, but it seems like it."

He laughed at the talk show reference, but I turned my tone serious again. "I don't know why I'm really here, though. What they've told me doesn't make sense."

Cody nodded. "I get you, but that's the kind of thing we need Aus for. He would be able to figure it out."

I sighed. "I've just been trying to learn as much as I can about magic until I can figure out a way to get back home."

"That's probably the only thing you can do right now. I mean, even if you did run, they would just pull you back through one of those portal things," Cody told me with a shrug.

"That's not what I wanted to hear." I told him. "I'm frustrated just sitting here and cooperating like a good little captive. I want to do something."

Cody smiled at me. "I like it when you get feisty. But you have to be smart and pick your battles. We need to prepare to fight and choose a battle that we have a chance at winning."

I sat back in my chair with frustration. "I know how you feel." Cody told me empathetically. "But think of it this way: you want them to think that you're on their side. That way they'll relax their guard and make it easier for us to escape when the time comes. You don't want them seeing you as an enemy and throwing you in a dungeon." He paused. "I'm assuming this place has a dungeon?"

I shrugged. "I'd rather not find out."

Cody and I chatted while he finished lunch, but when he went to the bathroom to clean up, I reflected on what he said. Yeah, as far as plans went, it sucked. But that's all we had for now.

Chapter 13

Caleb

I put Eeyore back into the playpen area that the twins had helped me put together for the pups. I tossed the two little dogs some bones to keep them busy while I went back to work. Anytime I let them out of their pen they ran right to Anna's room to look for her and then downstairs to see if she was there.

I took a sip of my coffee and grimaced at the lukewarm temperature, placing the cup back on my desk in distaste. A new window popped open on my screen, showing that Emerys was requesting a conversation. I had sent him a message earlier asking for help.

The fae were new to me and the rest of the pack. The only thing I knew about the fae were old nursery tales, and who knew how much truth could be found in those? For the most part, I had always thought the fae were just fairy tales. I had never expected to run into one in real life.

But Emerys was an immortal lamia and had connections to other immortals. If anyone could get us information on the fae, it would be him.

When I asked Emerys what he knew about the fae there was a pause.

Why would you want to know about them? Has one been seen in our world?

Yeah. They took our girl.

Shit. Arminius needs to know about this. Hold tight, I'll get back to you.

He broke our connection before I could get anything else out of him.

I clenched my fists in frustration. I was more than tired of sitting here helplessly while Anna was missing. My technical skills were all but useless in the struggle to get her back. If she had been taken by humans I would be able to search satellite images, security cameras, and traffic footage to track her down. But taken through a magical portal? I had nothing for that.

I was working on re-tasking a satellite so that we could monitor the area of northern Canada, where Austin suspected Anna was born originally. When James had gone up north to investigate Anna's past, he had discovered more mystery than he had uncovered.

Ingrid had told James that there was 'something' in the north that was not spoken of and had hinted that Anna's mother had been banished for breaking the rules. She had given James an old photo that we suspected was of Anna and her mother due to how similar they looked. Anna now had that photo framed at her bedside.

We didn't know for sure that Anna had been taken up north, but I was willing to bet on it. I really wanted to see what they were hiding up there.

I worked on that along with a few other projects for hours until Emerys reached out to me again. The window popped up on my screen to show that he was requesting contact, so I brought up our chat screen.

Arminius cleared me to share some intel...

I leaned forward in my chair eagerly. Finally! I was getting some answers.

The lamia and fae made an agreement centuries ago after the last war. They agreed to stay in their world and we agreed to stay here - it was an uneasy truce. The exception to that were a few of the minor fae who were mostly powerless, and only had enough magic to shift forms.

My jaw dropped – their world? It had never occurred to me that there could be other worlds out there. And was he saying that wolves were descended from fae? I had never thought about our origins before, I just assumed we were a race unto ourselves.

Our council is going to be meeting to figure out our next step. I have to warn you though – their main concern is going to be keeping the fae out. They aren't going to care about getting your girl back. They might even bargain with the fae and let them keep her.

Rage bubbled up inside of me. Anna was not a bargaining chip, and letting the fae keep her was not an option.

And if the wolves disagree?

Would the wolves be willing to take on the fae and lamia to save one girl?

I already knew the answer to that and I didn't want to think about it.

You know our females are precious to us, letting them come here and take our females whenever they want isn't an option.

Understood. But I think this situation is larger than you and me. You consider yourselves completely separate from the fae, but the older ones among us don't necessarily see it that way.

I swallowed nervously. This situation had gotten out of control really quickly. Emerys signed off again, and this time I didn't try to stop him. I needed to report this to Austin as soon as he got back, but I also needed more information.

I went back to working on the satellites. There were tons of satellites out there with low security that I could get into. The problem was finding one that could be useful. Some of them were 'high res' and could get me a picture of what someone was eating for breakfast, but those could only get an image about twice a day. That wasn't really helpful for monitoring an area for a missing girl.

Other satellites were 'high revisit' and cover more ground, taking pics up to every twenty minutes. The problem with those was that they were very low res and an image of a car would show up as about one pixel. That also made finding a missing girl difficult. Plus, there were also not very many satellites originally tasked to monitor the northern part of Canada. Why spend money to monitor a mostly empty area?

I needed to hack into a multitude of satellites that could monitor for any unusual activity in the north and then be able to take a detailed snapshot once I located an area of interest. Emerys had said that they were supposed to stay in their own world, but that obviously wasn't the case. The pack in northern Canada had hinted that there was more up there than anyone knew, so my guess was that there was some kind of a gateway up there.

If the fae were using a point in the Arctic to get in and out of our world, I needed satellites that could pick up on movement and activity where there shouldn't be any. I hurriedly gulped down the rest of the disgusting lukewarm coffee, so I had enough fuel to keep me moving. I needed to buckle down and figure this out. Anna needed me.

Chapter 14

Anna

Airmed had come to my room while Cody was still in the bathroom and we were now sitting awkwardly in complete silence, waiting for Cody.

I cleared my throat. "So... how many other healers are there?"

Airmed looked at me as if I had just insulted her. "They have me."

I nodded nervously. "I just meant, that humans usually have a lot of different healers so that the burden isn't so much on just one."

She gave me an irritated sigh. "Humans are fragile, short-lived little things, magic doesn't work well on them anyway."

"Really?" I asked curiously. "Have you tried? Why doesn't it work?"

Airmed looked at me as if I were a moron. "I don't need to try. It won't work because they don't have magic to begin with."

"Um, okay." I doubted that what she said was accurate. If she never tried then how would she know? And hadn't Froston told me that there was magic in everything around me? I would imagine that included humans as well. It sounded more like Airmed just wanted an excuse so that she didn't have to work on humans.

The bathroom door creaked open and I stood up, grateful for the interruption to this painful conversation. Cody stood in the doorway with a too-small towel wrapped around his hips and water still dripping from his hair. The water was dripping onto his shoulders and slowly down his very muscular chest. I licked my lips at the sight but shook myself out of it when Airmed gave an irritated sigh.

"Cody, I'd like you to meet Airmed. She's the healer who has been teaching me."

"*Trying* to teach you," Airmed grumbled under her breath.

111

I ignored her comment and gave her a polite smile instead of rolling my eyes at her like I wanted to.

"Uh, yeah. Nice to meet you," Cody said awkwardly. "Any chance they might have some clothes in my size around here?"

I blinked and looked at him. Most of the male fae that I had met so far had been tall, but lean. There was no way Cody would be able to squeeze into any of their borrowed clothing. Even the guards, whom Caylee had told me were part human, weren't close to Cody's size.

Airmed stood. "You don't have anything I haven't seen before, wolf. Just lie down on the bed so we can get this over with."

Cody looked at me and I gave him an embarrassed shrug. "Maybe cover up with the blanket for now, and then we can ask Caylee to find you some clothes?"

Cody shrugged and unknotted the towel. I adverted my eyes to be polite but out of the corner of my eye I saw him rub the towel through his hair before heading to the bed. My eyes were drawn to him as if he were magnetic and after a quick glance to see him heading for the bed I forced myself to look at the ceiling.

It wasn't too quick for me to notice that his muscular back led to an equally impressive backside and thighs. I waited until it sounded like he was situated in the bed before looking back in his direction.

Airmed had her eyes on me, obviously amused. "I guess he does have something *you* haven't seen before."

I turned bright red as Cody chuckled from his spot on the bed. He winced painfully and inhaled a sharp breath, so he probably shouldn't have been laughing at me anyway.

I followed Airmed over to the bed where we stood over Cody. He just looked amused as we both stood over him but at least he had flung a part of the blanket over his man bits. His body was still covered in cuts and, but it looked like the scrapes had started to heal up nicely. His eye was still swollen shut and had now turned more of a purple color than the red that it had been earlier. That had to be painful.

Airmed crossed her arms and stared at me. "Go ahead."

I huffed in frustration. "Go ahead and do what?" I shook my head. "Airmed, I'm not trying to replace you as the healer here."

She snorted. "Like you could."

"Exactly," I told her earnestly. "I'll never have the expertise and talent that you do." I was really trying to soften her up now. "But my goal is to do something different."

She raised an eyebrow at me, but at least she was listening.

"My expertise is going to be wolves and other shifters."

She rolled her eyes. "They barely have any fae blood at all, they're almost as bad as the humans."

I blinked in surprise. Since when did wolves have *any* fae blood? That was off-topic. I could question my father about that later, but right now I needed to get her on my side.

Cody looked just as surprised as I did, but I shot him a warning look before he could say anything. "They might be beneath your level, but they're the perfect patient population for me."

Airmed started to look interested. "That's probably true, I doubt you have enough talent in you to heal real fae. You definitely should never be given the opportunity to heal the prince or any other royalty."

I nodded in agreement. Was that why she's been so rude to me? She's been worried I would take her spot? "I fit in better with the wolves than with the other fae, anyway."

She looked me up and down. "True."

She meant for that to be insulting, and maybe it was. I needed to keep in mind that my goal was to get her to help me. If convincing her that I was inept did the job, then so be it. Yet, it was still infuriating that she considered the shifters to be beneath her notice.

I took a deep breath to calm my rising temper. "So… I would appreciate it if you could teach me how to heal wolves like Cody."

She stared deep into my eyes as if she was really considering it. I saw a flicker in her eyes when she made her decision. "I suppose."

I hid my smile and looked down at Cody. His injuries were more than enough to somber me up quickly.

Airmed reached for my hands and I gave them to her with surprise. She had never deigned to touch me before, was she really going to try to teach me this time?

We linked hands over Cody and he stared up at us apprehensively. This kind of magic was not something that wolves had much contact with, so I'm sure he must have been a little nervous at being my test subject. Especially since he knew I could barely function as a wolf, and now he was trusting me to use my fae magic on him.

"Draw your magic," Airmed instructed me. "I'll help to guide you in the right direction. Your goal is to smooth and soothe everything back into place."

I nodded and focused on my magic. I was surprised when I felt her guiding me, even though we weren't connected like the prince and I would be during our lessons together.

"You want to use the magic that's already inside of him, merge it with your own, and then use it to heal the damaged tissues," Airmed instructed me. "His body will accept the healing better if it recognizes the magic as his."

Airmed poked and prodded me in the right direction more than she guided me, but her instruction was helpful. I was so focused on what we were doing that I didn't realize how much time had passed until Cody let out a loud snore.

I giggled and Airmed gave me a small smile. I was shocked, I had never seen her mouth even twitch in the direction of a smile before. I used my magic to poke Cody in a now-healed part of his abs, startling him awake. He gave me a sheepish grin when he realized that he had fallen asleep. I smiled at him to let him know I wasn't upset.

He raised a hand to his face and gently felt around his previously injured eye. "It feels much better!"

I was going to just let go of how surprised he sounded. After all, I hadn't thought I would be able to do this either.

Airmed let go of my hands. "Yes, Anna did a good job for her first time." She raised her eyes to me. "I didn't think you would be able to do anything at all. It looks like you might have a future healing lesser creatures, after all."

I gritted my teeth. Lesser creatures?

Airmed raised her chin and took a step back. "I'll see you down in the training area tomorrow morning. I'm sure we will have some guards lined up that you can practice on. If you can manage to heal them, then I can stop wasting my time on the half-breeds all together."

She didn't even wait for an answer from me, she simply glided out of the room.

"Well, she's delightful," Cody said with a straight face.

I laughed. "She's one of the more delightful ones."

Cody made a face. "Great. I can't wait to meet some of the others."

I sighed and sat down on the bed next to him. I was exhausted, magic really took a lot out of me.

Cody patted the bed closer to him. "C'mere, Anna."

I hesitated but decided to just snuggle up to him. I hadn't been as close to Cody as I had with the twins, but now that I had been away from all of them for so long, I realized that was a mistake.

Cody reached his arm around me to pull me close and I cuddled in closer to his warmth and his scent. Before Cody had gotten here, I hadn't realized just how empty and alone I had been feeling. Caylee had been keeping me company, but it wasn't the same as having my pack all around me. I had gotten really attached to always having the guys close.

Cody moved his thumb in small circles on my lower back. "I missed you," he murmured into my hair.

"I missed you, too," I mumbled back, trying to hide the tears that I felt prickling at my eyes. There's no way I wanted to confess just how scared and alone I'd felt since I was taken from the pack, I didn't want Cody to think I was a wimp.

His thumb stilled for a moment. "You're not going to leave us now that you're an uber powerful fae princess, right?"

I picked up my head to look at him incredulously. "I've been worried that the pack wouldn't take me back... now that you know that I'm some kind of freak."

Cody laughed out loud, and I was a little insulted at first, but then I saw the humor in it all and laughed with him. I elbowed him in his now-healed ribs. "And I'm not a fae princess."

"The little redhead and the guards all call you 'my lady'. So you're some kind of royalty." Cody answered with a frown.

I shrugged. "I just want to go home and leave all this behind."

Cody gave me a squeeze. "You and me both."

I wiggled around to get comfortable but when I moved my hand on his abs I suddenly remembered that he was completely naked under the small corner of the blanket that he had strategically placed over himself.

I blushed, and Cody must have picked up on my thoughts because I could feel his grin as he gazed down at me. He could have teased me, but instead he just gave me a kiss on the forehead. "Once I get some clothes, do you want to give me a tour?"

"Oh, I'm not supposed to leave the room," I informed Cody. "Not unless I'm with my father, or the prince."

Cody frowned. "You *are* a prisoner here?"

I shook my head. "Yes and no. I'm... an unwilling guest?"

"Your father hasn't welcomed his long-lost daughter?" Cody questioned me with an unreadable look on his face.

"He's... confusing," I told Cody. "He's friendly sometimes, but I don't think he wants me around him most of the time. If he did, he wouldn't be keeping me hidden in a dark corner of his stone castle."

Cody gave me another squeeze. "I'm sorry, Anna. That must be rough on you. I know you were hoping for more when you found out you had family out there somewhere."

"Yeah," I said sadly. "I guess I was."

Cody gave me a grin. "What if we decided to explore on our own?"

I thought about it. I was nervous about my father's warnings about leaving my room, but I was getting better at magic and I knew how to shield myself. Plus, I wasn't alone anymore. Not many of the guards would want to take on Cody. The combination of the two of us together should make it okay.

I perked up. "You know what? Let's do it."

I hopped out of the bed. "But we don't need clothes."

Cody raised an eyebrow.

"I need to know if I can use my magic while I'm in my wolf form," I told him seriously. "Let's explore the castle as wolves."

Cody laughed out loud. "How will the fae feel about us 'lesser creatures' wandering their halls?"

I shrugged. "Who cares? The prince is off doing prince stuff, and the rest of the fae here should all fall under my father's authority. Let's just do what we want."

Cody looked at me with surprise and respect in his eyes. "You've changed since you've been away from us."

I shrugged, a little embarrassed. "I'll change in the bathroom. You can change here but crack the door beforehand so we can get out without hands."

Cody gave me a grin. "Yes, my lady."

I rolled my eyes but went into the bathroom to change. It had been too long since I had indulged my wolf half. I had been spending all my spare time moping around in a depression. It was time for me to run free.

Once in the bathroom, I slipped off my dress and stared into the mirror for a moment. I saw the same blond hair and green eyes that I had been looking at my entire life. But the girl that I saw in the mirror now had more strength and determination than I'd ever seen before.

I had gradually been becoming more confident in who I was, but now I had the strength to back it up. I would never have to cower in front of anyone like my uncle ever again. I was strong enough to protect myself and felt confident that I could take on most of the bullies like him back in my world.

My father and the prince were two of the strongest fae in this world and I was learning from the best. I intended to take in every lesson that they had to offer. I might not like everything that they had to teach me, but I was determined to find a way to use this power for good.

I gave myself a nod in the mirror and then shifted. I shook out my white coat and gave a wolf grin when I felt the cool stone beneath my paws. Not only was I a vicious Arctic wolf, but I was on my way to becoming a badass fae, too.

I ran out into the room and pounced on Cody. He tried to wrestle me to the ground, but I used some of my fae magic to throw the fight in my favor. Saying that he was surprised when I pinned him down with a paw on top of his head was a huge understatement. I had been practicing holding things in place with my magic and was pleased to see that it worked just as well on giant wolves as it did with apples.

I let him up and backed away, not sure how he would feel about being pinned down by a female wolf half his size. I didn't have to worry, because as soon as he got up he gave me a happy grin and a lick on the face. I nuzzled him affectionately before turning and racing for the door.

I nudged it the rest of the way open with my nose and squeezed through, Cody following behind me. The hallway in front of us was completely empty, and perfect for racing. I gave Cody a challenging look before darting ahead. He quickly caught on to the game and raced to get ahead of me.

We were neck in neck while coming up to a corner, so I used the opportunity to smush him into the wall and dart ahead. He didn't let me get far because he grabbed ahold of my tail with his teeth and gave a tug. It wasn't rough enough to hurt, but it was enough to make me turn around and pounce on him again.

We played in the hallway for a few minutes, wrestling and nipping at each other until we heard a crash. Caylee was ahead of us and had dropped a platter full of tea cups and a pot that she had been carrying. She was backing away slowly with a look of complete horror on her face.

I realized what she must think and quickly shifted to my human form, covering the important bits with my hands and hiding behind Cody. "Caylee!" I whisper-shouted. "It's just me and Cody."

Her jaw almost hit the floor. "My lady?"

Cody thankfully realized that I was using him to hide my nudity and didn't turn to look. He kept his eyes forward on Caylee.

"Cody and I were just looking around the castle," I told her quietly. I heard more footsteps in our direction and quickly shifted back to my wolf form. It was one thing to be naked in front of Caylee, but a stranger? Nope.

An older human woman stopped when she saw Caylee in the hall with the spilled dishes. "You little-"

I started to growl as soon as I heard her talk to Caylee in that tone of voice. Caylee was *mine* to protect. The older woman's eyes found me and Cody in the hall and she gasped.

I crept toward her slowly and she backed away.

"Mrs. Pendleton, it's just Lord Froston's daughter and her...companion." Caylee assured the frightened woman.

I placed myself in between Caylee and the mean woman, still not liking the situation. Cody stood next to me and Mrs. Pendleton looked even more terrified. Cody was large enough that his head came to Caylee's shoulder, so I'm sure he made a much more intimidating picture than I did.

"My lady was just asking me to show her around the castle," Caylee said quietly. "They surprised me when I came around the corner and I dropped the tray."

Mrs. Pendleton's mouth was still open. "Oh, well…"

I narrowed my eyes at her and let out a low growl again.

She swallowed nervously. "Why don't I clean this up and you can show Lady Anna around as she pleases?"

I relaxed and gave her a nod. That would be fine.

Mrs. Pendleton gave me a curtsy. "My lady." She lowered her eyes and waited for us to pass before starting to pick up the mess.

I waited until we had rounded another corner before giving a huff of amusement. Cody and I flanked Caylee so that she was in the middle. She kept giving Cody nervous looks, which was understandable. It's probably not every day that she's faced with a wolf almost as tall as she was and twice her size.

"My lady, it's probably a good day to explore the castle," Caylee told me without her usual bubbliness. I nudged her hand and she gave me a small smile. "Your father and the prince were summoned to court, so most of the fae are out of the castle until later tonight."

Cody and I exchanged wolf grins. This did sound like the perfect opportunity to explore.

"Why don't I lead you outside?" Caylee offered. "I don't think you've been out of the castle since you've gotten here."

I perked up. I hadn't even tried to go outside since I got here because I assumed it would be too cold. But now that Froston had showed me the trick to keep myself warm, Cody and I should be fine outside.

Caylee led us through the castle in what I suspected was the long way. We didn't pass more than one other person throughout the walk, so I think she wanted to lead us around any areas where she might have to explain why she was escorting two wolves around. The one person that we did encounter quickly turned and almost ran in the opposite direction.

Caylee paused in front of a set of doors and I hate to admit it, but when I caught the scent of fresh, cold, air from the outdoors, I pranced a little in excitement. But it was just a tiny bit of prancing, and it was barely noticeable. The two guards stationed at the door were too busy eyeing Cody warily to even notice.

I hurriedly wrapped Cody and myself in the barriers that would keep us warm, despite whatever freezing temperature awaited us outside. Caylee murmured to one of the guards, who turned to open the doors for us.

"I'll see about getting Cody some clothes while you're both outside," Caylee told me with a smile. I gave her a nod and barreled past Cody to get outside. The doors led out into a large courtyard, and the weather wasn't nearly as bad as I thought it would be. It didn't look like the castle was in the middle of the Arctic, after all. Was that just how Froston got from point A to point B? I was going to have more questions for him the next time we had a lesson together.

The stone paths through the courtyard were cleared of snow, but the surrounding ground had about a foot of powdery snow. Cody stopped when we got outside and cocked his head at me in question. I gave him a wolf smile when I realized he was probably wondering why he was still nice and warm despite the snow surrounding us.

I plunged off the path and charged through the snow, delighted at the way it flew all around me. I ran a circle around Cody and then nipped at him before darting away. It wasn't long before I dropped the barriers around us all together. It really wasn't that cold out here and we apparently weren't actually in the Arctic.

Cody chased after me and we spent hours playing in the snow together. I was pleased to discover that my ability to use magic was not hindered at all by being in my wolf form. I was able to use it to throw snowballs at Cody and chase him with little snow tornadoes. He thought it was a fun game to catch the snowballs in his mouth as I threw them.

The cloudy skies had darkened even further while we were outside and small flakes of snow started to drift gently down. At one point we had a small audience of people who found it amusing to watch me tease Cody, but they had all gone back inside. I nuzzled Cody tiredly to let him know I was done playing for the day and then trotted back to the doors. I scratched on the doors to let the guards know that I wanted back in and Cody followed me.

I didn't really care that much about being seen by other people right now. I was tired and hungry after all the exercise and magic use. I followed the scents of cooking meat and led Cody down to the kitchen.

This was the first time that I had been down here, but word must have spread through the castle about the two wolves wandering around. All of the people in the kitchen were humans and most of them backed away as Cody and I trotted in. I sniffed around, looking for the source of the delicious scents.

One of the humans didn't seem that intimidated by us and handed us each a big piece of ham. I eyed Cody's piece, which looked a lot bigger than mine, but decided I was satisfied with what I had. I made sure I had a good grip on my prize before trotting off to find somewhere Cody and I could enjoy our dinner together.

We had barely made it out of the kitchen when Caylee came running towards us, out of breath. "My lady. I heard you might need my assistance?" Had the humans in the kitchen sent for her?

Caylee led us back to my room and I was relieved to see that she was back to her usual bubbly self. She was chattering away about some of the clothing she was having made for Cody. Apparently she hadn't had much luck finding anything in his size. I tuned most of what she said out. I was too focused on the delicious ham I was carrying back, and couldn't wait to devour it.

Caylee left Cody and I alone in my room and we enjoyed our ham in companionable silence. I was glad that the two of us had decided to spend the day together in our wolf forms. Somehow, the world seemed so much simpler this way.

I was licking the last of the salty goodness off my paws and eyeing Cody, still gnawing on his ham bone, when my door slammed open. My father stood in the doorway and his anger quickly faded to amusement.

"When the prince told me he had brought you your lover, this isn't what I expected to find," he laughed.

I sat up straight and curled my tail around me. What gave him the right to burst in here like an angry father? He had all but pushed me on the prince, knowing the prince's reputation.

Cody crouched and gave a low growl, looking like he wanted nothing more than to take out some of his frustration on Froston. That didn't surprise me, Froston was the one who had taken me away from the pack to begin with.

Froston narrowed his eyes and flung a hand at Cody, freezing him in place. I flicked my tail in irritation and focused on breaking Froston's hold on Cody.

"Not now, Anna." Froston chastised me. "I need you to change into your human form, so we can have a discussion."

I looked at Froston defiantly, swishing my tail irritably. If he wanted to talk to me, he was going to have to be nice to Cody.

Froston rolled his eyes. "Cody, I'll release you, but I need to trust that you can act in Anna's best interest. And believe me, attacking me is *not* in Anna's best interest."

They locked eyes and must have come to an understanding because Cody was released from Froston's hold. Cody stalked to the other side of the room and stared at Froston with some hostility.

I decided that this was as good as it was going to get for the moment and slipped into the bathroom to change. The dress that I was wearing earlier was still hanging over the edge of the bathtub where I had flung it in my haste to get out of here.

I changed back into my human form and took a minute to clean up before putting my dress back on. I hesitated at the door but took a deep breath before going back out there.

Cody and Froston were still having a stare-down, and neither of them had moved. "You wanted to speak with me?" I reminded Froston.

Froston broke eye contact with Cody and turned to me. "Yes, Anna. I had intended on returning Cody to your pack immediately upon finding out about his presence here, but the prince has other plans," he grimaced.

I smoothed my dress down nervously. "What other plans? Is Cody safe here?"

Froston sighed. "I can't guarantee anything when it comes to the prince, but my priority is keeping you safe."

I frowned. "Then I need to keep Cody with me at all times."

Froston laughed. "That's not appropriate." He moved towards the table and tiredly sat in one of the chairs.

I shrugged. "It's not appropriate for people to keep being kidnapped from their homes either."

"Anna..." Froston said in a warning tone, rubbing a hand over his face.

I tilted my chin up. "He stays with me."

Froston shook his head but his eyes softened. "It looks like you inherited your mother's stubbornness."

I just nodded. "I'm the only person in this world who is dedicated to keeping Cody safe, and I'm not willing to let him go."

Froston sighed in exasperation. "Fine. I would move you to a larger suite of rooms, but I want to keep you as far away from the other fae as possible."

That was fine with me. After my dealings with Morpheus and the prince, I didn't want to be anywhere near other fae.

Froston looked at me thoughtfully. "I'll have a cot delivered for Cody."

"Cool, thanks," I told him flippantly.

"Anna…" Froston said softly. "Despite what you think, I do want what's best for you."

My heart softened towards Froston. He might be going about this all the wrong ways, but I did think that deep down, he was a good guy. He was the man that my mother had fallen in love with, the man who bought an island just to see the woman he loved smile. I did recognize that the prince had put him in a difficult situation, but I wasn't willing to trust him or give him a piece of my heart just yet.

"I just need more time." I told Froston honestly. "We got off to a bad start and you still haven't earned my trust back, yet."

Froston gave me a solemn nod. "I understand." He glanced at Cody. "I realize that you might be considered an adult in your world, but in this world you're still just a child."

I rolled my eyes. "I promise you that *Cody* always has my best interests in mind."

"If I didn't believe that, he wouldn't have remained in this room for more than a few seconds," Froston told me seriously. "I know how important pack is to your wolf side and how much you're probably hurting right now being away from them."

I decided not to inform Froston that I wasn't actually bonded with the pack. I was willing to let him think that my well-being was dependent on Cody's. Hopefully, that would give him some incentive to keep Cody safe.

Froston turned to Cody and his voice hardened. "But understand this, you're here because I think my daughter needs you. If you hurt her, you will *not* remain here, regardless of what the prince may want."

Cody gave him a wolf-nod to indicate his understanding and the two of them stared each other down again. "He understands," I interrupted, wanting to get the male posturing over with.

"The important question is why did the prince really bring him here?" I asked Froston. I pulled out a chair and sat at the table, still tired from all the magic I had used earlier.

Froston frowned as he watched me. "He thinks your magic might be enhanced by your pack. But I think he is also looking for more ways to manipulate you."

I sighed sadly. "The chances of him sending me home to my pack…?"

"Possible. But not likely to happen anytime soon. He's under pressure to prove himself to the king," Froston said darkly.

I paled. "When am I going to have to meet with the king?"

"Sooner than I'd like," Froston told me.

I could see the concern in Cody's eyes as he came over to me and laid his head on my lap. I gently stroked the silky hair on the top of his head as I worried.

"It won't be alone," Froston assured me, watching Cody thoughtfully. "I'll be with you the entire time. And the prince has a vested interest in you now."

I groaned. That was more worrying than reassuring.

Froston said goodnight after a few more threats directed at Cody. I was a little surprised that he did leave the two of us alone, but I think he realized just how much I needed Cody here with me.

I looked into Cody's blue eyes as I ran a finger along the super fine hair that lined the edge of his ear. He flicked it in irritation and I grinned. "I don't have clothes to offer you just yet. But I can make you a toga."

He cocked his head in interest as I went to the bed and tossed aside the blanket. I left the fitted sheet on the bed, but pulled off the flat sheet and held it up to Cody. "Do you want to change back to your human form?"

He shifted, and I kept my gaze very carefully on his face. It took all of my self-control not to let my eyes flicker away from his face as I directed him on how to wrap the sheet around himself. I gave a sigh of relief once he was covered up, but helped him make some adjustments to the toga so it would stay in place.

I grinned at him once I stepped back to admire my work. He placed a hand on his hip and struck a majestic pose. "How do I look?"

I giggled. "Like you belong in the Roman Senate."

He gave me a playful scowl. "I was hoping for something more along the lines of impressive, imposing, or maybe even... hot?" he teased me.

I blushed, not sure what to say. Cody and I had a flirty type of relationship, but he had never been overt about it before. I wasn't sure if he really liked me like that, or if he was just flirty with all females in general.

I saw a flicker of disappointment in his eyes when I didn't answer right away so I gave him a sassy grin. "I don't want to inflate your ego - the room isn't that big."

There was a knock on the door, and true to his word, Froston had a cot delivered for Cody. The two men who delivered it gave Cody some odd looks, but he acted like hanging out in a toga was totally normal. I waited until the door closed behind them before letting out a giggle.

Cody looked at me curiously, so I decided to explain. "You know we just hurt the reputation of wolves everywhere?" I giggled again. "Everyone here is going to be talking about wolves that play in the snow during the day and dress in togas made from sheets during the night."

Cody laughed along with me. "I doubt the council would approve of our performance as ambassadors for our kind."

I eyed the small cot that the men had set up for Cody. It was small enough that his feet would probably hang over the edge. "If anyone asks, that's where you slept," I told Cody before hopping on my bed and gesturing for him to join me.

If I had been alone, I would have probably just gone to sleep, but now that I had Cody here with me, sleep was the last thing on my mind. I could fight through my exhaustion for some quality time with him. If we were home, I would have suggested putting on a movie, but the fae hadn't embraced that much human technology. I jumped back up when I remembered the deck of cards that Caylee had left here. She had brought them to entertain herself one day while I had been practicing my magic.

Cody raised an eyebrow when I sat back on the bed with the cards. "Strip poker?"

I rolled my eyes. "That probably wouldn't work out too well for you since your toga is one piece of clothing. I was thinking more along the lines of 'go fish'."

Cody laughed. "That's probably a better idea."

I shuffled the cards as he watched. "I don't think I've ever played a card game that didn't involve alcohol or money," he told me thoughtfully.

I looked up at him in surprise. "What about as a kid? You didn't play with your friends or at school?"

He shrugged. "I was that annoying kid that wouldn't sit still. It was a much better idea to send me outside to play than try to make me sit still with a stack of cards."

I smiled at him as I dealt the cards, trying to imagine a little Cody. "I can picture you as a little troublemaker with shaggy brown hair and bright blue eyes."

He laughed as I dealt our cards. "You have the shaggy part right. I had an aversion to haircuts until I joined the military."

I picked up my handful of cards to see if I got anything good. Nope.

"What made you decide to join the military?" I asked curiously. "That would have meant leaving your pack, right?"

Cody looked through his cards. "That was the point. I was being stifled by a small town and a small-minded pack master who got off on forcing his dominance on other wolves. I wanted something more out of life."

I nodded, understanding exactly what he meant. "What about your family?"

He shrugged. "My father was killed in a dominance fight that went wrong when I was a kid. My mother found two other mates within a month."

My jaw dropped. "That must have been difficult for you. To lose your father and then have your mother move on so quickly?"

"She was only with him because of how dominant he was in the pack," Cody said bluntly.

I had no idea what to say to that. Obviously, I knew that parents weren't always the kind and loving people you saw on television. But

Cody was kind, hard-working, and spent his life helping other people. I had just assumed that meant he came from a loving background.

"Four?" I asked awkwardly.

Cody gave me a small smile. "Go fish."

I pulled another card and added it to my hand. Nothing useful. I couldn't think of a good way to ask 'did you like your new dads?' so I stared at my cards as if I was considering my next move. Because go fish was a complicated game like that.

Cody saw through my subterfuge. "Finding new mates was a necessity for her," he explained. "Without a mate, she would have been fair game to any male in the pack."

I looked at him in horror and he gave me a grim smile. "Not every pack is like Austin's. In a lot of packs, the strongest wolves take advantage of the weaker. Eight?"

"Go fish." He pulled a card from the stack and then paired it with one already in his hand. Looks like he was having more luck than me.

I think Cody felt the urge to soothe me because he continued. "The new guys weren't bad. Together they were enough to keep me and my mom safe. Plus, they were willing to keep me around as long as I wasn't too annoying."

My heart hurt for Cody. That would have been a really difficult childhood. I can see why he would have taken any opportunity to get out of there once he was an adult.

"Do you still keep in touch with your mom?" I asked quietly.

He flinched. "She got pregnant when I was over in Iraq. Her and the baby didn't make it."

I set my cards down to give him a hug and he hugged me back in surprise. "Sorry, Anna. I didn't mean to be a downer on game night."

I squeezed him a little harder before letting him go. "You're not. The more I hear about other wolves, the happier I am that you guys are the ones that found me."

"Me, too," Cody said quietly.

"Two?" I asked hopefully, going back to my cards.

He started to hand over a card and I reached for it happily, but he pulled it back at the last moment. "I think we should add some spice to the game."

I raised an eyebrow. "What are you thinking?"

"Anytime you get a card, you have to answer a question in return," Cody suggested with a smirk, still holding my card hostage.

"That goes for you, too." I told him with a smile.

"Of course," he said agreeably. Cody tapped the card as he thought. "Were you happy growing up?"

My eyes widened in surprise and I considered lying for a moment. I was so used to pretending that everything was fine it almost came naturally now. But this was Cody, and he had just shared about his shitty childhood.

"No," I said honestly. "I don't remember the original couple that adopted me. After they were killed in an accident, I hated almost every moment of my life."

Cody narrowed his eyes. "Your uncle?"

I hesitated, unsure of how much to tell him. "He hated having to take care of his own kids and was very bitter about being stuck with me. But he had to keep up public appearances, so no one would have believed me even if I told."

Cody looked angry when I told him that. "I haven't seen any of them since I turned eighteen," I told him. "I want to leave my past behind and focus on my future."

Cody gave a sharp nod before handing over my card. "I can understand that. But Anna, I don't understand how anyone could be cruel to you. You're so..." He waved a hand in my direction.

I made a face. "And I don't understand how anyone wouldn't love a shaggy little wolf with a penchant for getting into trouble."

A corner of his mouth lifted in a smile. "Touché."

He looked down at his cards again. "Three?"

I looked through my cards as if I didn't have each of them memorized, and then held up my three. I waved it at him while I thought of a good question. "Why did you pretend it was a date when we first met? Why not just tell me the truth?" I tried to hide it, but I think a tiny bit of hurt bled out into my voice.

Cody looked startled and then blushed. "I guess..." He ran a hand through his hair. "I knew you wouldn't give me a second look once you met Austin if I had brought you straight there. I guess I was being selfish." He hesitated. "You're smart, sweet, pretty, and way too good for me. I just wanted..."

He looked up to see me staring at him in confusion. This wasn't at all what I was expecting to hear. He reached for my hands. "I wanted a little time alone with you before everything changed."

"Cody." I looked into his gorgeous eyes. "When we first met, I thought that *you* were too good for *me*. I didn't understand why a guy like you would even give me a second look." He looked at me incredulously. "I was kinda hurt when I realized that you were just sent after me to bring me to your pack master. But I was angrier at myself for thinking that I could ever have a chance with you."

We looked into each other's eyes for a moment and I think I was the first one to laugh and Cody joined me. We laughed way to hard about something that wasn't even that funny. But I think that our laughter was a release from all the stress and anxiety. After a minute, we both calmed down and I shook my head. "We make a great pair."

"Glad you agree." Cody grinned at me. "My card?"

I handed him the card that he had won, and he proudly put it with his other pair. The next few rounds just resulted in us drawing more cards from the pile.

"Jack?" Cody asked hopefully.

I grinned and held up a jack. This time I had thought about my question ahead of time. "I know you adopted the twins when they were teenagers," I started out, trying to feel less awkward about what I was about to ask. "But is it weird for you that I'm dating them?"

Cody grinned. "I thought you would get around to asking me that."

I blushed but waited for his answer.

"The truth is, the twins are more like my brothers than anything else." Cody told me seriously. "My buddy, Mark, and I met over in the Middle East. We were in the same platoon and bonded as the only wolves in a group of humans. We always had each other's backs whenever we went outside the FOB, and he talked about his mate and pups."

Cody hesitated. "I didn't meet them until they were around twelve or thirteen. Mark had left me a letter that I received after... he had passed." He looked down at his cards. "I checked in on them occasionally and I thought they were okay." He shrugged. "But their situation bugged me because it was so much like my own was when I was growing up."

He sighed. "I was back from a deployment when they both showed up on my doorstep one day. Mason told me that they left home and weren't going back. He asked if they could crash there for the night while Jason just glared at me."

Cody chuckled. "I called their mother, of course. But when she made it obvious that she didn't give a fuck where they went, I decided they would stay with me."

"I was sharing a house with four other marines at the time and the place was a shithole. I took a look around and realized that this wasn't a place for two young wolves." Cody swallowed. "Lucky for them, I was up for reenlistment and declined. I took my terminal leave and moved back home to my old pack. I got them in school and did the best I could..." Cody shuffled through his cards distractedly.

"Those two little fuckers didn't make it easy on me," Cody laughed. "But once I made it clear that I wasn't looking to replace their dad, they relaxed."

I smiled, trying to imagine Cody with two rebellious teenagers to take care of. I had a feeling that the twins had been even worse than two regular teenagers would have been.

Cody looked up at me. "The truth is... they saved me."

I was surprised to see a sheen covering his eyes and he rapidly blinked as if trying to get rid of it. I wrapped my arms around him and leaned my head on his shoulder.

He slid his arm around my waist. "When I lost Mark, I went into a downward spiral. I didn't give a fuck if I lived or died. I just wanted to drink and fight. I was ready to sign up for another tour in Iraq. I wanted to go out in a blaze of glory – taking out our enemies and earning a spot in Valhalla."

Cody sighed. "The twins showed up and I couldn't just leave them. I had to give them the chance that I never had." I rubbed his back and he buried his face in my hair. "I made a mistake bringing them back to my old pack, but I didn't think I had any other options. I didn't want to raise them as lone wolves, I wanted them to have the option to join their own pack when they got old enough."

Cody raised his head to look at me. "I don't know when things changed for me. But at some point, I stopped thinking that I just had to make it until the twins were grown, and I started thinking about living life again. It became the three of us against the world, a band of brothers."

I smiled. "And then you met Austin?"

Cody nodded. "And then I met Austin and my life changed again." We sat in silence for a few moments. My life had changed when I met Austin as well; I thought about what would have happened if I hadn't and I shivered. Nothing good. That's for sure.

Cody kissed the top of my head and broke the silence. "I think you owe me a question after that one."

I laughed. "Fair enough."

He gently brushed my hair back from my face and looked into my eyes. "Would you ever consider me as a potential mate?"

I smiled at him. "Yes."

Cody let out the breath that he had been holding and gave me a huge grin.

I raised my face to his and our lips met in a gentle kiss before I pulled away. "But I would want to talk to the other guys about it first. We haven't really talked things through, but I wouldn't want them to get hurt."

Cody smiled down at me. "We've already discussed it."

My eyebrows rose. "You talked about it with the twins?"

Cody nodded. "With all of them."

I turned bright red. 'All of them' sounded bad. I felt a flush of guilt run through me, but then I realized what he had said. "You talked about me with Mason and Jason and who else?"

Cody blushed. "Not like that. We just met to get things out in the open and declare our intentions, so there wouldn't be any jealousy or fights."

"And you didn't think to invite me to the meeting?" I asked slowly.

Cody looked surprised. "Well, it was kind a guy thing..."

I pushed away from him. "So, a bunch of you guys met, and you decided what you were going to do with me? Who could date me? Who else was at the meeting?"

Cody looked guilty when he realized I was getting upset. "It was Austin, James, Caleb, and the twins. No one else."

I crossed my arms over my chest. "Do you see why I might be a little upset?"

"Umm…" Cody looked at me as if I had just asked him a trick question.

"It's because if I decide to be in a relationship with any of you, I expect to be an equal partner in it," I told him firmly. "If there are meetings about how to manage our relationship, then I deserve to be a part of it."

Cody nodded sheepishly. "Yeah, I get what you're saying. It won't happen again."

"So, what did you discuss at the meeting?" I asked, still feeling a little hostile.

Cody ran a hand through his hair nervously. "Well, we all just agreed that we had a common goal of making you happy. Austin wanted to make sure that we all had your best interests at heart."

My heart softened a little. "Well, I think we should have another meeting when I get back. I think it's a good idea to get everything out in the open. But how would you feel if I called a meeting with all the guys, except you, in order to talk about you?"

"I would be pissed," Cody admitted.

I sat back and picked up my cards again. "Six?" As far as I was concerned, the matter was settled until we got back home and I could address it with the rest of the guys.

Cody looked at me for a second before picking up his cards. "Yep." He dangled it in front of me but then handed it over. "This one's a freebie."

I smiled at him as I paired it with the card I already had and set them aside.

"Queen?" he asked, still watching me thoughtfully.

I held up a queen but sat it down between us. "This one isn't a freebie." I told him with a smile. "You haven't mentioned love or any females you might have been in a relationship with. Were you leaving them out on purpose?"

Cody laughed and gave me a wry grin. "Not on purpose. I haven't really had any relationships worth mentioning."

I raised an eyebrow. "Should I be worried that you don't see females as worthy of conversation?"

He shook his head. "Sure, I've…" he gave me a look. "…dated females before."

I rolled my eyes. "I'm not five. I know what happens when a boy and girl really, really like each other."

He chuckled. "Never been in a serious relationship. It's always been just for fun."

I frowned. "Is that how you think of me?"

He looked alarmed. "Anna, no." He struggled for words. "You're different."

"How so?" I asked curiously. "Have you dated other female wolves or just humans?"

"Just humans," he told me. "But that's not the only reason." He looked contemplative. "I've actually been thinking about this a lot since I met you." He gathered up his hand of cards and stacked them in a neat pile in front of him, setting them aside for now.

"When I was growing up, all I thought about was getting out of there. When I was in the marines, I was always thinking about my next deployment or my next duty station. After Mark-" He swallowed and looked away. "You already know that part."

I gave his hand a squeeze to encourage him to continue. "I never considered bringing a human woman into my old pack. That would have never ended well. My point is – I've never thought about a female having a permanent place in my life. Not until you."

Cody shrugged. "I think a part of me tried to stay detached from women that I might... date. I think subconsciously, I also sought out women who I wouldn't feel bad about walking away from. I never would have dated a girl like you. I was nervous just talking to you when we first met."

"A girl like me?"

"Sweet. Kind. Capable of love," he told me earnestly.

I think my heart melted a little when he told me that. "It makes me sad that you've never been in love," I told Cody. "I feel like you're one of the good guys out there who deserve it."

He shook his head. "I don't know if I deserve love. I definitely don't deserve you." My heart was now completely melted into a little pile of goo.

"Don't sell yourself short, Cody. I think you're one of the most amazing guys out there," I told him seriously and we shared a smile.

"What about you?" Cody asked. "Who was your first love?"

I shrugged, a little uncomfortable that he had turned the tables on me. "I've never been in love before," I said softly.

Cody brushed aside all our cards and pulled me close to him. "Why not?" he murmured to me in a low voice. "A man would have to be insane not to want you."

I forced a grin on my face that didn't make it to my eyes. "You know what they say though. One man's trash is another man's treasure."

Cody ran a hand along my back to cup my hip and bring me closer to him. "I'm not going to lie, Anna. I want to murder any man that made you feel like that – like trash."

I laughed bitterly and hid my face against his shoulder. "Me, too," I mumbled. He rubbed my back and I enjoyed just being pressed up against him for the moment. Cody exuded a warmth that was more than just his body heat. Now that I was more attuned to magic, it was obvious that part of that warmth was his magic. I was enveloped not just with Cody's scent and his body heat, but also part of his essence.

"I'm really amazed at how strong you are," Cody murmured to me. "After everything you've gone through, you came out sweet and kind. A lot of other people go through similar things and come out hateful and bitter."

I pulled away from him reluctantly. "I don't want to give you the impression that my life was all bad." I realized that most of what we had talked about so far was the negative.

"I used to desperately wish that I had a 'normal' childhood and would be jealous watching my peers go home to their families." I shrugged. "I couldn't understand why I was so unlovable."

Cody opened his mouth to speak, but I shook my head. "But I don't want pity and I don't think I would be where I am right now if my circumstances were different. If I hadn't been so desperate to earn any type of approval, I wouldn't have been so motivated to get perfect grades. I wouldn't have pushed myself so hard to succeed. I wouldn't have felt the endless drive to prove everyone wrong and make myself into someone that mattered."

I smiled at him. "And if anything in my life had been different, I might not have ever met you and the other guys. So, while parts of it might have sucked, I wouldn't want to go back and change it. I'm a better person after everything I've gone through, and the best is yet to come."

Cody gave me a warm smile. "I believe you can do anything you set your mind to, Anna. But you matter, regardless of what degrees you have or what your job title is."

I laughed. "It matters to me that I earned it on my own and I can be independent. I don't need anyone to take care of me. My degrees might be just pieces of paper, but they represent years of sacrifice and hard work. They're soaked in blood, sweat, and tears."

Cody chuckled. "I get it. I just don't want to you to think you have to hold a title to have the pack respect you. I want you to feel like you have the freedom to pursue whatever your heart desires. I don't want you to feel like you're obligated to bring it a certain amount of money."

I blinked in confusion and Cody continued. "What I do doesn't bring money into the pack at all," he explained. "I run volunteer services to help guys transition out of the military, which actually costs Austin money. I have a lot of other responsibilities in the pack to help balance that out, of course."

I nodded. Cody had previously spoken about what he did on base, so I knew how passionate he was about it.

"It would kill me to give that up and work a nine to five job just to collect a paycheck," Cody told me.

I smiled. "Luckily for me, I do like my job most days. I feel like I'm able to do a lot of good and I enjoy helping people."

Cody nodded. "That's all I needed to hear."

I sighed in relief, happy that he was dropping the subject. The twins had tried to pressure me into quitting my job before, not understanding how important it was to me. I was glad that Cody realized it was more than just a paycheck.

My heart squeezed when I thought about just how long I had been gone from my job though. Austin had submitted some paperwork to show I was on medical leave, but how long would that hold my job for? Would I still have a job waiting for me at the hospital by the time I managed to get out of here? It seemed like my life had turned into a series of disasters that pulled me out of my old life.

Despite my worry, a yawn still managed to sneak out. Cody smiled at me. "Ready for bed?"

I gave a tired nod before gathering up the rest of the cards to put them away. Cody picked up the cards that had scattered on his side and handed him to me. "I can sleep on the cot, if you'd be more comfortable with that?" Cody offered.

I shook my head at him. "I feel better having you close."

Cody gave me a pleased look before I excused myself to get ready for bed. I was a little embarrassed when I realized that I only had silky nightgowns to sleep in. Sweats and t-shirts didn't seem to be standard fae apparel. I sighed, but made sure the lights were off before going back into the bedroom.

Cody had already pulled up the covers for me to slip under. "Apparently, togas aren't really comfortable for sleeping," Cody said after a minute. "You okay if I take it off?"

I was glad it was dark in the room so that Cody couldn't see my blush. "Yeah, that's fine." I heard rustling before he settled down again with a sigh. "Much better."

I squirmed a little and then buried my face in my pillow, knowing he was only inches away and completely naked. "Hey, Anna?" Cody said softly.

"Yeah?" I mumbled.

"As far as kidnappings go, this one doesn't seem that bad. Not now that I'm here with you."

I grinned in the dark. "Back at you."

He scooted up to me, keeping the blanket between us, and wrapped an arm around me. I snuggled into him, enjoying the way that his large body fit around mine. My exhaustion finally caught up with me and I drifted off to sleep, content to have Cody's scent and warmth enveloping me.

Chapter 15

James

I stretched out my legs and surveyed my team. Austin had sent me along with Trevor, Rich, Mike, Sam, and Davis to Canada. Our mission was two-fold. First: find any information that could lead us to Anna. Second: help Ragnar regain control over the Montreal Pack. The Montreal Pack must be flush with cash, because Ragnar had sent a private jet to Virginia to pick us up and bring us north.

Normally, we would stay far away from any inner pack squabbles, but Ragnar and Ingrid were willing to work with us to find Anna. And I doubt Anna would appreciate hearing that Ingrid, her mother's twin sister, was murdered while we stood by and did nothing. My fists clenched at the thought of the battle ahead.

I looked over my team. Trevor was reclined in his seat with his eyes closed, but I could tell he was awake and aware of everything around him. Part of the reason for that was sitting in the seat across from him. Sam was a marine here with us while she was on convalescent leave. She was about average height with dark hair and golden skin who had intrigued the majority of Trevor's team. It wasn't every day that you find a panther with military training.

Austin had decided to send her up north with us in lieu of Quinn because his loyalties were still in question. I had disagreed with Austin's decision to send her with us. Sam was a wildcard as far as I was concerned, she was new and her loyalties were definitely unproven. She had appeared in Seaside through a stroke of luck, and appealed to Anna's sense of kindness to bring her into the pack. Austin had a soft spot for service members down on their luck with depressing back stories, and Sam checked both of those boxes.

I didn't trust her.

The overly smiley flight attendant came over to ask us to buckle up. We were going to be landing in a few minutes. Trevor gave Mike a kick to wake him, and Mike gave Sam a gentle shake to get her up. I narrowed my eyes at that. Sam couldn't be a fully functional member of the team if they were going to baby her. She had better not be one of those females who were incapable of pulling their own weight.

Rich and Davis murmured quietly in the seats behind me, talking about the plans after we landed. As far as I knew, we were going to have representatives from the Montreal Pack meet with us here before they took us deeper into pack lands. The last time I was here, I had met with their pack-master and heir apparent in their headquarters. Ingrid and Ragnar had surprised me with a late-night visit to share some information about Anna's mother that the pack-master had wanted kept quiet.

I idly wondered what this visit would entail as the plane slowed in anticipation of landing. We circled the airport and started our descent as I looked out the window.

"So, boss," Sam piped up. "What's the plan?"

I glared at her for being irritatingly cheery and growled my answer. "The plan is we do whatever it takes to get Anna back."

Sam nodded and swallowed nervously, avoiding my eyes.

"Asshole, much?" Trevor sent me via the pack bond.

"Would you have cared if it were Rich?" I shot back at him.

Trevor gave a slight shrug and settled back in his chair as the plane landed. I scowled, he knew I was right.

I grabbed my bag after we had gotten the all clear and made my way to the exit as the others gathered up all their shit. Leif and Erik were waiting for us on the tarmac with the same SUV they had used the last time I was here.

I grimaced. "They told you there were six of us this time?"

Leif gave me a feral grin. "The trunk is quite roomy."

The rest of the team trailed off the plane and I gave Trevor a look as I communicated the situation.

"Right. Rich, you're in the back," he barked out.

The drive was completely silent with all of us jammed into the vehicle along with our luggage. This time when we got close to the village, Sam let out a gasp as the mysterious fog enveloped us. "How did you all manage that?" she asked our tour guides.

Leif ignored her completely, but Erik turned to smirk at her. "We have quite a few powerful pack members here. It would be best if you remember that."

Sam gave a sharp nod and looked out the windows, fascinated by the fog. I watched her for a moment. Austin had confessed his suspicions to me that Sam was more than just a panther. He had called her in while Anna was in her magical coma, despite my objections. After being left alone with Anna for several hours, Anna woke up, completely unharmed. Sam denied that she did anything but hold Anna's hand at her bedside, but we all had our doubts. It was obvious that Sam knew more than she let on.

The fog cleared as we entered the village and Leif parked the vehicle in front of the same house I had been in before. I was hoping that Ragnar would prove to be a better ally than his father had, but only time would tell. As a last resort, I planned to use Anna's connection to Ingrid to force their hand.

Leif and Erik led us into the house and Ragnar greeted us with a solemn frown. I made the introductions and Ragnar greeted my pack mates politely.

"Perhaps I might have a few words with you in private?" Ragnar asked me. "Before your plane is ready."

My eyebrows rose. I wasn't aware we would be getting back on another plane after arriving here, I assumed this was our destination. I held my words, and instead followed Ragnar into an office. His gestured for me to sit, but my patience was already wearing thin.

"I can assume that you know the truth about Anna by now?" he asked, sitting behind a large mahogany desk.

I nodded. "I've pieced together as much. Unless you've been hiding more?"

He gave a slight smile. "Ingrid and her sister were tasked with protecting us from the fae. Astrid failed and sided with the enemy, becoming pregnant and making plans to abandon the pack. I can only assume that my father gave the order for Astrid's death, but he always denied it."

Ragnar leaned forward and steepled his fingers. "I am not my father, hiding behind plots and innuendo. If I have something to say, I say it."

"I'm the same," I said bluntly.

Ragnar smiled. "And that is why you're here now. I'll be blunt with you. My wife is the only white wolf we have left in the pack and none of our pups have inherited her power. The world is defenseless against the fae without a team of white wolves here to run interference."

I frowned. "Taking Anna from us isn't an option."

Ragnar tilted his head. "I've heard that she isn't the only white wolf in the states, that there may be more."

I nodded. "I've heard the same. There were a few names that came up during my investigation into her past."

"In exchange for our help in locating your mate I require your assistance in subjugating some rebel wolves in the north, along with a list of names that you have procured of potential white wolves."

I narrowed my eyes at him. I certainly hadn't claimed Anna as my mate just yet, but that wasn't the issue. "You won't maintain the respect of your pack if you use outsiders to eliminate your challengers for you."

Ragnar shrugged. "They aren't challengers, they're wolves controlled by the fae, sent here to create dissent and destabilize our pack. I suspect that they were responsible for the murder of my father and his mate."

I held in the growl that wanted to emerge. The fae were a bunch of fuckers. The more I learned about them, the more I hated them.

I held Ragnar's eyes. "What will you be providing us in return for our help?"

"I'm having a plane prepared now to bring you to our northern outpost. We have a very small settlement close to the gateway that allows fae to enter our world. Normally, it would be monitored by several of our white wolves and their support team, but almost all of them have met with their end due to mysterious circumstances over the last few years. The outpost is now abandoned by us, and I suspect it is being used as a base by the enemy."

I nodded. Destroy an enemy base and take it for myself so that I could use it to find Anna? I could do that.

"My team will need supplies," I agreed.

Ragnar gave a broad grin at my statement. "I'll provide you with everything you need and more."

"And I'll provide you with the list of names when we retrieve Anna and bring her home."

Ragnar's grin dimmed. He didn't think I would give them up that easily, did he? I wanted to keep him motivated to keep us alive and well.

I sat forward in my chair. "And now that Anna's secret is in the open between us – I want a promise that you and the rest of your pack will not try to harm her again. Your father tried to have her killed as a babe, don't think I've forgotten that."

Ragnar nodded solemnly. "My father always denied it, but he was a vindictive man. If Astrid hadn't planned to abandon our pack and join the fae, perhaps things would have turned out differently. But after she blatantly told him that she was in love with one of them?" He shook his head sadly. "I don't think there was anything any of us could have done to prevent that tragedy."

"My previous visit here must have made him realize Anna could be Astrid's daughter." I said quietly. "Is there any possibility-"

Ragnar cut me off. "My father is dead."

"And his death?" I asked quietly. "I received a visit from the fae that claimed to be Anna's father. He seemed to still have some affection for her mother."

Ragnar clenched his hands. "He's probably behind all of this," he snarled.

I watched him quietly. This is why blood feuds never ended until everyone involved was dead. Each side would continuously pick off members of the other, making the feud worse with every death, until no one even remembered the original reason for the feud at all.

But if someone harmed Anna, I wouldn't wait twenty-six years to take my revenge. It would be instant and bloody. Everyone involved would die, myself last of all. We were missing something about this whole situation. What had Froston been doing for the last twenty-six years? Why wait until now to murder Astrid's former pack-master and take Anna? If he was even the one who murdered them. Were there other players in this game?

"Did your father have any strong connections to any of the other packs?" I asked Ragnar, watching closely for his reaction.

Ragnar's eyes darted to the side briefly before coming back to meet mine. "He did," Ragnar admitted. "He had recently been in regular contact with Zilker's pack."

"Austin's father?" I asked in surprise.

Ragnar nodded. "My father had reached out to him for assistance in getting Anna for our pack. We are desperate for white wolves, and my father believed that the council would give her back to us."

I frowned. Not only had Austin's father never said a word of this to Austin, he had given no indication that he knew anything about Anna's past. "Austin's father is missing," I told Ragnar. "He is being accused of betraying us and using his position as a council member to bring harm to other packs."

Ragnar nodded grimly. "I'm not completely isolated here. I've heard that his name was dishonored. But I don't believe that the father's sins transfer to the son, so I'm willing to work with Austin and your pack."

Ragnar and I hammered out the specifics of our agreement. He was providing us with weapons and equipment but expected our team to do the heavy lifting to clean out the cancer in his pack. I had no problem taking out anyone who was an obstacle to getting Anna back, or who might be a threat to her future safety.

After we shook hands on our agreement, I went to find Trevor and the rest of the team. The plane that Ragnar had chartered to take us to our next destination would be here soon, and I needed to get the team briefed and prepared before takeoff.

Chapter 16

Anna

I woke up in the morning with Cody's warmth at my back and the weight of his arm over my waist. We were both tangled in the blankets, but even through the layers I could tell that he was happy to be pressed against me.

After last night, I felt closer than ever to Cody. Now that I wasn't too exhausted to move, I turned to face him and snuggled close. His face looked so peaceful, with his thick dark lashes and his full lips.

He must have felt my stare because his breathing changed, and I could tell that he was awake. A smile slid across his face before he opened his eyes to look at me. "Sleep well?"

I nodded. The truth was that I had slept better last night than I had slept the entire time that I was here. Having Cody nearby helped me to relax completely and I was happy that I had a dreamless sleep last night.

I scooted a little closer to Cody and we looked into each other's eyes.

"You're beautiful," he murmured, gently brushing my hair off my face.

I made a face. I'm sure I was lovely with my blond hair sticking up all over the place and my eyes filled with sleepiness.

Cody grinned and leaned in for a kiss. His lips met mine with just a gentle brush before he pulled away with an unsure look on his face. It made me smile. Because of Cody's confessions last night, I doubted that he ever felt unsure when kissing a female. I kind of liked that I threw him off his usual game.

I leaned towards him this time, and my kiss was nowhere near as gentle as his had been. I put all of my emotions into my kiss. I wanted him to feel how much I had missed him, how glad I was that he was here, and how close I felt to him. I felt my magic tangling with his as we reached for each other with more than just our bodies. Being enveloped in Cody's warmth and love gave me a sense of belonging that I had never felt before.

Our kisses grew more urgent and I pushed away the blanket that was forming a barrier between us. Cody groaned and pulled away, squeezing my hip and looking into my eyes. "Are you sure?"

I smiled at him and cupped his face as I slid one of my legs up against his. "I'm more than sure."

He licked his lips and I pulled his head down for another kiss. "The question is, are you ready for me?" I teased him, biting his bottom lip.

I felt more confident in myself than I ever had before. I was comfortable in my own skin. I trusted Cody with my heart and my body, and I was more than ready to see him in his own skin. There was no room here for the old Anna's doubts and insecurities. My body was being flooded by desire for Cody and every inch of my skin tingled in anticipation of his touch.

I pushed him to the side and straddled him with a grin as my exposed skin pressed up against the bare skin of his abs. His eyes widened in surprise before trailing down my body to take in my curves. The thin silk nightie that had been left for me in my wardrobe didn't cover much, and with the way I was sitting the tail end of the silk must have been tickling his more sensitive areas. My nipples tightened under his gaze, aching to be touched and adding to the need that was throbbing through me.

He ran his hands up my thighs and under my nightgown, resting them on my hips. I leaned forward for another kiss, running my hands up his abdomen and to his powerful shoulders. Cody's eyes were full of heat and his lips devoured mine with a passion that I was more than happy to match.

My breath hitched as he moved his hands from my hips to cup my bottom, making my insides quiver. I searched Cody's eyes, and seeing nothing there but heated desire made me even bolder. Before I could let even a smidgen of my usual self-consciousness ruin the moment, I pulled my nightie off in one smooth movement.

Cody looked at me almost reverently, trailing his hands up to cup my breasts. "Anna, you're more beautiful than I could have ever imagined." The way he looked at me made me feel powerful and desirable.

I surrendered completely to the sensations of Cody's attentions and couldn't stop myself from rubbing my lower body up against him. My movement caused me to move lower and his erection brushed up against me.

Cody gave an animalistic growl and flipped our positions so quickly that I wasn't even sure what happened until my head bounced on the pillow. He was now kneeling in between my legs and the cool air that brushed up against my exposed sensitive bits was driving me insane.

He had a dark, almost predatory look in his eyes as he kissed one breast before giving my nipple a gentle bite. I gasped in pleasure and my reaction definitely pleased him because he gave me a wicked grin. "I have been thinking about this moment for so long, I'm going to enjoy every second of this."

I wrapped my legs around his waist and squeezed to bring him closer to me. He let me do it and didn't object when I grabbed a handful of his hair and pulled him roughly to my mouth. I ground my body up against his and the feel of his erection pressed in between my legs was almost too much to bear. I *needed* him. Now.

We kissed and teased each other, exploring each other's bodies and wrestling the way that we did while we were playing in our wolf forms. But this time, I let him take the dominant position over me once I had enough teasing.

Cody knelt in between my legs and grasped my hips, pulling my lower half off the bed. This gave me a really good view of all of his muscles on display and his rather large erection teasing me at my entrance.

I moaned. "Please Cody, I need you now." I reached for his cock and teased it up against my clit, causing him to groan. He held me in place with one arm as he lined up his cock at the correct angle to push inside me. My legs were over his shoulders as he slowly inched inside of me and my eyes rolled back in my head at the intense pleasure of my body accommodating him.

He started with small, gentle thrusts until my body relaxed enough to fit all of him and he could drive his entire length inside of me. He filled me so completely that I felt stretched to the limits in a delightful way. I had to ball my fists into the sheets as the pleasure grew to almost unbearable heights and I was crying out with every thrust, begging for release.

I slid a hand in between my legs and the added sensation of having my clit stimulated caused my body to go over the edge and explode. Cody grunted as I contracted around him and caused him to climax.

He collapsed beside me on the bed and we both stared up at the ceiling, panting, before he turned to drop a kiss on my shoulder.

"Anna, that was…" He seemed at a loss for words.

"Beyond amazing?" I added for him. I turned to look at him and we shared a smile. There weren't really any words to describe what had just happened and I was okay with that. I was floating in a glorious afterglow, and was happy to doze off in Cody's arms.

I don't know what woke me a little while later, but I slipped out of the bed and grabbed a dress before padding to the bathroom. I had wanted to get an early start on the day, before Cody and I had taken a delightful detour. I smiled at his sleeping form before closing the bathroom door.

Now that Cody was trapped here with me, I had even more motivation to get out. Cody was here because of me, it was my responsibility to get him home safe. I needed a game plan and I needed to get a hold on my magic.

As I got ready for the day, I realized that I needed to confront the prince. He was giving me lessons on how to use my magic, but I needed to know exactly what was required from me. Both the prince and my father had been incredibly vague on my purpose here. I wasn't going to accept their brush-offs any longer.

I exited the bathroom just as Caylee was knocking on the door. She entered the room with an older woman following behind her who was carrying some clothing. Cody sat up in the bed and rubbed a hand through his hair.

"Good morning, sunshine," I greeted him. "We have some clothing for you!"

The older woman left the pile of clothing on our table with a sniff before heading out the door without a word to any of us. Caylee made up for the woman's silence with happy chatter, and Cody sniffed as the scent of food drifted over in his direction. He wound a sheet around his waist and made his way over to the table to see what Caylee had brought for breakfast.

"The whole castle is talking about you!" Caylee told us with a grin. "Everyone says that your love story is so romantic."

Cody stopped chewing and looked at me. I just shrugged. "What love story?"

"You know," Caylee said. "How you were taken from your love and he risked everything to come here after you, just so you could be together." Caylee sighed happily.

"Um, that's not exactly what happened," I told her, pushing my breakfast around on the plate.

Her smile faded a little. "But it's not too far off," Cody said with a grin and a wink before going back to his food.

"What does the prince think about that?" I asked cautiously. The prince had been hard to read so far, he had been swinging back and forth between trying to seduce me and being frustrated with my inability to use my magic the way he wanted me to.

Caylee just shrugged. "I don't think the prince really cares about what we commoners have to say."

I just sighed. "But he's going to be here today? For my lesson?"

Caylee nodded. "The kitchen is in a tizzy about finding some herbs for his lunch today. If you want to finish your breakfast, I can help you look presentable for him."

Cody gave me a strange look and I shrugged in embarrassment. "That's alright, Caylee. I think I'll just go with the natural look today."

Caylee made a face at me, taking in my messy bun. "Maybe I could help you brush out your hair at least?"

Cody smirked at me from across the table, but I ignored him. When I first got here, I was too depressed and exhausted to do much but sit at the vanity and let Caylee primp me to her heart's content. But now that I was free of Morpheus's nightly torments and I had Cody here to keep me company, I had no desire to sit there for an hour or more while Caylee played with my hair. I was ready for some action.

"Maybe just a quick braid?" Caylee coaxed me. "I can do it while you finish your breakfast."

I sighed, unwilling to hurt her feelings. "That would be great, Caylee. Thank you."

Caylee jumped up with a huge smile and kept chattering as she did my hair. I blushed when Cody watched the process curiously. Cody and I were finished breakfast by the time that she had patted the last hair into place. Caylee's 'quick braid' was more of a thirty-minute masterpiece that resulted in an intricate braid that resembled a crown placed on top of my head.

Caylee left us alone in the room, promising to come back when the prince requested my presence. Cody looked at me for a minute. "You look beautiful, but I have to admit that it's a little intimidating, the way that people treat you here."

I frowned at him. "The whole 'my lady' thing?"

He nodded. "Yeah, you have servants, a castle, and spend your afternoons with a prince. I feel like you've been slumming it with us in the pack."

I rolled my eyes. "I don't have any of those things, my father does. Plus, I hate spending time with the prince, I just want to go home." I walked over to his side of the table and cupped his face in my hands. "I don't want servants, or castle, or a prince. I want you." I gave him a small kiss. "I want our pack." I gave him another kiss. "And I want to go to Greenies for a burger and a beer."

Cody grinned up at me. "I can make that happen if you can get us out of here."

"Deal." I gave him another kiss and he pulled me into his lap.

I wiggled around to get comfortable and he groaned. "I'm not going to be able to behave myself if you keep doing that."

I nipped at his luscious lower lip. "Who says we need to behave?"

Cody chuckled. "Unfortunately, I do."

I pouted but he gave me a serious look. "You're here to learn magic, right?"

I nodded, curious to see where he was going with this.

"But a huge part of who you're is a wolf. I think that maybe the reason you're struggling is because you're still not comfortable with that part of yourself. You still think of yourself as a human and a wolf separate from one another."

I cocked my head at him thoughtfully. "You're right. I do still have that divide, but I've been working on it. I even used my magic last night when I was in my wolf form. I wasn't sure I would be able to do it."

Cody grinned at me. "Yeah, that was amazing. But you have the fae teaching you how to use your magic. Let me teach you how to be a wolf."

I realized that Cody needed to feel like he was doing something useful here, just like I did, so I agreed. "Okay, Cody. Put some pants on, and let's see what you got," I teased him.

He laughed, but nudged me off his lap so he could go through the pile of clothing that Caylee and her companion had brought by. Some of the pieces of clothing looked like something that 'peasant number one' would be wearing if we were filming a medieval times movie. Luckily, there was a pair of jeans and a shirt down near the bottom of the pile that must have come from the human world and looked vaguely Cody's size.

He took his clothing into the bathroom to get ready for the day while I sat at the table to think. I had been doing better with my wolf side, but if I was honest with myself, I still wasn't completely whole. Cody was right, I still had more work to do.

Chapter 17

Anna

I smiled at Cody as we sat opposite each other on the floor. He gave me a chastising look. "Don't try to distract me, concentrate."

I closed my eyes again and reached out for Cody with my magic. He was trying to show me the different kinds of things that an alpha wolf could do with their power. The twins had tried to teach me 'wolf stuff' before, but they hadn't mentioned anything about what Cody was doing now. I hadn't realized that there was more to being an alpha wolf than just holding a position of authority.

Cody had explained that the twins were still young and hadn't developed a lot of their power yet. They had the capability to be alpha wolves here in the pack, but were still transitioning from pup to wolf. Apparently, it took a lot longer for a wolf to reach maturity than it did for humans.

Cody pulsed his power and I felt it like a weight against me. "I'm going to reach out to you," Cody told me. "As an alpha, I can reach for the magic that makes you change. I'm not going to actually trigger your change, but you will feel me touch you."

I tried not to tense up as I felt tendrils of Cody's power reach for me and gently caress the well of magic that I would use to trigger my change. "If I wanted to make you change, I would tug on that well of power." Cody explained.

I exhaled as I felt him withdraw. "Now, try to do the same to me," he instructed. "Reach out and find the magic inside me."

I reached for him and clumsily fumbled with my magic. I could feel the warmth radiating from him, telling me that he had power, but I wasn't sure how to go about this. "You want to find the core," Cody coaxed me. I delved deeper into Cody and looked for his center, where his warmth was radiating from. It took me a few minutes, but my eyes snapped open when I found it.

"Good job," Cody praised me. "If we had a pack bond, this would be much easier. But you're doing really well."

I grinned at him. "How would a pack bond make it different?"

"The pack is all connected," he explained. "You can sense your pack-mates around you. The stronger you're as a wolf, the farther the distance you can sense them. You can also communicate with them by locating them and pushing your thoughts in their direction."

Cody leaned forward. "If you're a strong alpha, like Austin, you can do a lot more. He can influence the emotions of the pack, or call pack-mates to him."

I frowned. "Against their will?"

Cody shook his head. "Yes, but not like you're thinking. For example, if you have two pack mates get in a fight, Austin can pull them apart and soothe their angry emotions without ever touching them."

"Austin wouldn't use those powers to harm anyone," I said slowly. "But other pack masters?"

Cody grimaced. "I hate to say it, but you're right. There are pack-masters out there that abuse their powers. There are pack masters who use their powers to manipulate females, to subjugate males, and to rule their pack with an iron fist."

"Humans do the same thing," I said softly. "But instead of magic, they use money and power to manipulate the people around them."

Cody nodded. "There are good and bad people in any race or species that you look at. You can't let power corrupt you, you have to always focus on how you can use your power for good."

I nodded. "I want to learn to use my power to be a healer."

Cody smiled at me. "I can see you being very good at that. You already have a lot of medical knowledge. Once you get a handle on your magic, you'll be unstoppable."

I smiled at him. "I was thinking though…" I paused nervously, not sure if I was ready to confess my thoughts. "I went to school to be a pharmacist for a lot of different reasons, but my first choice was to be a doctor."

Cody looked at me in surprise. "What changed your mind?"

I grimaced. "I'm embarrassed to admit this – money."

Cody looked flabbergasted. "Money?"

I gave an embarrassed nod. "I had scholarships for my undergrad years, but there aren't really scholarships for medical school. I would have needed fifty to sixty thousand dollars a year for four years to make it through, then be able to afford working as an intern/resident for a couple more years." I shook my head. "I couldn't get approved for enough student loans to make it through all four years, and even if I did, I wouldn't be able to make the minimum payments once I got out. You don't start collecting the doctor paychecks until a few years after you graduate and finish your residency."

Cody looked at me thoughtfully. "But you could get the loans for pharmacy school?"

"Yeah, it was a lot less money. Plus, you have enough free time to have a job while in pharmacy school. That's not really an option for medical school."

"And now?" Cody prompted.

I blushed. "Now… I think now that I have magic, I think I might be able to do more good as a doctor." I hung my head. "But I still haven't paid off my loans from pharmacy school." I had been tossing this idea around in my head since Airmed had started to try to teach me how to heal. But the thought of borrowing money from the pack when I already owed so much to them made me nauseous.

Cody shrugged. "Honestly, you would have to talk to Aus about our pack finances. He would be honest with you about what we could do."

I looked up at Cody. "I was thinking… it wouldn't be difficult to make back his investment. What I really want to do is have a clinic, just for shifters." I started to get more excited as I spoke. "Especially for pregnant females. I haven't been a part of the community for that long, but everyone knows that pregnancy is dangerous for the female and the baby. What if I could figure out why? What if I could use my magic in combination with human medicine to make pregnancy safer for us?"

Cody's eyes lit up. "If anyone could do it, Anna, it would be you. If you could save our females…" He shook his head. "Shit, Anna. There is no way to put a monetary value on that, you could save our race."

"It would take a lot of time." I told him quietly. "Four years of medical school and then three to seven years of a residency. Plus, however long it takes to learn how to heal with magic. And all that is *if* I can even get into medical school."

Cody smiled at me. "Is medical school a necessity for someone who uses magic to heal?"

"Well…" I stared at the floor as I thought about it. It's always been ingrained in me that in order to be something, you need to go to school for it. But did Cody have a point?

"When I was on rotation with the medical students, their focus was diagnostics." I tapped my finger thoughtfully. "But using magic is different. I don't need lab tests or x-rays, I could feel what was wrong with you. I was putting things back the way they were supposed to be, it was…"

"Like magic?" Cody suggested.

I grinned at him. "Like magic."

"Maybe human medical school isn't what you need," Cody suggested gently. "Maybe you need more hands-on experience using your magic."

I sighed. "Airmed isn't going to teach me what I need to know."

Cody snorted. "No, she isn't. But Anna, I believe in you." Cody reached out to take both of my hands. "You need to believe in yourself."

I gave him a shy smile. It was a little overwhelming to know Cody had that much faith in me. What if I was too arrogant and I messed up? What if I hurt people by not knowing what I was doing? I had spent weeks with every moment of my day being spent on learning how to use my magic and I was barely proficient at basic tasks. How long would it take me to become as skilled and knowledgeable as Airmed?

I frowned at him. "I've been kind of afraid to ask, but what is the average life expectancy of a wolf?"

"A male? A few hundred years assuming he's not killed in a dominance fight." Cody answered. "But females?" He shook his head sadly. "Once you get your clinic up and running, it will probably be the same."

I grinned at him, happy that he could share my vision. "There are so many ifs to this plan," I said honestly. "But I want to try."

Cody nodded, getting a more serious look on his face. "Step one is getting our asses out of here."

I laughed. "Step one is actually getting Airmed to teach me how to use my magic to heal. Once I can successfully heal a broken bone, I'm going to start harassing her to learn more complicated healing."

"You're going to be the most popular doctor in the world," Cody told me with a grin.

"In the shifter world, maybe." I smiled back at him.

Caylee interrupted our plans for world domination with a knock at the door. My mood went from high in the sky to down in the dumps. It was time to go spend time with the prince again.

I hopped up, but Cody stumbled as he tried to stand, bracing himself with one arm on the floor. My heart sunk, that was not normal for Cody. I rushed over to him as he shook his head in confusion.

"Are you alright?" I asked as I knelt beside him.

He forced a smile and looked up. "Fine, I just need a minute."

My gut was telling me that something was not right here. "Did we use too much magic?" I asked Cody. I always was exhausted after trying to use too much magic.

He shook his head with a grimace. "We didn't really do anything that I don't already do on a daily basis."

I looked at Caylee who was hovering nearby and wringing her hands. "Does being in this world have any negative effects on non-fae when they get here?"

She shook her head with wide eyes. "No…"

I narrowed my eyes. "Caylee, do you know anything about this?"

Caylee shook her head. "Sometimes the guards are tired after being healed." She leaned in closer to whisper. "You know, because they don't have much magic to begin with?" She looked at Cody nervously, as if she was worried that she had just insulted him.

Cody laughed but stood. "That was weird. I just had a moment of weakness, but I feel fine now." He swung his arms around and then jumped up and down a couple times to show he was doing okay.

I watched him carefully. "Maybe you should take it easy for a little bit?"

He shrugged. "We don't really have anything to do here, anyway."

Caylee looked nervous. "The prince is waiting, and you know how he can get…"

I sighed. "Cody, do you want to stay here and rest?"

He scowled. "And leave you alone with him? Absolutely not." He stepped forward to put his arm around me and give me a kiss on the side of my head. "I'll stay by your side no matter what."

I wrapped my arms around him in a tight hug and rested my head against his chest so that I could hear his heart beating. "Promise not to engage him in an argument? Even if he tries to bait you into it?"

Cody gave me another kiss, this time on the top of my head. "I promise. But if he even thinks about hurting you, I *will* step in."

I moved my arms down to rest at his waist and tilted my head up for a kiss. I loved it when Cody got all alpha male, but I didn't want him to take on the prince. "I can handle him."

"I don't doubt it." Cody gave me another kiss before rubbing his nose against mine in an Eskimo kiss.

I smiled at him and grabbed his hand as I pulled away and headed for the door. "Let's not get Caylee in trouble for being late."

Chapter 18

Mason

I leaned against the wall and crossed my arms over my chest, looking out over the baggage claim area. Austin had decided to send me and my brother to get Gemma from the airport. At first, I was pissed. Then, I realized he had given us an opportunity to get a lead on what might have happened to Anna. She had already been missing for a couple days now and I was going insane.

A group of people startled to trickle into the area, and luggage came down the conveyer belt so the plane must have landed. I pushed off the wall and scanned the growing crowd for the woman we had been sent to get. Gemma was a halfling from the Canadian pack up north. Her pack master had been killed and the pack was being torn apart by a civil war as different factions battled for dominance. She had requested sanctuary in our pack until things settled because she was half human and unable to shift.

I shuddered at the thought of not being able to shift into my wolf form. Being trapped in just a human form for your entire life was a horrible fate. It also left you vulnerable to the other pack members – Gemma would always be the weakest of the pack and stuck at the bottom of the hierarchy.

I felt a mental nudge from Jason and saw him start to circle around from where he had been waiting on the opposite end of the baggage claim area. He had spotted her coming down the hall and she came into my view once she entered the large room. She was a petite brunette, walking with her head down and shoulders slumped forward.

Jason and I both headed towards her and she looked up in alarm as we approached. We exchanged glances as her eyes darted between the two of us and she took a hesitant step back. She resembled a frightened rabbit more than a wolf. It made me nauseous to think about how she must have been treated to react like this.

I gave her a friendly smile. "Hey, Gemma? I'm Mason and this is Jason."

She gave me a nod and then looked at the floor, her hair covering her face. Jason looked at me and I just shrugged. "Did you have any luggage?" I asked her gently.

She peeked through the curtain of hair. "No." Her voice was so soft I would have struggled to hear her if I had been human. I eyed the shoulder bag that she was carrying – it didn't look much larger than the bags the girls carried around on campus for their books. I doubted that she could fit much in there.

Jase and I stared at each other for a second. This hadn't been what we were expecting. I wished Anna was here. She would know exactly how to handle this.

"Uh, can I carry your bag for you?" Jason offered. Girls usually liked stuff like that, but this girl didn't. She shook her head no and hugged the bag even closer to her as if it contained something precious.

Jase looked helplessly at me for direction but I just shrugged again. Maybe she didn't like crowds and would relax a little once she was in the car. "This is a small airport," I told Gemma. "So the car isn't far."

She gave me a small nod but kept her head down and her eyes on the floor, waiting for us to move forward before trailing behind us. I felt like a jerk, having a girl walk behind me like that, so I stopped to try and beckon her forward. She halted the same time that I did and just stared at my hand confusedly.

"Come walk with us." I gave her what I thought was an inviting smile. She just stared at me, so I must have fallen short on delivery. There were people still streaming around us, so I was careful with what I said next. "You don't have anything to fear from us, we're not going to harm you."

She looked at me as if I had two heads, but shuffled forward to stand between Jason and I. Gemma held her bag to her stomach, with her arms pressed in close, as if she was afraid to accidentally touch either one of us. I was clueless on how to start a conversation here, usually human girls were friendlier.

We awkwardly walked to our Jeep as a group and I opened the front passenger door for Gemma, leaving it up to Jason to drive.

Gemma looked surprised that I was offering her the front seat but didn't argue.

Once we were all settled, Jason kept urging me to try and start another conversation via our bond. I rolled my eyes, he always left this shit to me.

"So, Gemma..." I cleared my throat. "You live in Canada?"

She squeezed her bag close and answered softly, "Yeah."

I felt Jason's frustration before he burst out, "With white wolves, right? That's where Arctic wolves are from?"

I gave him a warning glare. Obviously, it would be better to ease into an interrogation with her, not just shout questions at her.

Gemma gave Jason a shy smile before her eyes darted away. "Some of the wolves are, most are just regular."

"Is that where you grew up?" I asked curiously, leaning forward to hear her response over the noise of the engine and the highway.

She nodded. "My father was in the pack, but my mom was human. My mom and I had a little house just for us."

"That must have been nice," I told her. "My brother and I grew up in shitty packs that were nothing like the one here."

Her eyes met mine in the rearview mirror and I saw a spark of curiosity.

Jason noticed it as well, because he kept it going. "Yeah, the wolves in our first pack were a bunch of real assholes. Our second wasn't much better, but we had Cody to look out for us then. Not many wolves were willing to try and fuck with him."

I flinched when he cursed, but Gemma didn't seem to mind. She seemed too shy to ask any questions, even though she might want to. I decided talking about our history a little might make her feel more comfortable opening up to us. She listened as I spoke and Jason occasionally interjected. The more I told her about how Austin ran his pack, the more curious she seemed to be.

"What about humans or halflings?" she asked quietly. "Does your pack have any?"

"One of our wolves, Tony, had a human wife when he was in his last pack," I started to explain. "His son, Alex, is a halfling."

"He's a cool guy," Jason added. "He's going to go to school to be a nurse."

Gemma's jaw dropped. "He's allowed in school?"

Jase and I exchanged glances. Her last pack sounded like it was pretty fucked up, and she hadn't even told us anything yet.

"Yeah," I told her gently. "Jase and I are in college now, getting a business degree so we can help out with the pack businesses."

"But Alex isn't a wolf?" Gemma asked with a furrowed brow.

I shook my head. "He can't shift, but that doesn't make him any less of a pack member. He's still just as much a part of the pack as Jase or I."

Gemma stared at me for a moment before lowering her head in thought. I met Jason's eyes through the rear view mirror. It sounded like this girl had it worse than we had it growing up. We communicated with our pack bond and we were both in agreement. Our mission might have started out as 'operation: get info from the Canadian pack girl' but now it was 'operation: convince Austin not to send her back to hell.'

"Are you hungry?" Jason asked Gemma.

She bit her lip nervously and looked at the floor. She probably was hungry but was too afraid to say so.

"Because we're starving," I informed her. "We've been working all day and need a little bit of a break before we go back." That wasn't true at all. Austin had told us to bring her back without any detours, but we needed some more time alone with her. Maybe sharing a meal together would get her more comfortable with us.

"Catch31?" Jason suggested.

I nodded. That was a good choice. "Have you ever been to the beach before?" I asked Gemma.

She shook her head with wide eyes. "I've always wanted to see the ocean."

I grinned. "You'll like this place. It's right on the oceanfront so we can take you on the beach first. Plus, they have really good seafood there."

She gave me a shy smile. "That sounds nice."

We found decent parking down at the oceanfront since it was a cold day in November and let Gemma free on the beach. She was fascinated by the sand and the waves of the ocean. She even took her shoes off to wade into the shallows and splash in the small waves despite the frigid temperature of the water. Jason and I watched as she tilted her head back and the breeze played with the ends of her hair.

When she finally turned back to us, there was a lightness to her step that hadn't been there before. She gave us the first genuine smile I had seen from her so far. "Thank you."

I smiled back at her. "Ready to eat?"

She nodded, and we walked back onto the boardwalk so she could have a seat on one of the benches there and put her shoes back on. The Neptune statue loomed over us and she gazed up at it curiously. "I thought humans only worshipped the Christian god?"

Jase and I glanced at each other. If she hadn't been allowed in school, had she ever had interaction with humans before? The Montreal Pack was pretty well known for keeping themselves isolated from humans.

"Most of the humans in this country are Christian, but there are all different types of religions here. This statue is more a tourist thing than a religious thing, though," I explained.

She blinked and then stood. "Huh."

"Do you want me to get your picture with it?" Jason asked as he held up his phone. "Tourists come from all over to do that."

She nodded with a shy smile. Jason took her picture and she seemed fascinated when he showed her the result on his phone. Just how isolated were the wolves of the Montreal Pack?

We walked over to Catch31 and asked for a table for three. The waitress gave Jase and I a flirty smile, but Gemma was too distracted to notice. She looked at everything we passed as we walked through the restaurant as if she had never seen anything like it before. I pulled out a chair for Gemma and the waitress turned all of her flirtations onto Jason. I guess she had decided that Gemma and I were an item.

The waitress, Amy, left us with our menus and Gemma stared at hers.

Jason cleared his throat. "The seafood here is really good, they get everything daily from local docks."

"Oh, I'm a vegetarian," Gemma said absentmindedly.

Jason and I stared at each other in shock.

"Willingly?" Jason asked in disbelief.

Gemma turned red and I kicked him under the table. I've never heard of a wolf or halfling being a vegetarian either, but there was no need to be rude. He gave me an apologetic shrug, but I motioned over to Gemma, who was now completely hiding behind her menu.

"Um, they have oyster soup?" he said tentatively.

I rolled my eyes. "Vegetarians don't eat any living creatures, right Gemma?"

"Yeah," she said softly.

Jason just sighed but kept his mouth shut. "Would you try some boardwalk fries if we got some for an appetizer?" I asked Gemma.

She peeked over the edge of the menu at me and smiled. "That sounds good."

Gemma started to warm up to us after the fries came and she chatted about her life in Canada. She lived with a small pocket of wolves in the center of Canada, far from the pack leadership in Montreal. I hadn't realized just how huge their pack was- their pack territory encompassed all of Canada and included Alaska.

Their pack had small groups of wolves all over their territory with the pack-master and other leaders only making occasional visits. Unfortunately for Gemma, that meant that she had very little interaction with anyone outside of her small group. There were less than twenty wolves in her little village, and she was the only halfling. Her mother had died years ago, leaving her alone in a pack that treated her little better than a slave.

She spent her days cooking and cleaning for the full-blooded wolves. She told us that she almost never left the village and had only met a handful of humans in her life. Her pack didn't give her access to internet or television, so the only way she knew about human culture was from reading books.

Jason and I were so engrossed in her story, that neither of us thought to steer the conversation towards the Arctic wolves until we were almost finished with our meal.

"I think you're going to like staying with us," I told Gemma. "We'll bring you to class one day with us, our professors won't mind."

Gemma's eyes lit up and she gave me a shy smile. "That would be nice."

Jason finished the last bite of his meal and set down his fork. "Yeah, we can bring you whenever we go out and do human stuff, too."

Gemma nodded enthusiastically and took another sip of her drink. We had ordered her one of those fruity drinks that girls always seemed to like and Gemma had been absolutely delighted by it.

"So, Gemma," I started out, wanting to switch to more serious conversation now that she was more relaxed. "Did you know our girl, Anna, might be from your pack?"

Jason nodded. "She's an Arctic wolf, pure white coat."

Gemma's face closed off. "Her type would never interact with someone like me. She would have been sent to the pack master once she was born."

Jason and I glanced at each other. "Anna's not like that, she's cool." I told Gemma. "But she was adopted by humans when she was a baby, so she didn't grow up with wolves."

Gemma's jaw dropped. "That's impossible, the pack would have never agreed to that. The white wolves are the most precious wolves we have, they're the ones who-"

Jase and I leaned forward eagerly but Gemma eyed us nervously. "I'm not even supposed to know about any of this, if anyone found out that I told you…"

The waitress picked that exact moment to bring us a check and try to flirt with Jason again. Gemma was quiet as she watched Jason fend off the waitress's advances but then bluntly told her that he had a girlfriend. I left the waitress cash – with an extra tip for dealing with Jason's rejection.

Let's be honest, six months ago, one or both of us would have taken the waitress up on her offer. But now that we had Anna, all the other women in the world just seemed…less. None of them had her warm smile, her bright blond hair, her soft skin, her laugh… The whole world just seemed duller without Anna. I felt lost without her.

I snatched the Jeep keys from Jason as we walked back. He scowled but didn't argue. After we all got into the Jeep, I put the keys in the ignition, but I didn't start it. Instead I turned back to Gemma. "Anything you tell us, stays with us. Anna is everything to us and we just want to get her back."

"You love her?" Gemma asked softly, searching my eyes.

I nodded. "We both do. With every part of our souls. We will do anything to get her back."

163

Gemma took a deep breath. "No one tells me anything, but they forget that I'm around sometimes. I'm beneath their notice, just like a piece of furniture."

I gave her hand a squeeze. "Not anymore. Our pack isn't like that."

She gave me a small smile. "We'll see." She looked off into the distance as if gathering her thoughts. "The white wolves have magic, unlike the rest of the pack." She looked at us both to gauge our reactions, but I just nodded. It didn't surprise me that Anna was special.

"They go to Montreal once they are born to get special training and responsibilities," Gemma told us.

"What about Anna's mother, Astrid?" Jason interrupted. "Was she one of those wolves?"

Gemma paled again. "Astrid was banished... we're supposed to pretend like she never existed."

"But she did exist," Jason pressed. "And she had Anna."

Gemma nodded slowly. "The pack was very excited when two twin white wolves were born almost fifty years ago. They considered it to be very lucky, and both were sent to Montreal to grow up. They were the source of a lot of gossip, as they were more spoiled than any of the other wolves in the pack." Jason and I exchanged glances. One of them must have been Anna's mom.

"They were sent up north once they were old enough and finished training." Gemma hesitated. "You already know our real mission, right?"

Jason and I both nodded, unwilling to give away that we were clueless.

Gemma seemed satisfied with our answer and continued. "Our pack guards the world from the fae. The white wolves are the only ones who can truly guard, the rest of us support them. The pack master stations the white wolves near where the fae come through into our world."

My ears perked up at that. Anna had been taken by one of the fae who claimed to be her father.

Gemma leaned towards us to whisper. "Rumor has it that Astrid met one of the fae. She failed in her duty to protect us and sided with one of *them*."

My eyebrows rose. "Astrid's daughter? She's fae?"

Gemma shrugged. "I don't know anything about a daughter, just that Astrid was banished and her sister, Ingrid, was sent home to mate with the pack-master's son."

Jason and I looked at each other through the rearview mirror before I reached down to start the Jeep. Hearing that Anna really was part fae and not a purebred wolf didn't change anything for me. Anna was still Anna. But for everyone else? Would that change anything? The council thought she was incredibly valuable because she was a purebred white wolf. But how would they feel once the truth came out? Would they leave her alone to be with us? Or would they consider her an enemy?

"What makes a white wolf have magic though?" Jason asked with a frown. "What makes them different from us?"

I just shrugged, and Gemma gave him a strange look. "That's just the way it is."

I gave Jason a look. It didn't seem like Gemma was the type to question the status quo or ask questions, but we were. Austin or Cody would probably have more answers for us. I glanced down at my phone, I had texted Cody a couple times since this morning, but he hadn't responded to me at all. That was really not like him.

The last time I saw Cody was last night after the pack meeting, when he was on his way out to work with some of our other pack members. I was going to talk to Austin once we got back, I had a feeling in my gut that something was off.

Chapter 19

Anna

Today, the prince had decided to conduct our lesson outside in the courtyard. That meant that Cody and about a dozen of the prince's guards were watching us, making me feel even more awkward than usual.

Cody was trying to chat up some of the guards along with Caylee, but he very obviously was keeping me in sight. Which was good, because I wanted to keep *him* in sight, too.

The prince had already tried taunting Cody, but had given up when he didn't get the reaction he was looking for. Cody was playing it cool, he already knew how to handle a guy like the prince.

Right now, the prince and I were standing three feet apart, facing each other. "Today we're going to focus on increasing your elemental strength," the prince told me seriously. "I want to see just how much magic you can handle."

I took a deep breath. "Isn't that dangerous?"

The prince laughed. "Not while I'm here. If it gets to be too much, I can just siphon the magic off you. Let's start with water. There's plenty of snow around here, see if you can gather some up and melt it."

I frowned. That was a complicated order. I was going to have to gather up the snow somehow – with air? Or water? And then create a heat source to melt it. I closed my eyes so that I could focus and tried to forget about all the people who were staring at me, waiting for me to do something impressive. At least this didn't involve using precise little bits of magic like compulsion or healing did.

I had created little snow tornadoes the other day to chase Cody around the courtyard, maybe I could make a bigger one to gather up some snow? I delved into the magic inside of me and made a little snow tornado, trying to sweep up snow with it.

The prince laughed. "It's going to take you all day to clean the courtyard with that puny little thing."

My hackles rose. *I'll show him puny.*

I spread my arms out wide and tried to sense the world around me like Froston had attempted to show me. My eyes were closed in concentration so that I could focus on everything around me. I dipped into my pool of magic to create a much larger wind to sweep around the entire courtyard, but I remembered what Froston had told me. I should have a connection with the elements around me. I shouldn't need to use my magic like a giant pair of hands, I should be able to simply connect with the elements themselves.

I switched from using my magic to create wind to move the snow, to simply trying to move the snow itself. I felt the difference when I switched my focus; I could feel all the tiny snowflakes around me like little pinpoints. I decided I was going to go big and see just how much of it I could move. I cast my awareness all the way around the rather large courtyard and raised my arms as I lifted the snow.

I staggered as I struggled to lift the heavy weight, but Cody wrapped his arms around me from behind. His presence gave me the boost I needed and I used the wind to form a swirling mass of snow above the courtyard. There were shouts from the guards as the wind and snow whipped through them and they ran to take shelter. I created a barrier around Cody and myself, so we stood unaffected in the middle of the giant snow tornado I was creating.

The weight of keeping tons of snow up in the air as well as the strain of keeping the wind moving was quickly draining my strength. The assignment had been to clean the courtyard of snow, which I had done. But if I let go, all my work would be undone. I wanted to melt the snow, and hopefully drench the prince in the downpour.

I swallowed nervously. I had used fire in very small amounts, but nothing like the night when James was injured. I needed to repeat that feat now. I needed to get over the emotions that came along with this and just do it. I couldn't let anything cripple me.

I gathered all of my hate, anger, and frustration that I had felt since being kidnapped and held here against my will. My anger that I was taken from my pack, my frustration at not being able to contact them, my hate for the prince when he casually manipulates humans as if they were nothing, my hate for Morpheus for plaguing me with nightmares and siphoning my magic. All of that went into the heat that was building inside of me.

I turned to hold Cody protectively, the way that I had held James that night. Squeezing him tightly, I stoked the flames burning inside me to almost unbearable heights before letting all of my rage out in the form of a massive inferno. The fire exploded out of me and went skyward towards the snow tornado. It blossomed out like a mushroom cloud, melting the snow as it was sucked into the wind keeping the tornado moving. I felt a moment of panic when I realized that this could go horribly wrong if I lost control of the wind and the fire.

I let go of the force I was using to hold the now-melted snow in the air and it pelted the barrier in a thunderous downpour. The fire petered from the rain, and I slowed the wind back down to the slight breeze it had been blowing at naturally before I had taken control.

I opened my eyes to see the prince laughing maniacally. I was disappointed to see that he had been completely unaffected by the fire, snow, and water behind a barrier of his creation. I had been hoping to have singed or at least splashed him. Further back, in the archway that led back into the castle, I saw Froston looking at me with horror etched on his face. He quickly hid it when he realized I was looking in his direction and pasted his usual pleasant mask on.

I let go of Cody and took a step back, watching his face nervously. I shouldn't have worried, because he gave me a huge grin before leaning forward for a kiss.

Cody's lips met mine in a brief touch before he pulled back and laughed. "Damn, Anna. That was crazy awesome."

I gave a faint laugh. Cody might have trusted me completely, but I didn't trust myself. So many things could have gone wrong with that, I was lucky that I hadn't hurt anyone.

The prince finally stopped laughing, and I shot him a glare as I pulled away from Cody. I was still a little shaky from all the magic that I had used, so Cody steadied me with an arm around my waist.

The prince stalked over to us with a gleam in his eyes. "I think you're almost ready," he told me as he circled around us. "The king is going to be pleased." He rubbed his hands together in glee which caused a pit of nervousness to form in my stomach. From my time with the prince, I had learned that he was usually most pleased when causing someone else distress.

"Froston!" the prince shouted and I winced.

Froston stepped out into the courtyard and walked in our direction. "We need to head back to court," the prince told him with bright eyes. "I have work to do."

Froston walked over to me and Cody. "Take the rest of the day off." He murmured to me before turning to Cody. "She needs to rest after that."

Cody gave me a squeeze and a kiss on the forehead. "No problem."

I was surprised when Froston narrowed his eyes slightly but didn't say a word about Cody's affection towards me. The prince ignored us completely, shouting orders at his guards.

Cody took my hand and we walked back inside as Froston created a portal for the prince and his guards. I focused on putting one foot in front of the other so that I wouldn't stumble or fall as we made our way back to my room. Caylee caught up to us, but Cody asked her to bring some food back to our room. She skipped off and promised to meet us in a few minutes.

As soon as we got back to the room I plopped down on the bed and snuggled up to one of the pillows. Cody sat next to me and stroked my hair gently. "Snuggle with me?" I asked with a yawn.

"I'm going to use the bathroom." Cody gave me a kiss. "I'll be right back."

I squeezed my pillow tighter and waited for him to come back. It was only a few minutes before I heard a crash. I jumped up and ran to the bathroom, shouting for Cody.

There was no answer, so I burst in the door. Cody was lying crumpled on the floor. It looked like he had been washing his hands at the sink but lost his balance and fell. I knelt next to him, panicking. What had happened?

I tapped Cody on the cheek, calling his name. After what seemed like an eternity, he started to respond. "Anna…" he said groggily. "What happened?

I nervously smoothed his hair back, my hand shaking. "I'm not sure, big guy. I heard a crash and ran in to find you on the floor, out cold."

He grunted and I helped him sit up. "This is serious, Cody. Something's not right here."

Had I made a mistake while healing him? Had I damaged him by trying something completely out of my depth? Let's be honest, when it came to magic, I was clueless. Tears came to my eyes, I just knew this was my fault.

"Hey," Cody said softly, brushing a piece of my hair back. "This is not your fault."

I smiled through the tears that were threatening to fall. "How do you know that's what I was thinking?"

He grinned. "Because I know you."

I helped him stand up and watched him cautiously as he stretched his back. "Anna, I'm fine," he said as he rolled his head, stretching his neck.

"You're not fine." I said firmly. "We need Airmed."

Cody groaned but let me take his arm and help him to the bed. That's when I knew that things were *really* not okay. There's no way Cody would lean on me unless he was hurting bad.

I sat down on the bed next to him. "Cody, tell me what's wrong." I demanded in a no nonsense voice.

He tried to shrug it off, but I wasn't going to let him off the hook that easily. "I'm serious, Cody."

Cody sighed. "I haven't been feeling one hundred percent lately. At first, I just thought I was still sore from the ass-kicking that I got. But I started getting these dizzy spells…"

"And you didn't think that was important to mention?" I asked incredulously.

Cody gave me an embarrassed shrug. "You're already under a lot of pressure right now. I didn't want to put more crap on you if I was just being a pussy."

I rolled my eyes. *Marines.* "Cody, telling me that you're having dizzy spells and passing out is not being a pussy."

"That was the first time I passed out," he said defensively.

"It's been getting worse?" I asked, trying not to let my panic show.

He sighed. "Yeah."

I stood up and paced. "This is what we are going to do. Caylee should be here in a few minutes. I don't want to leave you here by yourself, so I'll ask her to go get Airmed while I stay with you."

He put an arm over his eyes. "I'm not even hungry anymore."

My stomach sank. Cody didn't want to eat? This was not looking good. Maybe when the food got here, the scent would spike his hunger.

I started pacing again and rubbed my hands over my face. A dainty knock sounded on the door and I ran to open it for a surprised Caylee. I took the tray of food from her. "Caylee, would you be able to find Airmed? Cody's not feeling well."

"Of course, my lady," Caylee said, glancing worriedly at Cody. "I'll go right away."

I sat the tray of food down after Caylee ran off, but Cody didn't perk up. This was the first time I'd ever seen him ignore food. Airmed had better get here quickly.

Chapter 20

James

I trudged into the little house and stomped my feet, trying to get the majority of the snow off my boots on the mat in the mudroom before going further in. I was fucking tired of the snow and the cold, but I wasn't giving up. Ragnar had sent us to the outpost closest to the gateway that the fae used to get in and out of our world. I patrolled the area with my snowshoes daily, desperate to catch a scent or sign that would indicate Anna had been here. So far, I had found nothing.

Myself and the rest of the team had arrived here, ready to do battle with the wolves that Ragnar had spoken of. But after some surveillance and then an inspection, we had determined that no one had been here for close to a week before our arrival. We kept guard continuously, just in case they showed up unexpectantly, but none of us had seen a sign of anyone.

Ragnar had been disappointed at the news, but suspicious that the wolves had gone into the fae realm. He was convinced that the fae were behind everything bad that had befallen his pack. We agreed to stay here for the time being, just in case they came back.

Being in a small house with five other wolves, all of whom seemed to be in various stages of forming mating bonds, was driving me insane. I didn't want to hear Sam giggle, Davis flirt, or see Mike make sad cow eyes at Sam. I wanted them all out of my sight and hearing. I was especially frustrated because normally Trevor would feel the same. But more than a few times, I caught him watching Sam with longing in his eyes.

I took off my boots and the outer layers of clothing while still in the mudroom, slamming the door as I stomped into the house. This shit had gone on too long. I was staying outside as long as I could to patrol, but even with my superior abilities as a wolf, I couldn't tolerate the extreme temperatures for long.

Trevor met me in the great room with a frown. "We have news from home. Cody is missing."

I cursed. "Missing or taken?"

Trevor grimaced. "Probably taken. Robbie's body was delivered to the house along with Cody's phone. Looks like Robbie lured him out to a country bar for a meeting."

"And during the meeting, Robbie ends up dead?"

"With a hole in the head," Trevor confirmed.

"And Cody is nowhere to be found."

Trevor nodded. "We sent Henderson to the bar where they last met. He caught the scents of fae and wolves outside the bar. Cody and Robbie were definitely inside, along with the fae. The bar was boarded up and blood was found inside, but no sign of the owner or employees yet."

I cursed again. "The fucking fae again. Any sign of Anna?" I added, attempting to mask any emotion.

Trevor looked sympathetic and shook his head. "Not yet."

I clenched my fists, trying to keep myself from punching the wall. Austin was right, random acts of violence weren't going to help me get her back. Keeping my temper under control and thinking rationally would.

"The witches?"

"Not willing to come up here."

I nodded. I hadn't expected they would, but it was worth a try.

"The lamia?"

"Austin's working on it, but it doesn't sound good."

"Satellites?"

"Caleb has a few over the area, nothing is showing."

"So we have nothing?"

Trevor hesitated. "Will you call me a fucker if I offer hope?"

I just glared at him.

"Right. Food's in the kitchen."

Chapter 21

Anna

I hovered over Cody nervously as Airmed examined him for the fourth day in a row. Cody's dizziness and fainting spells had been getting worse and more frequent. At first, he would be fine within minutes after an episode. But yesterday and today it had been lasting for much longer. Each time Airmed examined him, she claimed there was nothing wrong and that maybe his spells were due to weakness from being a 'lesser creature.'

Cody had been coming with me to all of my magic lessons and we hadn't left each other's side in days. We ate the same food, drank the same water, and slept in the same bed. If it were an illness, I should have been affected as well. Cody and I were closer than ever, but I was in a panic over his state today. He was almost unresponsive and it had been over an hour since he had a dizzy spell. He should have been up by now and insisting that he was fine.

Airmed's eyes were closed and I could feel tendrils of magic extending over him and searching through his body. She had reluctantly agreed to see what she could do after Caylee brought her to the room to see me panicking yet again. While I was waiting for Caylee to bring Airmed, Cody had gotten even more unresponsive, reverting almost to how he had been when the fae first brought him in.

Airmed sighed and opened her eyes. "Physically, nothing is wrong with him."

"But something's wrong with him," I insisted. Airmed had ignored all of my pleas to the contrary in the last few days, but surely she could see that this was getting worse. This was something real

Airmed nodded reluctantly. Finally! She was willing to admit that he needed to be healed.

"I've seen this a few times before…" she told me. I could see the hesitation on her face, she was debating on what to tell me.

"Where have you see it before?" I asked aggressively. There was no way I was going to let her walk out of this room without getting some answers.

She met my eyes and held them. "One of the fae is an expert in using compulsion and he's able to invert his magic so that it can't be detected. But it does have side effects like the ones Cody is exhibiting."

"Prince Mandrake," I spat out. "Why would he do this?" I paced back and forth. The prince had reappeared the next day after his trip to court and been even more aggressive with our lessons. He had been pushing me as far as I could go every day. A part of me hated him for being such an asshole, but I couldn't deny the results. I had made huge advances in the way that I was able to use my magic and the amount of magic that I was able to handle.

I wouldn't call he and Cody friends, but Drake had lost interest in trying to antagonize Cody after the first day and they had both kept their interactions professional. I hadn't expected to hear that Drake was behind this, I should have known that was suspicious.

"Never mind." I muttered. "I don't care *why* he did it. How do I fix it?"

Airmed tilted her head to watch me. "You won't be able to sense the magic that he used on Cody, only the prince can remove it."

I cursed. That damn prince had fucked with me for the last time. A knock sounded on the door and Caylee opened it to see one of the prince's guards standing there. Good. That meant that the prince was nearby, and I could get him to fix whatever he had done.

I stomped over to the door and Caylee scampered out of my way. "Where is he?" I growled at the guard.

"Downstairs, my lady," he replied with his eyes downcast. "He requires your presence."

"I actually require his." I snarled as he stepped back to let me through the doorway. He led me through the castle and to Froston's hall where we saw the prince striding towards us. I felt my magic swirling around inside of me and wanting to rise to the surface. I tried to stuff it back down but my anxiety was making it difficult. The more I practiced using my emotions to manage my magic, the more it seemed to be tied to them.

"Finally," Drake grumbled as he tried to take my arm. "We have somewhere to go."

176

I evaded his grasp. "No, you have something that you need to fix." I told him defiantly.

Caylee and the guard gasped and the prince's head snapped to them. "Get out!" he shouted.

I braced myself for a fight. Drake was going to reverse whatever he did whether he liked it or not.

"Cody hasn't been feeling well but I think you expected that." I accused the prince.

He rolled his eyes. "Oh, is that what you're so fired up about?"

I stepped right up to him so that the hem of my dress was brushing his boots, tilting my head up so that I could hold his eyes. "You. Will. Fix. Him."

Drake grabbed my upper arms. "We can discuss this later. Right now, we have more important things to deal with."

"There is nothing more important than Cody right now." I snarled. "If you want me to go anywhere with you, you're going to fix whatever you did to him."

The prince huffed. "Or I can have one of my guards toss you over his shoulder and carry you like a sack of grain."

"You can try."

The prince and I stared at each other but he was the first to break. "Fine," he grumbled. "We fix your wolf and then you come to court with me. But I expect you to be on your best behavior."

"Fine." I stomped to the door, glancing back to make sure that he was following me. He sauntered after me as if he didn't have a care in the world, which made me grit my teeth even harder. What I really wanted to do was let go of the tight control keeping my magic inside and lash out at the prince, but that wasn't going to help Cody.

Caylee met us outside the doors with a terrified look on her face, but Drake's group of guards just stared at me with stony faces. I could care less if they thought I was being disrespectful to their prince.

I led the procession back up to my room and motioned for the prince to step inside before me. He bowed elaborately. "Oh, after you, my lady."

The smirk on his face made me want to punch him, but I needed him to help Cody. I could always punch him later.

177

I stood next to the bed and smoothed Cody's hair back tenderly. He looked even worse than he did before I had left the room. The prince stood on the other side of the bed and scowled down at Cody.

"Why would you do this?" I asked him softly.

Drake met my eyes. "Isn't the more important question, what did I do?"

I didn't look away from him, meeting his gaze straight on. "It's compulsion, but with the magic inverted so that I can't sense it to remove it."

He smirked. "What would I use compulsion to do to your friend, here?"

My heart started to beat even faster. "Make him compliant? Like you did before?"

Drake laughed. "That was the easy compulsion that I showed you how to remove. This one was more complex and subtle. It's actually a shame that you can't see it, because it's quite the work of art."

I growled at him.

"Oh, all right," he sighed dramatically. "You seemed a little tense. Like maybe you needed to relax in order to get a handle on your magic. Imagine my surprise when I go into your friend's mind to find that he is completely in love with you, but doesn't have the courage to tell you. I went all the way to the human world to get your lover for you, only to find out that he isn't even your lover."

Drake shook his head. "I merely put a few suggestions in his mind to make him act on his feelings for you." He paused with an evil grin. "And, of course, do everything in his power to seduce you. The plan was for him to dump you after that, break your heart so that I would be there to pick up the pieces..."

Drake shrugged. "But things never got that far, so I guess that game's over."

"Just fix him," I spat out. Emotions were swirling through my mind. Cody and I had spent close to a week here together. He and I had become friends, lovers, and confidantes. Every morning I would wake up beside him and look into those gorgeous eyes of his – it still made me smile every time. We shared everything, and the thought of some of the things we did at night made me blush.

Had anything that I shared with Cody been real? Or had the prince's compulsion made him confess to feelings that weren't really his? I lowered my head. How was he going to feel when the prince removed the compulsion? Was he going to be disgusted and horrified? Was he going to be angry?

If someone had put me under a compulsion to seduce someone, I would be beyond angry, I would be furious. I was so embarrassed. How could I have not suspected that Cody wasn't himself? If he hadn't gotten sick, I would have never realized he wasn't acting like himself. What did that make me?

"Oh, relax." The prince rolled his eyes. "I can feel you worrying from here. I didn't make him feel anything for you, I just made him act on what was already there."

The prince placed a hand on Cody's forehead and closed his eyes. I became even more nervous as the seconds passed. What made me think that I could trust the prince to fix this? What if he made things worse? How could I stop him?

"Stop," I told him. "I need to see what you're doing."

Drake laughed. "Why not?" He grabbed my hand and connected. I felt a moment of worry when I realized that our connection was forming more quickly and easily each time we made it. How many times would we need to connect before it was permanent?

Instead of delving into my well of magic like Drake usually did, he pulled me towards him. My awareness changed as I was surrounded by his magic and inside of his mind. I could see his magic from his perspective, and the little bits of his magic inside Cody were obvious now. Being inside Drake's mind gave me a little insight into him. I could tell that he was impatient to get this done and eager to get somewhere. I tried to probe a little but he quickly shut me down.

Do you think you can undo it? Drake asked in my mind. I looked at the web of magic that was threaded all throughout Cody and doubt flooded me. This was Cody's mind, did I really want to take a chance at fumbling around with my clumsy magic? What if I did more harm than good?

Guide me. I felt Drake's amusement, but he did as I asked. He guided me through unraveling the complicated web of magic that he had woven through Cody's mind. This magic went deeper than any of the compulsion magic that I had seen before, the tendrils of magic were much smaller and woven all together in a delicate mesh that drew in parts of Cody's own magic. There was no way I would be able to do something like that, even undoing it was beyond what I could have done on my own. Drake had to step in several times to work with me when we reached a complicated snarl. Eventually, I was convinced that we had gotten all the magic out of Cody and I withdrew from Drake.

Drake took his hand away from Cody, but Cody didn't react. "Well?" I asked the prince nervously.

The prince smirked at me. "Consider him fixed."

I glared at him. "Last time I removed his compulsion, he sat up and was completely normal."

Drake laughed. "This compulsion has been affecting him for far longer, he just needs to sleep for a while so that his mind can heal."

I narrowed my eyes at him. "How can I be sure that you really fixed him?"

The prince shrugged at me. "How can you be sure that I didn't?"

I had more than enough of all of the fae. If I never had to see a fae for the rest of my life, I would be happy. Their callous indifference to the pain and suffering that they caused to the people around them for the sake of their own entertainment was infuriating.

I felt Cody's hand twitch in mine before he gave it a firmer squeeze. "Anna…"

I leaned over so I could murmur in his ear. "Cody, I'm here. The prince just removed his compulsion from you."

I could tell he was struggling to stay awake. "Anna… I just want you to know… I love you."

I felt tears come to my eyes and I gave him a kiss on his forehead. "I love you too, big guy."

His eyes closed again and his breathing was deep and steady.

"See? I told you he was fine. Now let's go," The prince said, holding out his arm. "Your father should be in the courtyard any moment to transport us to court."

I have never wanted to punch someone more in my entire life than right now. I took his arm but sank my nails into his flesh. "If I get back here and he isn't completely better you're going to regret the day you were born." I hissed at him.

Drake chuckled and watched me with heated eyes. "I love it when you threaten me," he purred. "But I promise that your lover will be just fine."

I held his eyes, debating on whether or not I could trust his word. Was I willing to leave Cody here and hope that he was healed by the time he got back?

"Airmed!" The prince shouted. She appeared in the doorway, her posture stiff.

"Stay with the wolf. Anna doesn't trust my word that he's healed."

Airmed gave a slight bow. "Of course, Your Highness." Her eyes dropped to our linked arms and she gave me a look of pure hate. I guess this meant that our temporary truce was over. Airmed was back to hating me again.

Drake and I made our way down and Froston met us in the courtyard. He ran his gaze over my airy purple dress. "Perhaps we should let Anna dress for court?"

"We've already wasted enough time," Drake snapped. "We need to do this now, before my brother-" he took a deep breath and looked towards the sky. "It's important that we do this now."

Froston and I exchanged glances. There was something that the prince wasn't telling us, and I didn't like it. I just wanted to get this over with so that I could get back to Cody.

Froston waved his hand and created a portal that led into another courtyard. This one was lacking in snow or ice, and had some plant life growing. I peeked through, curious as to what awaited us on the other side, but I couldn't see much.

The prince waved a few of his guards through the gateway and they spread out on the other side. Checking to see if it was safe for the prince? After a few moments, one of them bowed to the prince and said something to him in their language.

The prince grinned and strode through, waving for the rest of us to follow. I looked around with wide eyes once we reached the other side. The king's castle was definitely 'prettier' than Froston's. Where Froston's castle looked like it was built as a defensive structure, this one was art straight out of a fairytale. It was made out of white stone that glimmered in the sunlight, whereas Froston's was a dreary grey. This one also had towers and spires with glittering blue tops compared to the plain boxy shape of Froston's.

Servants rushed to fawn over the prince and offer him food, wine, and a bunch of other comforts, but he turned them all down and waved them away. He turned to me and held out his arm. "Anna, darling, this is your time to shine."

I swallowed nervously and gave him a glare, but I took the arm he offered after Froston gave me an encouraging look.

The prince tucked my hand in under his arm as if he was afraid I would try to get away. I just sighed. I knew better than to try and run - I wouldn't make it far.

I walked beside the prince with Froston following close behind, and the guards in formation around all three of us. We crossed through a large archway that led into the castle and it took a moment for my eyes to adjust to the shadowed halls. The inside of the castle was just as impressive as the outside with thick carpeting covering the stone floors and woven tapestries to decorate the walls.

As we walked, I tried not to look like a complete tourist, but I still received more than a few curious and some disdainful looks. "Court is already in session," Drake murmured to me as we strode down the hall. "We will be announced when we reach the throne room. Try your best to curtsy without falling down." He smirked at me and I rolled my eyes. I would probably end up embarrassing myself somehow, but a fall from an attempted curtsy probably wasn't going to be the catalyst.

We paused at two large doors and the prince straightened his clothes before taking my arm again. A fae dressed in some fancy clothes straight out of medieval times gave the prince a deep bow. "My prince," he said in a nasally voice.

The prince gave him a nod. "Geoff. You already know Lord Froston." He gestured towards my father. "And this is his daughter, the lovely Lady Anna."

Geoff gave my simple dress a doubtful look but the prince simply glared at him and he straightened up. "I'll announce you right away, my prince."

The guards pulled open the two large doors and we walked through an opening that was large enough for a dragon. Geoff tapped a long ornate staff on the floor to get everyone's attention.

And there were a *lot* of people in there; there had to be over a hundred fae dressed in fancy court clothes with servants darting between them carrying food and drinks. Everyone in the huge throne room stopped to stare at the sound of the staff echoing through the room. I tried to keep my cool, but there were way too many eyes focused on me to be comfortable.

There were fae like Froston and Drake – beautiful and perfect beyond belief. But there were also other fae that didn't fit what I had been expecting. There were fae with horns, fae with extra limbs, and fae with distorted features that would never be mistaken as human. I wondered if this had been what Caylee had spoken of – were these what she had called 'lesser fae?'

"Presenting Prince Mandrake, Lord Froston, and his daughter, the Lady Anna," Geoff called out. The whispers started as soon as we walked past the threshold and the guards tugged the doors closed behind us. They shut with a loud thunk that sounded ominously final.

I swallowed nervously but tried to keep my head held high as we strode through the room. The crowd parted as we walked closer to the throne that was the centerpiece of the room. I tried not to be obvious about staring at the fae as we walked through them, but I couldn't help it. Some of them were tall and lithe with an ethereal beauty that I had started to associate with the fae in general. But others had horns, tails, or extra appendages. Some looked like they had begun to shift into an animal form but gotten stuck in between. Others looked like they were made from darkness and shadows, only taking the most basic of human shapes. Not all of the fae were human sized either. I spotted what could have been pixies or sprites floating beside giants and ogres.

The room itself was a work of art with gold embossed paintings on the walls and an elaborate floor mosaic, all leading to a shining gold cupola that contained a dais to hold the king's throne.

If I had been expecting a glittery gold throne, I would have been disappointed. The throne that the king lounged on was dark and twisted, more like something out of a nightmare than a fantasy. But the king himself? Absolutely gorgeous. He was tall and lithe with blond hair and a golden tan. His cheekbones were high and defined, his lips full. But despite his physical beauty, there was something missing. As we got closer and I was able to look into his silvery eyes, I realized what it was. He was like a stone statue - perfectly beautiful but cold and hard. There was no depth or warmth to him

The prince paused within the empty semicircle of space before the king's throne and released my arm to perform an elaborate bow. I took that as a cue to perform my curtsy. Froston came up beside me to bow as well. The two men stayed bowing instead of rising, so I paused my curtsy halfway through. My legs trembled a bit as the minutes ticked by, and I realized that the princes warning not to fall when curtsying might not have been that far off.

I kept my head lowered just like Froston and the prince, but peeked up through my lashes to see what was taking so long. I was guessing that we were waiting for some kind of signal from the king. The whispers from around the room had stopped, and the silence echoed around us.

"You may rise," the kings melodious voice floated through the room and I was surprised at just how much it affected me. The prince had mentioned that his father was considered an incubus by humans, but I hadn't expected the raw sexuality that oozed from him.

The prince stood with a grin, seemingly unaffected by how long the king had made us wait for acknowledgment. "My king, it's my pleasure to bring you the project I've been working on." My brow furrowed. I was a project?

King Illian flicked his hand in my direction. "Lord Froston's daughter? Explain."

The prince circled around me. "Not just his daughter. She's also a product of the shapeshifters we left behind in the human realm thousands of years ago. They have developed a very strong connection to the earth and its magic in our absence."

"Hmmm." King Illian eyed me curiously.

The prince kept talking. "I've felt her magic for myself, it's not limited to one element or even a small range. She has access to every type of magic imaginable."

I heard murmurs start in the crowd around us, but the king just watched me without saying a word. "Drake speaks the truth." Another fae pressed through the crowd to stand near us. "She's not the first of her kind, the Summer Court has one of their own."

I couldn't keep the scowl off my face, they needed to stop referring to me as an object.

"That's what you've come to report, Fallon?" King Illian asked

"Yes, Your Majesty." He replied with a bow. "Brother." He gave my prince a nod and a smirk. "But I'm in the process of acquiring more females that have the same curious mix of fae and wolf magic, so that we will be able to breed a larger population than the Summer Court."

I looked at him in horror. Did he not realize he was talking about people?

Drake scowled. "Acquiring them from where?"

Fallon smiled triumphantly. "There are plenty of wolf packs that don't appreciate their females or treat them properly in the human world. With a little kindness for the females and money for the males, we can create a small army in a short amount of time."

The king didn't respond, but shouts started in the crowd around us. Apparently, not everyone here agreed that creating an army of creatures that had the potential to become more powerful than themselves was a good idea. The king held up a hand for silence after a few minutes of arguments and the room quieted down.

He gestured for me to approach where he sat on the dais. I smoothed my dress nervously, and after a less than subtle nudge from the prince, I started towards the king. He stood as I approached, and held out a hand to help me up the stairs.

I very cautiously placed my hand in his – the prince had already warned me that the king was what the humans would consider to be an incubus. I was worried about what power the king might try to use on me, but he merely assisted me to stand on the dais across from him.

A small smile curled across his lips as he ran his eyes over me from my head to my toes. "I see why my son is fond of you."

I blushed, but decided it was best not to respond to his comment. I was fine with letting the king think the prince and I were a thing if it kept me safe from his intentions. The king took both of my hands in his and I was surprised – and relieved – that I didn't feel any magic radiating from him, only the warmth that a normal human's hands would give off.

That thought had barely crossed my mind when the king's magic slammed into me like a freight train. I was completely unprepared and caught off guard, which is probably why he did it. The throne room had completely disappeared in a flash of light when the king attacked, and I was locked in my mind with him.

I felt like I was careening through space in a helpless spiral and I fought to get my bearings. Laughter echoed around me and I felt a hand reach through the darkness to grab my arm.

Light exploded all around me and the king stood across from me. Once again, we were in his throne room – but this time we were completely alone. The king roughly took hold of my upper arms and stared into my eyes. "Let's see what you're made of."

I realized just how gentle the prince had been with me as the king combed through my mind. He roughly pulled my memories from me, causing me to cry out in agony as my mind felt like it was being ripped apart. Memory after memory was wrenched from me for the king's perusal and then discarded. I tried my best to struggle against him, but the pain made me weak and my disorientation made it difficult to get a grip on reality. I was a quivering mess by the time he was finished with that and tore into my magic.

I cried out again as he shoved into the very center of who I was, ransacking my magic and taking it for himself. When Morpheus and the prince had taken my magic from me, it had felt like I was being drained. This felt like my very essence was being ripped away from me, leaving me a shredded mess of remains.

I thought the pain would never end, but after what seemed like an eternity, the king released his hold on me. Reality folded back around me and I tumbled off of the dais, unable to keep standing. The prince caught me with a look of pity and handed me over to Froston.

Despite all the eyes on me, I was barely able to keep the tears from flowing. Froston held me close to him and rubbed my back as I tried to keep my shuddering sobs inside. I buried my face in his shoulder, unwilling to let the fae world see my shame.

The king casually made his way back to his throne and sat, unconcerned with the trauma that he had just inflicted on me. The satisfied look on his face set a fire inside of me that replaced my fear and pain with anger. I still clung to Froston for support, but my tears dried up. I was not willing to let him destroy me like this.

"You've done well." King Illian told Drake. "I'm impressed with the potential that she has."

The prince preened at the praise and I couldn't hide my scowl. Now that my pain was fading, my anger was growing inside of me.

"Prince Fallon," the king called to Drake's brother. "I approve of your plans to acquire new females to create more of these." He waved a hand in my direction, making it clear that by 'these' he meant me.

I felt Froston stiffen with tension, but I was still too physically weak to stand on my own. "And my daughter?" he asked softly.

Dread radiated through me when the king was silent for almost a full minute before answering. "She is too old for my intents, and is already defectively formed. I need new, fresh subjects to mold into what I want. Your daughter has served her purpose for now, do as you please with her."

Froston relaxed and let out his breath. "Thank you, Your Majesty."

"But Lord Froston?" King Illian called. "I want her within reach if I have need of her again."

Froston gave a sharp nod and the king turned to address his subjects. "I've decided that we will be pursuing a new avenue in our fight with the Summer Court..."

My eyes narrowed at the king's words. I was defectively formed? He was going to need new, fresh subjects? It sounded like he wanted to take female wolves, breed them, and then take their babies to shape into killers. Innocent children would be used as cannon fodder for his stupid war against the summer fae.

I got angrier the more I thought about it. I wasn't going to let him get away with this. My rage set my veins on fire and I started to breathe heavier. I stepped away from Froston and tapped into my magic, letting what little I had left swirl around me.

Froston watched me curiously but didn't try to stop me. Several of the fae had drained my magic and I had just stood there and let them do it every time. I had been pushed and prodded and manipulated since I got here. But letting the fae and the King do the same to innocent children? I couldn't stand by and let that happen. Fury filled me.

I reached out my awareness and started to draw energy in, the way that Froston had shown me with the lightning. But this time, I wasn't drawing it from the world around me, I was drawing it from the fae who couldn't protect themselves from me. Magic whipped around me in a vortex that grew with the more energy that I took in. Shock was etched on the faces of the fae around me when they realized what was happening, and then the entire room exploded into motion.

Lesser fae ran for the doors, not wanting to get caught up in my magical tornado. I pulled harder on the magic that I sensed all around me and the fae who were already caught up in my maelstrom collapsed to the floor. All my rational thoughts were gone, I was completely consumed by my anger and a lust for more magic.

I saw Froston in the panicking crowd; he had enacted a barrier around himself, similar to the one he had taught me to protect myself from Morpheus draining me at night. He was watching me with an unreadable look in his eyes, but didn't seem to be interested in interfering with what I was doing.

Drake was standing back and watching me as well, with a similar barrier to protect himself. But he had a wide grin on his face and a maniacal gleam to his eyes. There were other fae that had used barriers to protect themselves, but they were quickly heading for the doors, seemingly unwilling to engage me in a fight.

Confident that I wasn't going to be getting opposition from the fae around me, I turned back to the king. He was the reason I was brought here. He was the one who saw my kind as disposable weapons, objects for him to use.

The king was standing strong in front of his throne, watching me with interest. "I wasn't expecting this," he said with an amused grin. "Just how much magic can you take in?"

I took a step towards him and snarled, "You're about to find out."

The king was untouchable behind the barrier that he had created, but I'd broken barriers before. The king casually walked down the stairs of the dais, heading towards me. I let him come, preparing myself for what I had to do.

No one else was going to stand up to this king. No one else was going to protect the females he wanted to go after. No one else was going to defend the helpless children against him. I was the only one standing here against the king. I was alone, but I could do this.

I pulled harder at the magic, drawing in everything from all around me. My awareness spread outside of the throne room, reaching the fae who thought that they would be safe outside of my sight. They weren't. I drew their magic in easily, the stone walls not hindering me at all. I didn't stop to question how I was doing this or even to think, I just did it.

My body felt like it was about to burst from all the magic that I had taken in. I felt like I was floating in the clouds and I couldn't stop a huge grin from spreading across my face. The king had made a huge mistake – thinking he could take me on now.

The king stopped a foot in front of me and reached forward to clasp my arms. I let him – I wanted to draw my prey in. I felt him as he connected with me and attempted to draw out my magic the way that he had before, but this time I was ready for him.

When I felt the tug of his magic pulling on mine I pulled back. There were a few moments of tug of war and a frown shadowed his face. I yanked as hard as I could and the frown turned to horror as his magic started to flow into me. He fought me with everything that he had, but it simply wasn't enough now that I had a good grip on his very core of magic. I ripped a metaphorical pair of claws through that core, shredding the fight that was left in him and causing him the same pain that he had given me earlier. His struggles became weaker and I didn't try to hide my elation.

I thought I was high before, but the king's magic was nothing like everyone else's. It was warm and golden like the sun's summer rays. Warmth filled me and the king staggered. I used my massive horde of magic to hold him in place and kept draining. I felt it the moment that he stopped struggling and gave into me completely.

With this much power humming through my veins I could do anything. I felt like a goddess. The king was gasping for breath, terror in his eyes but I kept draining. I kept consuming him until he slumped in my hold and there was only emptiness in his eyes. I let his body slump to the floor. The most powerful fae in the kingdom, who everyone was so afraid of, was now just an empty husk laying at my feet.

I threw back my head and laughed. I was high as a kite and I didn't care. My gaze drifted to Drake, who was looking at his father's corpse with glee on his face. Drake had hurt me, but he had also helped me. He felt my gaze and looked up at me with adoration. "Anna, you're more than I could have ever hoped for."

Content that he wasn't a threat to me, I turned to Froston. Froston's face was molded into the pleasant mask he used to hide his true feelings. I narrowed my eyes and strode towards him. Now was the time for me to get the truth out of him.

He held up his hands as I approached as if he were trying to calm a wild animal. "Anna, you need me to get home," he murmured.

I circled around him. Deep down, I had rational thoughts that were trying to surface through the haze of magic that clouded my brain. I shook my head to focus. I did need Froston to get home.

Home. Thoughts of home penetrated the hazy mist in my mind and memories of my pack surfaced. I needed to get back to my guys. Cody was waiting for me back at Froston's castle, but the rest of my pack was still searching for me in the human world.

"Anna," Froston called to me softly. "The fae are going to be regrouping and not all of them are going to be as pleased as Prince Mandrake at what you've done. We need to get you out of here *now.*"

Reality started to sink back in and I looked at the king's corpse again. My magic wasn't swirling around me in a frenzy anymore, it was slowly sinking back into me. But I felt uncomfortably full, like I had just indulged in a feast and was unable to get up from the table. I stared at the king's body, gauging my emotions. Yes, I felt some regret. But for the most part, I felt that my actions were justified.

But the king wasn't the only one who had nefarious plans for the wolves. Where was Prince Fallon? I looked around the throne room, at the bodies of the fae who had passed out from my attack, at the food and drinks that the servants had dropped in their hurry to run from me. I didn't see Prince Fallon anywhere.

"Anna," Drake said as he walked up to us with a pleased smile still on his face. "I have a feeling that Froston is going to offer to take you back to your world."

Froston gave him a nod of agreement but I watched Drake carefully. Was he going to try to stop me?

"I want to ask… would you consider staying?" Drake asked hopefully.

I looked at him as if he was completely insane. After everything that had happened? After everything he had done to me? After what he did to Cody? Why would I agree to stay?

I took a deep breath and tried to settle my mind. My buzz was fading, and my thoughts were becoming more like my own. I could feel the magic inside me, filling me up, ready for me to use. I relaxed and realized that I had been fighting my magic in the past, I needed to let it become a part of who I was. This time, the magic didn't feel like a foreign presence inside me, it felt a little more natural.

My silence made Drake frown. "Together we could best my brothers and take the throne. I need someone like you."

My eyes snapped open. "Like me?" I said in disbelief. "Someone for you to-"

Froston cut me off, which was probably a good idea. "I think it's probably best for Anna if she goes back to her world. Not many fae will be able to follow her there and those that can will be too occupied with fighting for the throne to chase after her."

Drake looked disappointed. "Is there anything I could say to convince you to stay? I don't…" He looked as if he was struggling to find the right words. "There isn't anyone else like you here. No one else is… honest with me."

I just stared at him. His gentle tone and exposed vulnerability had softened my anger towards him. Yeah, he was probably used to everyone just doing and saying whatever they thought he wanted to hear because they were afraid he would murder them. I was probably the only person stupid enough to treat him like a normal person on occasion. But was he trying to manipulate me now? Was he trying to get under my skin and appeal to my softer emotions because his offer of power didn't appeal to me? Or did he honestly have feelings for me?

"I don't belong here," I told him firmly. "This world would kill me. You don't need someone like me, you need someone who can stand beside you as an equal. Someone who will fight beside you, not against you."

"But that could be you," he insisted.

"No. That's not me." I answered with a tone of finality.

Drake stared at me sadly for a moment before putting his trademark smirk back on. "I didn't think you would, but I had to try." He shrugged and gave me a wave before sauntering out of the throne room. "Be seeing you, I have a throne to take."

I watched the prince with mixed feelings. It was impossible for me to tell if he was being honest or just trying to manipulate me. I hardened my heart and turned to Froston, he had promised to take me home.

"How many others can make portals?" I asked Froston as the prince left. If I went home to Seaside, would others follow? Would I put my pack in jeopardy?

"Any portal? There are as many as ten or so. But a portal into the human world takes more power and expertise. There is one other in the Winter Court, but several in the Summer Court," Froston answered me.

I frowned at his answer. I hadn't met anyone from the Summer Court. Would they leave me alone? Or would they come after me, too?

Froston created a portal back to his castle and helped me through. After it snapped shut we stood in his courtyard. He surveyed the long walk across the icy path to the entrance of his castle and sighed before turning to me. "You haven't seen the last of Prince Mandrake. He'll be occupied with the fight for the throne for a while, until he realizes that having you at his side might tip the scales in his favor."

I frowned. "He's probably already forgotten me."

Froston shook his head. "No one is going to forget about you after the amount of power you just demonstrated."

My heart sank. "You think they'll come after me?"

Froston sighed. "Drake and his brothers will be too busy fighting each other for the throne for the time being. But let's hope that Drake wins, at least we can count him as an ally."

Froston took my hands. "You have a good heart – and an honesty and an openness that most of us lose in childhood. Manipulation, coercion, and blackmail are things that the fae excel in from an early age. You have to if you want to survive court intrigue; that's why I didn't want you to grow up here."

I nodded slowly. "And you think that the prince is attracted to me for those qualities?"

"I think that's part of it, but what the prince doesn't realize is that if you were to stay here, you would lose the very things that make us all love you so much," Froston told me quietly. "If you didn't lose those qualities, you wouldn't survive here. And if you did harden your heart and completely become one of us?" Froston just shook his head. "There's more than one reason I wouldn't want to see that. The world is safer if you keep your kind heart."

I sighed. "So, you're taking me home?"

Froston gave me a warm smile. "I'm taking you home."

Chapter 22

Anna

I stood in the courtyard with a huge grin on my face. Cody seemed like he was healed and was standing next to me with his hand in mine. When I had gotten back to the room, Cody was upset with me for leaving him behind while I went into danger, but excited when I told him that we had permission to go home. I decided not to tell him the entire story of what happened until we were home safe. I also needed to talk to him about what the prince had said about putting him under compulsion.

As soon as I had walked into the room, Cody had told me that he loved and missed me. The compulsion should be gone by now, but I was still wary about any lasting effects. As soon as we could be alone I wanted to tell Cody everything.

Caylee was waiting for Froston with us and chattering about how we should come back for the next festival.

"I don't think we're going to come back that soon." *Or ever.* I thought to myself. I would miss Caylee's bright cheeriness and her big heart, but I wouldn't miss any of the fae.

I reached forward to give Caylee a hug without getting tangled in her mass of waist-length red curls. "Thank you for everything that you have done for me since we got here. I'm going to miss you."

Caylee's mouth dropped in shock and she gently patted my back. "Um... thank you, my lady."

I pulled back from her to look into her bright blue eyes. "Anytime you think you might want to come back to the human world, I have a place for you in my house. I can find you a job, or you can go to school, you can become anything you want."

Caylee tilted her head in confusion. "I don't want to go to the human world, I like it here."

I just smiled at her. I might disagree with her choice, but I had to respect her decision. I just wish she would give it a chance.

"I'm not sure what I'm going to do without you," I told her quietly.

She perked up. "Oh, you can always send for me if you need me."

Ideas started to percolate in my mind. Could I trick her into visiting and show her how awesome the human world was? Maybe I could tempt her into staying.

Cody squeezed my hand. "Caylee is probably safer here for now, we're not sure what we're going home to."

I nodded reluctantly. "You're right, Cody."

Froston stepped into the courtyard and made his way over to us. "Could I have a few moments with my daughter, please?" Caylee gave him a curtsey and then disappeared back inside. I didn't let go of Cody's hand, anything Froston had to say to me, Cody could hear.

Froston's eyes flicked down to our joined hands and a scowl shadowed his face, but he didn't comment. "Anna, I'm sending you back to your world so that you don't get caught up in the battle for the throne that is sure to occur here."

I nodded. I definitely wanted no part of that.

"But I'm not willing to send you back alone," Froston told me with a frown. "You need to keep moving forward with your magic. Learning should be easier when you're surrounded by your pack. Your connection with the pack will keep you grounded."

A sense of dread pooled in my stomach. "Who are you sending with me?" I asked reluctantly.

Morpheus and Talen entered the courtyard and walked towards us.

"No," I told Froston. "Absolutely not."

"Just Talen," he tried to assure me.

Talen hadn't tormented me the way that Morpheus had, but I didn't trust any of the fae. I glared at Talen as he took his time crossing the courtyard. "How do I know I can trust him?"

"You can't," Talen called to me cheerfully.

Froston gave him a sharp look as I ignored Morpheus completely and studied Talen. The first time we met, I was more concerned with

194

being kidnapped than I was at getting a good look at him. The second time, I was focused on Morpheus.

Talen was tall and lithe like all the other male fae that I had met so far. His dusky gold skin and black hair gave him the air of an Egyptian god, or Tariq Naguib. He was dressed in clothes that would help him to blend in back in my world – jeans and a t-shirt - but the ethereal beauty that seemed to be etched into the fae's DNA was going to make him stand out no matter what he wore.

"What kind of magic do you have?" I asked, trying to keep the accusation out of my voice. There was no way I was bringing a fae with dangerous powers back to Seaside with me.

Talen just smiled at me.

Froston frowned. "Anna, it's not polite to ask someone what kind of magic they have."

"It's also not a good idea to admit that you lack the basic ability to sense another's magic," Morpheus mocked me.

"Thank you, Morpheus. That will be all I require from you today." Froston told him with a flick of his wrist.

Morpheus's face tightened at being dismissed so casually. He probably came to see me leave so he could get a few last minutes of torment in before I was out of his reach. Hopefully, forever.

I extended my senses to get a feel for Talen. I had gotten in the habit of keeping that all locked down after the various attacks on me. What I felt from Talen surprised me. "You don't feel like anything to do with winter, death, or destruction," I said in surprise. Talen's power reminded me of the beginning of spring – when the ice first started to melt and green buds started appearing on trees.

"Talen's story is his own to tell," Froston told me cryptically. "But he has just joined our court recently." He glanced over at Talen. "In the last hundred years or so?"

Talen nodded, and Cody and I exchanged glances. The last hundred years or so was recently?

I stepped up to Talen and looked him in the eyes. He was only an inch or two taller than me, so I didn't even have to tilt my head up that far. "I'm not bringing you back with me without you making some promises first."

Talen cocked his head to the side with a sly grin. "I've already promised your father that I will not physically harm you or any of your pack members."

I shook my head. That was not good enough. "You will not harm anyone physically or emotionally. That includes my pack, other wolves you might meet, or any of the humans in my world."

Talen pouted. "And if I'm attacked?"

I frowned. "You can defend yourself against true threats to your safety." I felt like I was missing something. I wanted to cover everything I could think of because I knew how fae liked to mess with people, and they didn't care if people got hurt. Talen's power might seem benign, but I was sure that he was still more than capable of stirring up trouble.

Cody cleared his throat. "You should also include our other allies – we have agreements in place with witches and the lamia."

Froston and Talen both scowled when they heard the word 'lamia' but I nodded. "No harming our allies in any way." The last thing we needed was the fae coming back to our world and setting the races against each other.

"Talen is going to stay by your side," Froston informed me. "He'll keep you safe and help you with your magic."

I nodded in agreement but inside I was already starting to worry. He was going to have to stay in the pack house with me, but what about when I went to work? Could I trust him alone in the house with my pack mates?

"Do you have any healing skills?" I asked Talen hopefully. That was the magic that I wanted to learn.

"I can heal the earth."

I sighed and looked at Froston. That wasn't what I was hoping to hear, how was I going to progress with my healing skills? I wanted to talk to Austin about my idea for a clinic, but I didn't really have the skills to back up any of my plans yet. The thought of Airmed coming to my world to help me learn to heal wolves and humans was laughable. I'm sure she would prefer waterboarding.

I enacted barriers around Cody and myself to protect us from the elements. Froston had already explained that he had no choice but to open a portal in the human world in the Arctic because that's where the veil was the thinnest. Once we stepped into the Arctic, he could open a portal to anywhere in the human world and bring us back home.

I took Cody's hand and Froston's magic caused my skin to buzz as he formed a portal. I took one last look at the castle that had been my prison for so long and then happily stepped through into the mass of swirling wind and snow that waited for us on the other side.

Chapter 23

Sam

The sat phone did the beeping thing that let me know someone was trying to call in. I hurriedly snatched it up, eager for any news from the outside. The guys had all been driving me nuts in this little house, and James was seriously ready to rip someone's head off. I wasn't stupid – I was the most expendable person here, so it would probably be me.

I ran to the mudroom, skidding as I slid on the slippery floor. I shouted for Trevor, but hurriedly started to suit up without waiting for him. The phone's connection to a satellite wasn't strong enough to connect completely indoors, we needed to be outside under an open sky. The antenna was already extended, but the weak signal was fading in and out. Hopefully, being outdoors would clear that up.

Trevor walked into the mudroom just as I had pulled on the first outer layer that I needed to go out into the frigid temperature. "We have a call," I told him excitedly.

He gave me a brief nod and reached for his outdoor garb. James had already demanded that Rich and Davis help him out there with something, and Mike had just come off watch, so he was sleeping. I pulled on layer after layer, making it almost impossible for me to move comfortably. I covered my face with my scarf, put on my goggles, grabbed my weapon and I was ready to go.

It felt good to have a weapon in my hands again. When overseas, my rifle is within reach at all times. It never leaves my sight and it is usually in my hands. When I first get back to the states, I always feel naked for at least the first week without it. During the day, I'm never quite sure what to do with my hands since I'm not holding it. During the night, I'll wake up and reach for it, only to have a panic attack when it's not there. It takes me a couple of minutes to realize where I am and that I already turned in my weapon to the armory.

I had to wait another minute for Trevor to suit up before we were ready to head out. We made sure that the door to the main house was closed before opening the door to the outside. Freezing cold air blew into the room as we stepped out. We trudged a small distance from the house until the sat phone could pick up a steady signal.

As soon as we got the signal locked down, I made the call and held it in between myself and Trevor. Caleb answered, and I could hear the excitement in his voice. "We have movement! Take down these coordinates."

Trevor plugged the numbers into the GPS as Caleb shouted them out. He had to repeat them several times because our signal was unreliable. "What should we expect?" I asked Caleb worriedly.

The phone lost signal completely and I gave a sigh. If Caleb had been expecting danger, that would have been the first thing he told us, not the last. Caleb was probably hoping that this was Anna coming back to him, but my sixth sense was tingling. I had a feeling that this was not something good.

"I don't think we should be split up for this," I told Trevor seriously, after he had promised to report back to Caleb ASAP. "I don't like leaving Mike alone in the house and sleeping, he's vulnerable."

Trevor looked at me for a moment before nodding. Movement showed over the next hill of snow and I tensed. But it was James, leading Rich and Davis back to the house.

I waved frantically at James so that he would head over to me and Trevor, rather than to the house. His dark eyes weren't visible behind his goggles as he trudged over to us, but I could feel the black mood wafting over him.

Trevor explained the situation to James and got a sharp nod in return. "Davis, back to the house with Mike. The rest of us will check it out."

We waited until Davis had made it back to the house safely and shut the door behind him before following the coordinates that Caleb had given. They were very close to us – just over the next hill in the opposite direction that James and company had just come from.

As soon as we crested the hill my eyes opened in disbelief and I brought my weapon into firing position. Four men, dressed completely inappropriately for the weather, were arguing amongst themselves in their language. None of them had weapons, and all of them looked like they were dressed for a summer renaissance fair. They were definitely fae. Further away I saw what looked like a small group of shifters – probably wolves if they were up here. Were those the wolves that we had been sent after?

James held up an arm for us to stop. If these guys looked over in our direction, they would easily be able to see us. But this was our only chance – these guys had to be the fae that had taken Anna. Who else would just be wandering through the Arctic?

"We attack, but leave one of them alive for questioning," James ordered.

Trevor and I looked at him in shock - they didn't have weapons. And those hadn't been Austin's orders at all. He didn't want to start a war with the fae, he wanted to reach Anna's father and bargain to get her back. There was no guarantee that these fae had anything to do with Anna's abduction and captivity. Murdering fae could set off a chain of events that we wouldn't be able to stop.

James felt our indecision because he growled, and I could feel the pulse of his power roll over us. James was powerful enough that he could have been pack master of his own pack – but I think he was aware that he lacked the temperament to be a leader like Austin. I wasn't officially in their pack, so I wasn't as affected as the others, plus I had a little extra protection that they weren't aware of.

I guarded myself against the wave of power that James had sent out, but Trevor and Rich both raised their weapons, ready to fire. Unfortunately for us, one of the suspected fae caught sight of us at that moment. James was the first to hit the trigger and the rat-tat-tat of the weapon made it obvious he had it on automatic.

A fae dressed in bright red breeches and a matching top embroidered in gold waved his hand and our guns went flying. None of the fae were hit by any of the bullets, but we had their full attention now. My ears were ringing from the sound of the gunfire but I could make out that they were arguing even more intensively now. The shifters grouped more closely around the fae, looking nervously in our direction. I was completely unable to move as if I had been frozen in a block of ice. None of the other guys were moving either, so they must have been held by the same magic.

I squinted at the bonds that held us. I could barely make out the magic that was woven to hold us in place, but my parents had shown me how to undo basic things like this as a child. I hadn't done it in years, but I started to pick at the bonds, trying to get a grasp on a piece of magic I could use to unravel the whole thing. My magical abilities were almost non-existent, but that's what made me able to stay under the radar and avoid anyone able to pick up on power signatures.

A flash of light made me look up to see a portal opening right next to where the fae were standing. They looked up in surprise and I hurriedly worked on the magic encasing myself and the other guys while they were distracted. The first person that stepped out of the portal was what I thought was another fae, but he was dressed in jeans and a t-shirt. He immediately caught sight of the first group of fae and shouted. They started flinging magic at each other as more people came out of the portal. I finally pulled at the right combination of magical threads and the hold fell apart.

A man dressed in white and silver came through next to join the battle. James had immediately hurried through the snow to get one of the weapons that had been tossed away from us, so he missed who stepped through next. I gave a happy shout when I recognized Cody and Anna.

They were also inappropriately dressed for the weather but didn't show any signs of being cold. Anna stepped in front of Cody and I saw the faint glimmer of magic surround them that indicated that she had put up some kind of barrier.

That was new.

I went for my weapon as quickly as I could but was frustratingly slow through the snow. The first group of fae stumbled back through a portal, carrying one who looked like he had been wounded in the battle. The group of shifters followed close behind and barely made it through before the portal closed behind them. James had retrieved a weapon and was trudging through the snow towards Anna and the others. I pitied anyone who tried to get in the way.

Cody murmured into Anna's ear and she gave a happy cry when she saw James heading towards them. I saw James waver for a minute, deciding on whether to greet Anna or go after Froston. Anna made the decision for him by running up to him and flinging herself on him. I had to laugh when she actually took him down, and the other guys joined in. The relief that came after surviving a battle always made me a little giddy and I found myself giggling almost uncontrollably.

Chapter 24

Anna

I was crammed into the little house in the Arctic along with six wolves, two fae, and a panther, all of whom were glaring at each other in silence. I gave James's hand a squeeze to try and get him to relax – it had no effect. When I had first clasped his hand in mine he had looked down at our hands and blinked in surprise, but he hadn't objected or pulled away, so we were making progress.

I cleared my throat. I could tell that managing this group was going to be up to me since I was the common denominator. "Thank you for bringing Cody and me back, Froston." He gave a tight nod but didn't take his eyes off of James – I already had to break things up once between them.

"And Talen, thank you for agreeing to come back to Seaside with me to protect the pack." Talen gave me a *look*. I doubted that he had volunteered for this, and he definitely wasn't here to protect the pack, but I was trying to put a positive spin on things.

"James." I squeezed his hand for attention. "Froston and Talen have already agreed to come back to Seaside with us to protect our home against other fae." I reminded him.

I think Froston was more interested in protecting his investment and preventing other fae from snatching me up and using me against him. But once again, I was trying to stay positive.

There was still silence in the room, so I brought James's hand up to my mouth and gave it a bite hard enough to leave an indent but not draw blood. That got his attention.

"James," I said softly. "I know you accepted a mission from Ragnar to come up here, but there's no way you can defend yourselves against the fae."

"The real mission was to get you back," he grumbled irritably. Reminding James that he wasn't the biggest bad in the room was usually not a good idea, but in this case I think that he needed to accept it so that we could move forward.

I smiled at him. "Mission accomplished."

The rest of the team watched James carefully. He was going to decide if they all went back or stayed here. I knew that James still had the need for vengeance burning in his heart, but I was hoping that his love for me would win out.

"My agreement with Ragnar isn't complete," James admitted reluctantly. "My team needs to go back to Montreal briefly before we can go home to Seaside."

I gave a sad sigh. "Froston can make a portal for you to bring you directly back to Montreal." Froston and James glared at each other. "Right, Froston?" I prodded.

He gave a sharp nod and James ripped his eyes away from Froston to focus on me. His eyes softened so that I could see his affection for me shining through. "I hate to be away from you any longer, Anna. But now that I know you're safe I can follow through on my duty to the agreement."

I nodded. I didn't like it, but I understood it. Duty, honor, and commitment were hardwired into James, once he made a promise like that, he didn't break it. I went up on my toes to give him a peck on the lips. I knew it was difficult for him to show affection to me in front of others, so I did it for him.

James held my eyes for a moment and the corner of his mouth turned up in the beginning of a smile. Before it could spread completely over his face he looked away and his expression hardened again as he surveyed the team. "Trevor, Davis, I want you on guard outside to make sure no one else comes out of a fucking portal to surprise us. Mike, Sam, pack up our shit. Rich, you're outside with me while I report to Austin."

"I'll watch Froston and Talen in here," I volunteered quietly.

I saw a twitch of amusement cross James's face so briefly that I wasn't sure if I had imagined it or not. "Good idea, Anna. You can watch Cody, too." There was definitely a slight twinkle of amusement in his eyes this time, I didn't imagine it. But I did think I was the only one who saw it.

Sam pulled me to the side while the guys were occupied. "Anna, we need to talk when I get back to Seaside." She glanced at James which made me curious. Did something happen between them?

"What happened?" I murmured to her.

Sam just shook her head. "Later."

The team scattered in different directions and Talen scowled. "How long is this going to take?"

"You're stuck with me for the time being," I told Talen firmly. I turned to Froston when a thought lit up in my brain. "I think that Talen should report directly to me while he's here."

Froston arched an eyebrow.

"Our pack follows military structure," I explained to him. I'm sure that as a powerful lord of the fae with plenty of minions to order around, Froston would understand the importance of chain of command.

Froston looked at me and then at Talen. "The fae follow more 'might is right' guidelines, but after your display at court, I think Talen will agree that he doesn't wish to challenge you."

Talen scowled but reluctantly agreed. I watched him carefully, I had a feeling that he would be testing me in the near future to see what he could get away with.

"Since we are here for a few minutes, let's talk about the fae that were outside," I said strongly.

"Summer fae." Talen snarled.

"And wolves," Cody added quietly. "The wolves followed them right back into their world."

I reached for Cody to give his hand a squeeze. "Apparently, the prince isn't the only one using the wolves."

Froston shrugged. "Well, technically the wolves are part of Summer."

Cody and I stared at him.

"Wolves are the descendants of lesser Summer fae shifters that stayed in the human world when the rest of us left. They didn't have magic to do anything other than shift, so they thought they could create better lives for themselves here," Froston explained.

I frowned. "Are there still these wolf-fae in the Summer Court?"

"Yes," Talen growled. "But they aren't like you. Being in the human world and breeding with *them* has changed your kind into something new."

I exchanged a look with Cody. Talen made it clear that he wasn't that fond of humans, how was he going to do here in the human world?

Sam and Mike came back into the room, carrying multiple packs of gear. Cody went over to help them but Talen and Froston just watched without expression. Cody shooed me away when I went over to help but I just rolled my eyes. If Sam could carry that stuff, why couldn't I? Granted, she was in much better shape than I was. As a marine on deployment she would have been walking miles every day through a desert while carrying a thirty-pound bag filled with military gear.

James stuck his head in through the door of the mudroom and shouted for us, indicating that it was time to get going. Everyone else suited up in their outdoor gear, but I put the barriers around Cody and myself and the fae did the same.

We trudged outside into the snow and Froston reached for me. "I'm testing my limits by making this many portals, Anna. Lend me some of your magic?"

I narrowed my eyes at him suspiciously but gave him my hand. "How much magic are you going to take?"

Froston gave me a sad smile. "I know your experiences have been negative up until now, but I don't need to *take* anything from you. You can give it to me willingly and stay in control of the flow."

I closed my eyes, so I could focus better on my magic. I still had an excess that was swirling around inside of me, so I really did have some to spare. I felt Froston open up and I pushed some magic towards him, my nerves on edge. A part of me was waiting for him to try to grab ahold of my magic like the king and Drake had and I was tensed for a potential battle. But Froston just accepted the amount that I had given to him and withdrew.

I let out the breath that I had been holding and opened my eyes to see Froston's broad grin. I still didn't fully trust him, and I wondered if he had truly needed some of my magic, or if he had just wanted it.

He opened a portal in front of us and Davis and Mike went through first. Mike stuck his head back out and called an okay.

Sam and the other guys went through one by one, but James hesitated. He grasped Trevor's shoulder. "Can I trust you to complete the mission?"

Trevor gave him a wide grin. "Of course. I would have questioned your sanity if you were willing to leave Anna this soon."

"Keeping her safe is my top priority."

I rolled my eyes. I think that at this point, James should have been asking me to take care of everyone else. I was the only one here that had a chance of standing up to another fae attack. Although, the magic battle from earlier did make me doubt myself a little. The fae had been flinging magic at each other faster than I could follow. I couldn't even tell what some of those magical weaves were meant to do if they reached their opponent.

I may have bested a fae in a magical tug of war, but I was still a clumsy child when it came to using my magic for more advanced things. Somehow, I doubted that any other fae would be giving me the opening to drain them of magic again, they wouldn't underestimate me as easily. If I had to fight to get past one of their barriers to drain their magic, I'm not sure if I would be able to. I would have to let them think that they had a chance to drain mine.

After Trevor had passed through the portal and it closed behind him, Froston opened another one. My heart sped up in excitement as I saw the familiar view of the wide expanse of our back lawn that led up to the patio. I was right on Froston's heels as I walked through the portal and tugged Cody behind me.

We stepped through and I dropped the barriers that had protected Cody and I from the harsh elements of the Arctic, but were also preventing me from taking in the scent of home. I breathed in deep, smelling the fresh cut lawn, the scent of the forest almost fifty feet away, and the very faint scent of an ocean breeze beyond that.

James started pulling off layers of gear that had protected him from the Arctic cold now that we were in a more temperate climate.

I heard a happy bark and turned to see my two little pups running full speed for me. I couldn't stop the huge smile that spread across my face and I knelt to greet them. "Oh, my sweet babies! I missed you so much!" I wasn't even embarrassed to use the super high voice that I reserved for my pups.

Cody chuckled but the fae had looks of distaste on their face.

"Those don't look like wolves…" Talen said in confusion.

I just gave him a glare and then turned to see Caleb heading for us. He must have been taking the pups outside for a potty break while we had appeared.

"Caleb!" I ran to meet him and wrapped him in a tight hug as the pups danced happily at our feet, begging for more of my attention.

"I missed you," Caleb murmured to me, giving my forehead a kiss before turning his attention to the fae.

"This is Froston and Talen," I told him as I stepped back from our hug. "Talen is going to be staying with us for a little while."

"Austin approved that?" Caleb asked in surprise.

"Well…" Technically, I hadn't asked Austin before agreeing to my deal with the fae. But if that was part of the conditions required for me to return to the pack, would he object? Cody had been there for our negotiation. Surely, he would have spoken up if he thought Austin would disagree.

I bit my lip and looked at Cody worriedly.

"Don't worry, I think I can speak for Aus when I say that we would rather have you back with an extra fae than have to live without you," Cody assured me.

Froston just shrugged. "Anna, dear. I will be back to look at the wards that Talen helps you put up. For now, I have important matters that need my attention."

We stood there awkwardly for a minute. I didn't feel like our relationship was strong enough to warrant hugs, but he was my father… Froston looked amused when I held out my hand. "Thanks for bringing me back home," I told him with a firm handshake.

I could tell Cody was hiding a grin, but Caleb looked as awkward as I felt. What was the protocol for thanking your kidnapping fae father for bringing you home?

Froston shook his head in amusement one last time before creating another portal, giving us a wave before stepping through.

Talen gave a sigh. "Can you at least offer me some refreshments before we start on the wards?"

"I was just working on dinner when I got the call from James." Caleb told us.

"I'm going in to update Austin," James grumbled as he walked away.

"Are Austin and the other guys inside?" I asked eagerly, following behind James and picking up the scarf he dropped.

Caleb gave me a smile. "Austin is off the premises, but he'll be back as soon as we let him know you're here." He gave Talen a suspicious glance so he probably didn't feel comfortable being more specific in front of our guest.

Cody gave me a nudge to turn around. "The twins should be here any minute."

I saw a flash of brown fur in the woods across the lawn and grinned. I took a few steps forward and tore the delicate fae dress at the neckline before shifting. I wiggled out of the torn remnants of the dress and shook out my coat before running to meet my twins as they burst out of the trees. I gave a happy yip as I crashed into Jason and we rolled into Mason. I was the first to jump up and bounced around them excitedly. I couldn't get enough of their scents and happily took turns pouncing on both of them alternately.

They were both rotating between getting my scent and licking my face, so it was a frenzied mess of a greeting. After we had all calmed down a little, I gave them each an affectionate nuzzle. If I were in my human form, I probably would have cried with joy. But I embraced who I was as a wolf and gave into my instincts, letting out a joyous howl. They both joined in and I heard the answering howls from wolves around the property. Austin had even more pack members on guard duty than ever before, judging by the answering chorus.

I leaned my weight up against Mason and gave his face one last lick before trotting back to where Cody, Caleb and Talen waited for us. I saw the longing in Caleb's and Cody's eyes – they would have joined in the celebration if it wasn't for the fae that was currently scowling in one of our patio chairs.

Talen had flung himself into a chair with a petulant look on his face. "Are you done, yet?"

I growled and snapped at him, letting him know that I was the one in charge here. The twins circled around Talen as they growled, backing up my threat. Talen's eyes widened a little when he realized he was surrounded by the three of us, and I was glad to see that he did have the sense to be afraid.

"Let's go in," Cody suggested. "Caleb and I'll watch your friend while you get changed."

I hesitated at the doorway. One of Austin's rules was no wolves in the house, but this was a special circumstance and my paws were relatively clean. Although, if Austin found white wolf hairs in the house, there was going to be no doubt who they were from. The twins seemed torn between following the rules, sticking close to the stranger, and not wanting to leave my side.

After a moment of hesitation Jason leapt into the house after me. Mason gave Talen one last growl and followed him into the house. I started to head for the stairs but turned to give Talen one last warning. He held up his hands in defense as I snapped at him and held his gaze, making my threat clear. "I understand, Anna," he murmured. "I'll wait right down here and behave myself."

I glared at him for a moment longer before trotting off with my head and tail held high. The twins raced me up the stairs to my room and shifted to their human forms. I only hesitated for a split second before shifting. This was Mason and Jason. My twins. My loves.

Jason enveloped me in a tight hug the second I was fully human and Mason followed suit. "Fuck, Anna," Jason murmured into my hair.

I gave his neck a bite and he started to laugh. Mason pushed aside my hair and gave my neck a bite and then we were all laughing. Both of the twins released their death grips on me and took half a step back. Before I left, I would have been freaking out on the inside about being naked in the same room with naked men. But now? I was just happy to be back with my twins, they had both seen all of me before, and I wasn't going to hide any part of myself from them.

Mason mussed my hair. "You've gotten feisty since you've been away."

Jason grinned. "You're more wolf than ever."

"I'm more Anna than ever," I told him seriously.

They both gave me matching grins and my heart started to beat faster. Having their naked bodies close to me was giving me more than just a 'welcome back' vibe. Instead of withdrawing or trying to hide my feelings, I pressed my mouth to Mason's. Living with Cody had made me realize that a lot of my fears and insecurities were unfounded and that I needed to live in the moment.

Mason froze in surprise but then returned my kiss passionately. We devoured each other with our mouths, words not necessary to communicate our feelings. I had felt like a piece of me had been missing the entire time I was in the fae world, and now I was complete.

Jason groaned and pushed my hair aside to kiss my shoulder. "Now this is how a reunion should go."

Mason pulled away from me with a smile. "May I suggest a shower?"

I grinned back at him. "You gonna wash my back?"

"Something like that," Jason murmured as he gave my bottom a squeeze.

I gave a throaty chuckle and Mason licked his lips expectantly. Jason surprised me by picking me up and throwing me over his shoulder. "You're all ours now, Anna."

I smacked his very nice, firm bottom, of which I had a really good view of. "That's what you think. You're actually mine."

"I'm okay with that." Mason told me with a grin as he followed Jason into my bathroom.

Jason turned on the shower and ice cold water shot out to hit my butt and the back of my thighs. I squealed in surprise and both of the guys laughed. "You're going to regret that." I threatened him. I think they would have taken my threat a little more seriously if I wasn't helplessly dangling over Jason's shoulder.

The thought of using my magic to get the upper hand briefly crossed my mind, but I wanted a little more 'normal' time with them. I wanted to go back to the easy camaraderie that we had before I left. I wasn't ready to reveal just how much of a fae I had become.

Mason stepped into the shower first to test the water before Jason set me down gently. Even though the mansion had absurdly large rich-people showers, it was crowded with three people, especially when two of them were large men over six feet tall.

Jason leaned against the wall to watch as Mason squirted some of my body wash onto a loofah. "I want to spoil you a little." He murmured as he took hold of my arm and started to wash me.

I looked at him suspiciously for a moment, expecting this to turn into a prank. But my skin wasn't turning blue from the soap and Mason was gazing at me lovingly as he gently washed.

"I missed you." I told him as I got on my tiptoes to give him a kiss.

A smile spread over his face and I took the loofah from him. It was erotic the way that my soapy skin slid over his, my nipples hardening with my arousal. "You should let me wash you." I said in a husky voice that sounded deeper than usual.

"Nope." Mason told me with a grin. "We already decided it was spoil Anna day, there's no changing it now."

"Let me in on this." Jason said as he stood up and stepped into the shower with us.

I stepped back to let Jason all the way into the shower but bumped into Mason. "Guys, I don't think the logistics of this is going to work out."

Jason gave me a wicked grin. "I know how we can make this work."

Mason pulled my hips so that my bottom was flush against him. "I can definitely make this work." He murmured into my ear before kissing the side of my neck. His erection was pressed up against me so I couldn't help but wiggle against him. He groaned but moved his hands up to cup my breasts.

Jason surprised me by dropping to his knees in front of us. I had to lean my weight completely against Mason when Jason pulled one of my legs over his shoulder.

Jason looked up at me to watch my reaction as he teased me with a finger, circling around my clit, but not touching. I was throbbing with need before he even lowered his mouth to me. He slid his tongue along my slit in one long lick before focusing on my sensitive bud. The sensation of his tongue tasting and teasing me was almost too much to bear.

"Get her ready for me, Jase." Mason murmured as he played with my breasts, teasing my nipples.

I panted as desire flooded through me and heat pooled in my core. Jason was using his tongue to whip me into a frenzy and the sensation of Mason pressed up against me as he played with my sensitive nipples was almost too much to bear. My body was on fire with need.

"I'm so close…" I gasped out. "I need.."

Without warning, Jason sat back on his haunches before standing and backing up. I made a noise of complaint, but Mason was quick to spin us around and pin my back against the wall. He hoisted me up a few inches and I reflexively wrapped my legs around his waist. The tiles were cool against my back, but felt good with the heat of Mason's body pressed against my front.

I squirmed to rub against him, greedy to have him inside of my aching core. Mason reached down to guide himself into me but paused at my entrance. I could feel the tip of him pressing against me, driving me insane.

"Please, Mason." I cried out.

He inched his way inside with excruciating slowness, causing me to moan with pleasure. The sensation of him working his way into my needy core caused my lower belly to clench, I had never wanted him as much as I did now.

He paused again once he was fully inside me and my muscles clenched around him. "You okay, pretty girl?"

"I will be." I panted, I was overwhelmed with a sense of fullness but eager for him to really begin.

He gave a dark chuckle and started to thrust inside of me, starting slow but moving faster with each stroke.

My eyes met Jason's as Mason found a rhythm that was quickly pushing me to the edge. "I love the sexy little noises you make. Are you going to cry out my name when I'm pounding my way into you?" He fondled himself as he spoke and I licked my lips at the sexy sight.

The combination of Mason hitting exactly the right spot inside of me and Jason's dirty talk was enough to push me past the brink and send me into oblivion.

"Fuck." Mason panted. "I can feel you squeezing me."

He gripped my thighs harder and came inside of me with one last thrust. We held still for a moment and just basked in the pleasure of being together. Eventually he let go of my legs but they were too weak to hold me up. I slid slowly down the wall, my legs like jelly.

"I got her." Jason said as he pushed Mason back and took hold of me. He claimed my mouth with his and the feel of his body pressed against me caused another wave of heat to crest over my body.

Desire built up inside me once again as he turned me to face the wall and cupped a breast in his hand. "Anna, I want you so bad." He crooned as his erection pressed up against my ass. I ground up against him so that he was pressed between my cheeks and groaned. I was more than ready to have him inside of me.

I leaned forward to grasp the railing of the shower door and bent over, allowing him access to me. He moaned as he rubbed himself against my already slick center. "Don't be gentle." I urged him. Mason had gotten me more than ready to handle Jason being a little rough and I was eager for it.

Jason followed my request and shoved into me with one stroke, filling me completely. He grasped my hips and the angle at which he drove into me made it feel that he was even deeper inside me. He thrust into me relentlessly and I held onto the railing for dear life. The feeling of his cock pumping inside of me brought me to new heights of delirious pleasure.

I rode the wave of bliss higher and higher until an orgasm exploded through me, sending shock waves through my core. Wave after wave of endless pleasure crested through me and I felt Jason let go with a strangled cry.

He slid out of me slowly once the agonizing pleasure had faded into a satisfied buzz. He wrapped his arms around me tightly as I stood up completely. With his face buried into my wet hair, I felt his ragged breath against my ear.

"I can never lose you again." He said roughly. "I wouldn't survive it."

"You won't." I assured him, running my hands over his arms comfortingly as he squeezed me even tighter. I could feel his emotion as he clung to me and recognized his embrace for what it was. I had known for a while that the twins had abandonment issues from their past and losing me had triggered something inside of Jason. Something dark and desolate.

I tapped his arms to let me go so that I could turn to look in his eyes. "Jason." I said firmly as I cupped his face with my hands. "I'll never leave you."

He searched my eyes with a hint of wild desperation. "I know, it's just…"

"Even if we are physically apart, I'm still here with you in your heart." I lowered one of my hands to place it over his beating heart. "I'll always find you, and I'll always come back to you. I love you."

That seemed to calm him, because he took a ragged breath. "Anna, I love you too. I just don't have all the right words…"

I smiled at him. "You don't need to tell me with words."

He relaxed completely and gave me a more normal smile, the light coming back into his eyes. I squished his face to give him fish lips and he swatted me away with a huge grin.

The three of us finished our shower properly and cleaned up. But not without accidentally getting soap in each other's eyes and elbowing each other in the ribs multiple times. This shower was really not made for three people. "Next time maybe we should go for the hot tub?" I suggested with a grin.

Both of the guys perked up and gave me matching grins. "See, that's why we need you, Anna." Jason said with a smirk. "You're the brains of this operation."

I rolled my eyes as Jason stepped out of the shower and opened the linen closet for some towels.

While he was distracted, Mason grabbed my arm. "Thank you." He told me with a serious look in his eyes. "We both wanted to hear that, but Jason needed it."

My heart melted. I'm sure that Mason would have had his hands full while I was gone, but a part of me bled for him. He was the one who would have kept it together while Jason panicked and acted out. He was the voice of reason between the two of them, but that didn't mean that he suffered any less, or didn't feel everything that Jason did. It just meant that he hid his feelings deeper inside so that his brother would have someone to lean on. It had been that way since they were two scared little wolf pups locked in a cage, terrified that they would never get out.

I wrapped my arms around him. "I meant every word for both of you. I worried about you while I was gone."

Mason dropped a kiss on the top of my head. "I worried about you too, I'm glad you're back. I promise that we're going to keep you safe from now on."

I smiled at his words, but deep down I was worried. The guys couldn't protect me from the threats to come. They were going to have to learn to rely on me to take the lead and keep our pack safe. I felt a flicker of self-doubt but quickly chased it away. My guys needed me, and I wasn't going to let them down. I could do this – I wouldn't let anything stop me.

Chapter 25

Anna

I rubbed a towel through my hair and stepped out of the bathroom, but Jason stopped me with his hands on my hips. "I need to make sure you have enough of our scent on you still," he murmured as he rubbed up against me.

I giggled. "Maybe you should just give me one of your hoodies to wear."

His eyes lit up and he gave me a quick peck on the lips. "Be right back."

I rolled my eyes as I headed into my closet to find some clothes, but Mason trailed after me with a frown. "What about my scent?"

I flung a pair of my most comfortable leggings at him. "Can you put your scent on these?"

He rubbed them up against his face but still grumbled. "But you're going to wear Jason's clothes?"

I sighed as I pulled on my panties. "His hoodie… and one of your t-shirts?" I was pretty excited to be home to wear my own clothes instead of the fae dresses, but honestly, I liked being wrapped in their scents just as much. It gave me the feeling of safety and home.

Mason gave me a huge grin and tossed the leggings back at me. They hit me in the face because my hands were occupied getting my bra on. I pouted but Mace just kept grinning, so as soon as my clasp was secure I followed him out of the closet and threw a shoe at him.

He grunted when the shoe hit him right on his naked ass and almost ran right into Austin, who was just stepping into my room. There was a moment of tension when Austin froze at the sight of Mason leaving my room while completely naked. Emotions flickered over his face too quickly for me to read before they settled into warning. I could tell they were using the pack bond when Mason held his hands up defensively and a second later Austin gave him a reassured nod. Mason slid out the door and I had Austin to myself.

"Austin!" I shouted happily, wanting to break the tension. I was ecstatic to see Austin again, but nervous at his reaction to running into a naked Mace. I didn't think it was a secret that I had become intimate with the twins, but knowing something and having in right in front of your face were two very different things.

Austin's eyes widened briefly when he realized I wasn't completely dressed either, but this was a whole new Anna. My undies covered more than a lot of bikinis did, and I wasn't ashamed of what I looked like. Cody and the twins had been very vocal about just how much they enjoyed all of my curves, so I wasn't embarrassed to wrap Austin in a hug. Whatever issues he had with Mason had been worked out for the moment.

I could feel his hesitation for a split second, but then he relaxed into my embrace. I took a deep breath and inhaled *Austin*. He was warmth and strength, power and acceptance, the center of our pack. I laid my head against his chest, feeling the smooth fabric of his dress shirt against my cheek and listening for the comforting beat of his heart.

Austin kissed the top of my head and rubbed my lower back. "Anna, I need to apologize to you," he murmured quietly.

I raised my head nervously. "For what?"

His eyes were troubled as they met mine. "For failing to keep you safe."

Was that it? I smiled in relief and gave him a squeeze. "Austin, honestly there is nothing you could have done. Plus, things worked out for the best in the end."

He shook his head in denial and I could see the guilt in his eyes. "I promised to protect you. I promised that you would be safe here with my pack."

I pulled away to hold his hands in mine. "The fae are …impossible. But one of the reasons that Talen came back with me is to fortify our defenses against them."

Austin's face darkened. "Yes, we're going to need to talk about that. I've already spoken with Talen regarding the conditions for him staying here."

Jason burst back in the room and tossed a hoodie at me. Austin grabbed it out of the air before it could hit me in the face and handed it to me. Mason was only a few steps behind him with a t-shirt. Both of them were fully dressed, so it was just me that needed to make myself decent.

I pulled on the t-shirt as I went back in the closet for my leggings. "As soon as I get dressed, let's go down and get something to eat. I'm starving, and I have so much to tell you!"

"Let's be careful about what we say in front of our guest," Austin cautioned me. "We can discuss things in detail later when it's just us."

I stepped out of the closet, now fully dressed. "I kind of promised to keep him close," I told Austin sheepishly.

"Cody already told me about that." Austin gave me a warm smile as he put an arm around me to walk me out the door. "We can give him a room in the house, that's close enough."

The twins followed close behind me. "Cody said you can do magic now?" Mason asked curiously.

When did Cody have time to tell them that? Maybe with the pack bond?

"Do something cool," Jason urged me.

"You wanna see something really cool?" I asked with a grin, stepping away from Austin to get some space.

Austin looked almost as interested as the twins did so I formed a mini-fireball in my hands and tossed it back and forth until it fizzled out.

The twins watched with open mouths but Austin was more reserved. "I think we need a 'no fire in the house' rule," he told me seriously.

I just shrugged. I couldn't really think of a reason why I would need to use fire other than to light a candle while in the house anyway. I bounced down the stairs with the guys following behind. I glanced behind me when I reached the bottom of the stairs and frowned when I realized they were using the pack bond to talk – probably about me.

I whirled around and held out a hand to stop Austin when he was on the last step. He raised an eyebrow at me in question and I hid a smile. Austin wasn't used to me being assertive, but he was going to have to get used to the new Anna.

"I want to be included in the pack bond," I announced. "There's really no rational reason to exclude me."

I heard the twins make murmurs of agreement but they quieted down after a glance from Austin. He watched me for a moment and I started to lose hope. Had Austin changed his mind about me while I was gone? Was he having second thoughts?

Because Austin was on a step higher than me, he was even taller than usual. I had to tilt my head up to search his eyes. I tried to look confident and hide the fact that his hesitation was tearing me up inside.

"You're right, Anna." He finally told me with a sigh. "That was one of my biggest regrets after you disappeared. If I had let you into our pack bond sooner, then it would have been easier to locate you."

I let out the breath I had been holding but felt a little bad about pushing Austin when I saw the unhappiness on his face. I already knew that he was dealing with guilt about losing me to the fae. But being a full member of the pack was really important to me. I craved it with every fiber of my being.

"When?" I asked eagerly.

Austin gave me a smile. "With the six of us? Tonight. The rest of the pack can wait."

I bounced over to Austin and gave him a hug. I could tell that he was surprised – being physically affectionate was not something I had been comfortable with before. But he needed to get used to the new, fearless Anna. I had fully embraced who I was and a large part of that was my wolf half.

That part of me needed physical touch from my packmates. My week with Cody in the fae world had changed how I looked at myself and made me more comfortable with everything that made me a wolf. His lessons on wolves had made me realize that so much of what I suppressed was perfectly natural and acceptable.

After I pulled away from Austin, Mason mussed my hair. "Now we'll never lose you."

Jason grinned. "You won't be able to hide from us, even if you wanted to."

I just laughed and walked towards the kitchen, I could smell something delicious that was calling my name. Caleb had said he was in the process of making dinner, and I hoped that it was almost done because I was starving. All the stress and magic made me work up an appetite – not to mention the welcome back sex.

I turned the corner but stopped and stood still when I heard a feminine giggle. My eyes narrowed, and I stalked into the kitchen to see what female was in my territory. I recognized the deep tones of Cody's voice mixing with the feminine giggle and I started to see red.

My eyes were focused on the stranger when I entered the kitchen. What was a female doing here in *my* home with *my* wolves? She had better not think that she could take my place here.

Cody stood up to greet me. "Anna, this is Gemma." He gestured to a petite brunette with a shy smile.

"From the Montreal Pack," Caleb reminded me gently, looking a little alarmed at the steam that must be coming out of my ears.

That's right. I'd forgotten that Trevor had told us about the female halfling that wanted to visit. I relaxed and realized how aggressive I had almost gotten over a harmless giggle. What had gotten into me?

Gemma had definitely noticed my hostile attitude because she had taken shelter behind Cody. My vision tunneled on the hand that she had placed on his arm and I felt a surge of aggressiveness rise up again. *Mine.*

Austin put his arm around me. "Anna," he murmured to me. "It looks like you've become more in touch with your wolf instincts."

I blinked and shook off the weird emotions that were trying to overwhelm me. Is that what had gotten into me? Was this normal? "I'm sorry, Gemma. I guess I'm just a little sensitive about being replaced while I was gone."

Gemma gave me a small smile. "I understand," she murmured before lowering her eyes to the ground.

Austin wrapped his arms around me and gave me a kiss on the cheek before murmuring in my ear. "No one could ever replace you, you'll always be our top female."

I relaxed again and the guys took that as a signal to start grabbing plates and setting the table. The kitchen was full of everyone in motion but I still watched Gemma warily. My instincts were screaming at me that she was an enemy, but I pushed those feelings away. Gemma was obviously shy and I was being rude. I should be welcoming her into my home, not acting like I wanted to attack her. I thought about Reagan and shuddered. I did *not* want to become her.

I looked at Austin sheepishly but was surprised to see a little bit of pride in his eyes. "Your protectiveness shows that you consider us to be truly yours," he explained quietly in my ear as the rest of the group loudly went about getting dinner. I started to walk over to the stove to see what I could do to help, but Austin took my hand to lead me to the seat next to him. "Relax, you deserve a little bit of pampering now that we have you back."

I gave him a warm smile and he raised my hand to his mouth to give it a kiss. "We missed you."

"I missed all of you." I murmured to him. It felt so good to be here and be surrounded by my pack again. The warmth, the laughter, and the energy in the room made me feel more alive than ever.

Once everyone was seated Austin raised his hand for quiet. "Talen, thank you for joining us tonight. I believe that you'll have no problem following the pack rules we discussed earlier during your stay here."

Talen raised his glass of wine and gave Austin a nod.

"This is the plan for tonight," Austin continued. "After dinner, the twins can show Talen to his room and make sure Gemma is settled in for the evening. Then the seven of us have something important to do on the beach tonight."

I grinned at Austin. It was finally happening, I was going to be an official part of the pack tonight. I couldn't wait to be a part of the pack bond, I had a feeling that it was going to make my relationship with the guys even stronger.

"Anna, would you mind filling us in on what has happened to you during the days you were gone?"

I cleared my throat and looked around the table. "It may have been days for you, but it's been weeks for me. Time moves differently in the fae world…"

I told a generalized and slightly more positive version of the events that I had been through while in the fae world, and the guys listened quietly with surprise etched on their faces. A lot of my story seemed unbelievable, even to me, and I had been there.

I was careful about what I said about King Illian, Drake, and Froston because I wasn't really sure where Talen's loyalties laid. I could tell by the look in Austin's eyes that he realized I was leaving things out but he didn't question me. I had a feeling that there was going to be a lot of questions when we finally got our private meeting.

I had looked around while I was talking and my eyes kept being drawn back to Gemma. She seemed quiet and nice, someone who I should want to be friends with, but a part of me just did *not* like her. I saw James watching her as well with a look of suspicion on his face, but he looked at everyone like that.

I was torn between wanting to trust my instincts and feeling guilty about my Reagan-like behavior. Over the past few weeks I had been working really hard to get in touch with my wolf side and to indulge that part of myself that I had kept suppressed for so long. Clearly, letting my wolf side *completely* free wasn't a good thing, I needed to find balance.

Cody chimed in on some of the details I had skimmed over while James just watched me with his dark eyes unreadable. The twins still seemed a little in awe of my newfound powers and I looked at them nervously. Was this going to change how they felt about me?

Both of the twins gave me wide grins and Mason shook his head at me. "Don't worry, pretty girl. We'll make sure the pack doesn't spoil you, even if you are some kind of royalty."

I laughed. His words brought me back to the first night I had spent here at the mansion. Mason had promised me then that he wouldn't let the pack spoil me, after revealing how rare female wolves were. The twins had taken me in and made me a partner in their shenanigans.

I had been afraid that they would either think less of me for being fae, or put me on a pedestal for being able to use magic. I was glad to hear that nothing was going to change. I wanted them to see me as an equal and to accept me as one of them.

After dinner, Caleb helped me with the dishes while the twins were upstairs with Talen and Gemma. The other guys were preparing something outside for the pack bond ceremony. They had asked me to stay inside while they worked, so that it would be a surprise. I was nervous and excited at the same time and was almost jumping out of my skin with anticipation.

"Anna?" Caleb asked me quietly.

I set down the dish I had been scrubbing aggressively and gave him my full attention. "Yeah?"

"Have you considered that you were set up?"

I frowned at him. "Set up for what?"

Caleb set down the towel he had been using to dry dishes and took a step closer to me. "Froston and Drake – I don't think they were honest with why they brought you there."

I nodded slowly. "Yeah, none of their reasons or explanations made that much sense to me. Froston told me that he was forced to take me so that 'others' wouldn't. I assumed he meant the prince, but he never really said. I felt like I was missing something the entire time I was there."

"And Froston told you that the prince found out about you by sensing a flare of your power, right?"

I searched Caleb's eyes. What had he figured out that I had missed?

Caleb reached for my hands. "Anna, what if the prince felt your power and set you up to take on his father?"

I laughed. "Why would he think that someone like me would ever be able to take down an immortal, all-powerful fae that had ruled their world for hundreds of years?"

Caleb raised an eyebrow. "Because an immortal, all-powerful fae that had ruled their world for hundreds of years would be too arrogant to realize what a threat you were until it was too late. A king like that would have probably never let down his guard for another fae - he underestimated you and it cost him everything."

I thought about that. It still seemed a little ridiculous that I was able to take someone like him down, but was Caleb right? I saw how ecstatic Drake had been when his father fell. If I had failed, the prince wouldn't have lost anything. I would have been sent back with my father and no one would have guessed that Drake had any ill intentions towards his father. Drake had made me believe that he was competing with his brothers for his father's affection, did the rest of the court believe that as well?

"And you think Froston knew?" I asked him cautiously. Froston had shown me time and again that he wasn't the caring father I wanted, but deep down I still had a tiny kernel of hope that just wouldn't die. I really wanted to believe that he was a good guy, even though evidence kept showing up to the contrary.

"Did he try to stop you?" Caleb asked me pointedly.

I thought back to the moment in the throne room when I had started to take magic from the fae around me. Froston had realized what I was doing and stood by, not saying a word to stop me. "No." I said quietly. "He didn't."

Caleb nodded. "I think there's more to this than either of us realize."

I sighed. "I agree. When I first arrived in their world, my father told me that he was deeply indebted to the king, but he didn't say why. Maybe he thought this was his chance to get rid of his debt?"

"And maybe the prince made a deal with him." Caleb added. "Maybe Froston wants the future king indebted to him, not the other way around."

"There's no guarantee that Drake will be king." I mused out loud. "Froston said the three princes are going to be fighting over the throne."

"And who do you think Froston will be fighting for?" Caleb asked me pointedly.

"I just hope they leave us out of all of it." I told him tiredly. "I've had more than enough of the fae to last me a lifetime."

He laughed. "I hope so too." He paused and looked worried so I reached to give him a hug. I wrapped my arms around his waist and he embraced me in return. I inhaled Caleb's scent and relaxed in his arms.

"Catch me up on what I missed here?" I asked him softly.

Caleb laughed. "Not much, except for the entire pack being frantic and trying to get you back."

I gave him a shoulder bump. "Other than everyone getting an ulcer, though?"

Caleb shook his head. "Some serious stuff went down between Austin and the council. Emerys gave me some info about the lamia's relationship with the fae."

"Yeah, I picked up that there are some issues there." Froston and Talen had been hostile at the mention of lamia, so the two races were definitely not on friendly terms.

"Tell me about the wards that Talen is supposed to help with." Caleb said. "How are they supposed to keep us safe?"

"We're going to have two." I told him. "The first one is going to be only on the house, and it's going to prevent anyone from entering who means us harm. It's too complicated and involved to be able to put in over the whole property, so that's where the second one comes in." I paused to gather my thoughts. "I'm not sure how the one over our property is going to work, but somehow it's going to alarm us if anyone crosses the barrier line. That will give us enough time to get into the house and organize our defenses."

"That's smart." Caleb told me with a grin.

I shrugged and tried not to look worried. "It sounds really complicated to put in place. I'm not sure we can do it without Froston's help."

"And if we have Froston's help, the barrier won't protect us against him." Caleb surmised.

"Or Talen." I added. "I'm not sure what happens if we put up a barrier and the person that means us harm is already in here. It might treat them as someone who needs to be protected."

Caleb sighed. "Nothing is ever easy."

We held each other for a couple minutes and I just enjoyed Caleb's presence. I had missed the steady comfort that he always managed to give me so effortlessly. It felt good to be back here with him.

Caleb gave me a shy smile. "So, having magic is probably going to up the level of pranks you're able to pull on James, huh?"

"Yeah…" My eyes lit up. I hadn't considered that until now, but I was going to have to have a serious discussion with the twins. We had pranks to plan.

Caleb laughed and hung up the towel he had been using as I put away the last dish. "Let's get the twins and go out?" I suggested. I was eager to get started on the events planned for this evening.

The twins came in right on cue. But my eyes widened when I saw Jason carrying Evelyn's urn. I had planned on saying my final goodbyes to Evelyn multiple times now, but each time my plans had been derailed.

Mason cleared his throat. "We thought you might want to say goodbye first? Before starting a new chapter of your life with us?"

Tears came to my eyes and Jason looked nervous. "Or not?"

I shook my head. "No, that's perfect."

This was the perfect time to say my goodbyes to Evelyn. She had guided me through much of my life, and whether that was because she was being paid by my father or not wasn't relevant. I think that she had done the best she could, and I didn't blame her for what had gone wrong with my childhood. I believed what I had told Cody. It sucked, but I wouldn't be the person that I was now if I hadn't lived through it.

Letting the ocean breeze carry her ashes away would be cathartic and symbolic of me letting everything from the past go.

I wouldn't just be saying goodbye to Evelyn, I would be saying goodbye to my old life, to the old Anna, to all the memories and pain that had held me back for so long. I needed to let go of all of that before I could be free to live my new life with the men I loved.

I walked outside with Caleb and the twins, following the path that led us out to our own section of beach. Our spirits were high, and we laughed and joked the entire way. Cody, James, and Austin were already waiting for us around a bonfire that they had built while we had been inside.

I looked around at my circle of guys. Austin, our fearless leader, with the fire glinting off his dark blond hair. James, my dark warrior, watching the twins warily as they got precariously close to the flames. Cody, my giant wolf, making Caleb smile in spite of the nervous look on his face. My twins, my partners in crime, daring each other to jump in the freezing cold water. Caleb, my sweet wolf, waiting for me to join them.

Austin gestured for me to join him as the rest of the guys encouraged me.

This was it. I was home.

I took a deep breath and took the first step towards my new life.

Epilogue

Talen

I watched 'Gemma' carefully. She was good, but not good enough to hide from me. She excused herself from the wolves to use the bathroom and I slipped into the hall to intercept her. No one noticed me go, because no one cared about my presence to begin with.

I sauntered up to her and leaned a shoulder against the wall. "Well, well, well, *Deirfiúr bheag*. I'm debating on whether or not I want to reveal your secret to the group."

She dropped the innocent little victim act and stood up straight, pushing her shoulders back to confront me. "You won't." She told me confidently.

I shrugged a shoulder. "Why not? The ensuing drama should be enough to entertain me for a day or two."

'Gemma' laughed. "Because I can promise you entertainment for far longer than that."

I raised an eyebrow curiously. "Why are you here?"

She tsked at me. "What fun would that be?" She continued past me, but looked back. "See if you can figure it out."

"I hope you hid the body well." I called after her softly.

She flashed me a feral grin. "Don't worry, they won't be finding dear, sweet Gemma anytime soon."

NOTE FROM THE AUTHOR

Everyone has dark moments in their life that we sometimes wish we could erase or forget. But sometimes it's the pain and struggle that we have gone through that gave us our inner strength.

For me, writing started as a way to confront some of the demons of my past so that I could put them behind me forever. Most of my characters have a dark or troubled past and my books follow their progress as they emerge from the darkness that has held them down for so long.

As the darkness fades, hope for a better future starts to emerge (like the sun after a storm). A piece of my soul goes into each one of my books, and my hope and faith in a brighter tomorrow is reflected in each one of my characters.

Books have always been a source of escape and enjoyment for me, so I hope that my work can help others in the same way☺

-C.C. Masters

ABOUT THE AUTHOR

C.C. Masters lives near Virginia Beach with her two furbabies, the inspirations for Tigger and Eeyore. She enjoys long walks on the beach and loves to run through the forest under the light of the full moon☺

Books by C.C. Masters

Seaside Wolf Pack Series

Book 1: Finding Somewhere to Belong

Book 1.5: Finding Anna

Book 2: Finding the Fire Within

Book 3: Finding the Power Within

Book 4: Finding Truth Beneath the Lies

Book 5: Finding My Breaking Point

Book 6: Finding Hope

Hollow Crest Wolf Pack Trilogy

Book 1: New Beginnings

Book 2: The Struggle

Book 3: A Place to Call Home

Printed in Great Britain
by Amazon

81690938R00132